Truth Moon

by

Kay Freeman

Truth Moon

Cover Art by *Rae Monet, Inc.*

The Wild Rose Press, Inc.
PO Box 708
Adams Basin, NY 14410-0708
Visit us at www.thewildrosepress.com

Publishing History
First Edition, 2023
Trade Paperback ISBN 978-1-5092-4800-1
Digital ISBN 978-1-5092-4801-8

Published in the United States of America

The girl's eyes gazed left and right, considering her options. "Too early for running," I growled. "You just got here." I grasped her elbow, holding her near.

She wrapped the blanket around herself even more tightly, but she was still exposed from the thighs down. I walked in front of her, blocking their view. I rarely concerned myself with propriety or became emotionally invested, but for some reason this felt different than usual. I shouldn't feel anything. "Remove the jacket and pants, they're wet," I said. "I don't want water dripping on the steps and the cellar floor. Dangerous." A horrified expression appeared on her face, like I'd asked her to streak around the yard naked. "Now. Next time I won't ask."

Holding the cover with one hand and trying to maneuver the wet pants off with the other proved impossible. "Um…please," the girl said, stumbling and struggling. "Could you hold it?" She asked, her shoulders slumping.

I took the blanket and shielded the girl from my brothers while she removed her clothing. For a small girl, she was solid and muscular. She wore plain white cotton panties, the good-girl kind. Why did Cowboy bring a good girl here?

Praise for Kay Freeman

2021 Mentee, RAMP program from Romance Writers of America.

Her short story, Meeting, Matching and Dating was featured in the Rom Com Magazine, Meet Cute Press in March 2021. The editor of the magazine wrote, "What we loved about this story (besides everything): the opening line is one for the books. This piece hilariously captures so much of the bad about dating in the age of the swipe right: the overthinking, the nerves, the (bad) advice from friends, the pressure, and the picture filters."

She won a Geraldine Dodge Grant from the state of NJ in 1997 and 1999 for her paintings and a Mid-Career Fellowship from Princeton University in 2007 for her teaching.

Dedication

This book is dedicated to the man in my life, Barry Wilkins, and to anti-heroes everywhere—men with edges, men with bully tendencies, and the strong women who love them.

I also want to thank Romance Writers of America and the Ramp Program; A.R. Case (Calia Wilde), author of *Mahem*, *Where Evil Thrives, Truth as Poison, Down in Blood, Dreams in the Dark, Hope to Lie, Destroyer's Soul* and *Dead in the Water*, who mentored me through the editing process and so much more; and Jason Pettus and Morena Stamm for their editing assistance.

Writers seldom get where they are going alone. Thank you to John Fox at Bookfox, Writers Studio NYC, Catapult, Contemporary Romance Writers, Stanford Continuing Studies, Contemporary Romance Writers, and Passionate Ink for providing workshops, conferences and forums that educate and support writers.

This is a dark romantic suspense. It contains adult themes and may include triggers for some (non-consensual touching, near-rape, light BDSM activities, confinement, discussions of past sexual abuse experienced by the heroine, and references to the hero's war experiences.) It is not a gender neutral read with much of the plot occurring in an outlaw motorcycle club setting. Intended for 18+

Chapter 1

The Take Down

"Falling stars are Gods and Goddesses throwing kisses at the Moon." ~ Rory Riley

Rory Ducked. The box whizzed by her head, missing by mere inches, landing on the bamboo floor. *Bang.*

Lloyd barreled towards her, zooming in close, "You'll never get another job in Vegas," he sneered, his spit sticking on her cheek. "I know the owners of every yoga studio in this town." His arms flailed in her face like one of those tube men you see at car washes. He scattered yoga paraphernalia around the studio and shouted obscenities before picking up the gift he'd hurled and finally stalking away. Information on sexual harassment and effective responses had not been part of her 200-hour yoga teacher training curriculum. As Lloyd slammed the door on the way out, the feng shui bells hanging on the frame railed, crashed, and jingled until fading, a quiet uneasiness remaining behind.

"Are you alright?" Sarah, Rory's friend and colleague, asked through the open door linked to Rory's.

"He's totally cray. Would you believe he threw something at me? Luckily, it missed. His behavior is becoming more bizarre every day," Rory said. "All this because I won't date him and accept his chippie bling?" *I built one new life. I can create another.*

"He's a hit 'em and quit 'em kind of guy," Sarah replied. "I did him once, and he didn't act bonkers like this. What kind of gift?"

"For real? More like graft. A gold choker."

"Me too. I treated it like an initiation. You could have accepted it. I pawned mine."

"We're not Lloyd's harem," Rory said, re-stacking the foam blocks. "He must have gotten a deal and bought them in bulk, wholesale. If I'd kept it, he'd have expected something in return."

"Soul is a great yoga studio. I mean, it was voted best in Nevada last year! And overall, Lloyd treats us well, even gives us control of the schedule."

"Swell, he lets us do our jobs."

"Everything isn't always black and white, Rory. But no matter what, I'll always have your back."

"What Lloyd's doing is wrong," Rory said, organizing the paperwork on the counter. "It's sexual harassment. You need to be woke."

"I've got a number you can call to report him, but let me talk to him first," Sarah said. "It's going to cause a shitstorm. If he doesn't back off, then call the number."

"I'll call the law instead." An idle threat. *I can't go to them or anyone else.*

"Do what you need to, but get your students' phone numbers or email addresses, in case the school closes or he fires you. But I'll talk to him," Sarah said, patting Rory's shoulder reassuringly and hurrying to the room next door to teach.

Rory's phone beeped. She looked down at a text from her devil.

Lloyd—*Uneed 2come 2my house 2night—*
—Assist w/schedule—
—If udon't no courses 4u next quarter—
—NVM PTSD class for vets2.—

What a thirsty tool. Rory had designed the post-traumatic stress disorder course. She loved the veterans. She needed the money from the other courses to keep her apartment. Locating a new job in this town, where yoga instructors showed their asanas off on every corner, would be difficult. *Funny one, Rory. I'll join them and hold a sign—WILL DO YOGA POSES FOR FOOD.* She stuffed the phone in her bag and rushed out the door, ignoring Lloyd's nonsense. He got salty whenever he didn't get his own way.

****

The sun burned hot and high as she headed towards the VFW Hall, but then it magically disappeared behind a cloak of clouds. Her hands itched, bile pushed up from her belly up into her throat, and like a lush she heaved liquid on the pavement as people gawked. If she'd eaten today, the stress wouldn't have affected her as badly. No one wanted to imagine someone else losing it all in some casino. It was Las Vegas, after all. *Pathetic. I don't need to take a step into a casino to lose everything.*

As Rory reached the front of the VFW, her phone announced an incoming call. She looked at the number. Lloyd again. She remembered the only advice her mother had ever offered her: "*Worry about the shit you don't see coming, girl. That's the stuff that will bite you in the ass. Every time.*"

Rory entered the double doors and followed the red arrow on the posterboard sign. "Yoga for PTSD," it read, with more red arrows taped to the floor. Soothing music played in the low-lit, wood-paneled room, lined with rows of mats. A student stopped Rory and asked a question. She detected the foul bouquet immediately—lemons, nutmeg and musk. The only scent he ever wore. Heart pounding, her breath shortened. There was drumming in her ears, tingling in her fingers, and intense stomach pain creeping in. Her hands shook and she dropped the binder, stumbled out of the room, and raced down the corridor. The walls breathed in and out, then closed in, the floor spinning, her safe place transformed into a horror funhouse.

"He isn't here," she repeated, clutching the wall, then sliding and crashing down on her rump. Mustard and brown linoleum squares twirled. Today someone's aftershave had set her off, and the session hadn't even started yet. The hideous yellow illumination from the fluorescent lights blinded her. Slowly, once, twice, she inhaled and exhaled, continuing with her breathing exercise until the beating of her heart slowed. She filled a paper cup at the water dispenser and used her hair as a screen, bringing the drink to her lips. She squeezed the paper vessel too hard, almost collapsing it and spilling drops of water on the floor. She removed the coins from her pocket. *Clang, clang, clang, clang*—the sound magnified, hitting the bottom of the change pan, sounding like a bomb exploding. Rory wrestled the package from the vending machine, then almost dropped it. Her hands were weak and damp with sweat, slight bumps forming. Hives again? She gagged on the cashews. A problem swallowing too. *I'm a fraud. How can I help them when I can't help myself?*

Rory checked her watch. The class was about to start. She darted into the bathroom, splashed water on her face, pulled her hair into a ponytail, and returned to the class. "I'm sorry for cutting our conversation short. We can talk later," she said to the student, picking up the notebook. Her eyes connected and crashed with the vets throughout the session, her stomach twisted, and her face heating up. *I'm a weirdo. Other women aren't like me.*

At the end of class, music from Chaka Khan flooded from her phone. Sarah's image popped up. *Not Lloyd, thank God.* "How did it go?" Her friend asked immediately after Rory answered.

"Only one tonight, but Lloyd's still threatening me. He said he'd make me pay."

"It's all talk, don't trip. He won't do anything. At least I don't think he will," Sarah stammered. "I don't know what's wrong with him. He's never acted like this before. Maybe some kind of mid-life-crisis thing. Like we discussed, I'll talk to him."

"He's forcing me into a corner," Rory said, but didn't want to argue. "I've got to bounce. I need to keep my wits about me walking home."

"I wish you'd take a taxi," Sarah said. "A mile at night isn't safe, plus now it's raining. The bus is an option."

"I can't afford a taxi. Lloyd shorted my last three checks. And I don't know about waiting for a bus…better to be a moving target. Anyway, the rain's lessened."

"I'll pay for an Uber. I'll call for you," Sarah volunteered.

"I appreciate the offer. You're a loyal friend, but I can't. No worries. I'll be fine."

"Take your mace out and keys too. Spray your attacker, dropkick them in the balls, and gouge their eyes out."

"And you call yourself a yoga instructor," Rory teased.

"Be safe. Text me when you arrive home," Sarah said.

"Bye, Mom," Rory said, ending the call. *I've never had a friend like Sarah. I don't need to go through anything alone. Unfortunately, there are some secrets I can't share, even with her.*

Rory stood on the steps outside the VFW and looked across the street. A young girl with her mother stood there, holding hands. "The name Rory means 'Red King,'" her mother had once said. "Imagine my disappointment in not having one." Rory began walking, and when she reached the end of the street, the shadow of an elephant emerged on the side of the brick building. The elephant in the room from her past? Not because Rory wasn't a male. She ran as fast as she could, not turning back to see what was creating the foreboding mystery on the wall. *I didn't look back when the fire turned my old life into ashes either.*

There was a tingling on the back of her neck and a stabbing pain in her stomach. *Listen to your gut—something isn't right.* A mud-stained white van idled at the curb, dented on the passenger side with rusted spots on the roof. Its rubber blades squeaked, screeched, and dragged across the windshield until the driver slapped them off. A bumper sticker read *Defend the Blue, Support your Local Police.* They began pursuing her like a dog on the hunt, stomping the accelerator and speeding ahead, smacking a puddle, spraying torrents of water over her.

Rory screamed, spun, shook her hands and whipped

her hair back and forth. The van's windows were partially open, and the laughter of men faded away as the vehicle zoomed down the street. *Assholes.*

It was sultry for May. Maybe her clothes would dry by the time she reached home. All the stores were closed, leaving the alley dark and spooky. *Stop being a baby.* She wished she had a ride. Her mother used to say, "If wishes were horses, beggars would ride." She never understood the saying. Did beggars wish for horses, or did other people wish for the beggars to have them? All she knew was that her mother didn't want to hear anything about wishes, telling Rory to shut her mouth.

Under a streetlight on the next block, a figure appeared. Seconds later, the person dropped out of sight. *Creepy.* She reached a coffee shop wedged between two of her favorite hangouts, a bookstore and an art gallery. Lit in the enormous window was a featured book, *The Butterfly Garden.* She had started it but hadn't finished. It had triggered her. *Maybe after a few years of therapy, I'll be able to read it.* New paintings hung in the gallery window, women in all kinds of languishing poses. The hair on her arms stood. *Is it the paintings?*

A man in camouflage lunged from the shadows of the gallery. She side-stepped out of his reach, causing him to stumble and fall. A knife clattered to the wet blacktop, light bouncing from store windows onto the silver blade. Her attacker clambered up and peeled off a black mask.

"Lloyd? Why?"

"You're coming with me," Lloyd said, scowling. "If you don't, I'm contacting the cops."

"You attacked me and *you're* calling the police?"

"Call it a citizen's arrest. You got the job under false

pretenses. You can explain at my house."

"I'm not telling you anything," Rory said, straightening her sweatshirt. "I'm going home."

Suddenly a super muscular man with long white-blond hair, wearing a black leather jacket, emerged from the shadows of the coffee shop. He reached for her shoulders while another man with glasses pushed Lloyd into them, causing the blond one to loosen his grip. Miraculously, Rory broke free and ran. "Catch her!" the blond man yelled.

Rory ran down the block and cut down an alley she used as a shortcut sometimes, a large chain link fence greeting her. Rory loved to climb trees, and the climbing wall at the gym was her number one activity. *No different here*, she told herself. Fear surged as Rory propelled her legs up, wedged her feet into the wire, and climbed as fast as she could.

Halfway up, the blond man latched on to her ankle. Rory kicked back wildly, seeking to shake him loose, her bag jostling and spilling things below. Watching her cell phone go, she cried out, "Nooooooo." Then her favorite book fell, *The Heart of Yoga,* banging Blondie's head. Distracted by the wallop, Blondie looked away, and this time her kick connected—*whack,* right in his nose.

He dropped to the ground. "Bitch, you're dead!" he bellowed. Blood gushed from his nose as he paced back and forth, words pouring from his mouth, "&#%!@?! You'll pay for this when I—"

The guy with glasses interrupted. "*Sshhh*. Someone might call the police."

Rory hit the ground and popped them a nasty look, and they glowered back. She thought better about provoking them further and took off, jogging down the alley, debating what to do about the men. She couldn't go to the police. Too many questions. *Do they work for Lloyd?* She could call Sarah if she hadn't lost her phone.

Rory continued home, walking slowly and softly, glancing over her shoulder and listening. She couldn't believe Lloyd and the other two had attacked her. *Are they stalking me?* She stopped at the end of each block, waiting and watching until she was sure no one was behind her, then proceeded on to her apartment.

****

I'm home.

A three-story building, wood-clapped with chipped white paint and rotting siding. Rory had restored the front door herself, painting it cranberry red. Lit up by the streetlight, the color and sheen radiated hope, but she didn't feel hopeful now. She listened before turning the key in the lock. Thank goodness she wore her housekey around her neck, instead of in her purse. Her apartment was quiet. All the lights were off like she'd left it. She twisted the key and pushed the door open.

Two silhouettes ran at her. Air skimmed Rory's skin. Her many nights of learning how to maneuver around the space with the lights off was no longer for fun, or a way to save money on the electric bill. This was for real. She darted around them like a star quarterback and kept them from catching her. She sprinted to the bedroom, slammed the door, and engaged the lock, leaving the men still sliding, stumbling and cussing on the other side. *Fools.*

Whack. Thump. Sounds vibrated across the wood. "She wants us to dance for our supper," someone yelled. It sounded like Blondie again. *Bam bam. Wumphf.*

At some point, the door would give. *I should hide.*

9

Rory sprinted to her closet and opened it. Lloyd jumped out of it and sprung at her, his arm held high. He brought a hypodermic needle down and snagged her yoga pants, pushing it deeply into her thigh.

"Ouch, stop it!" she screamed.

"I know all about your lies," Lloyd said. This time he jabbed the needle in her arm.

"AHH!" she cried, pushing him away. "Why are you doing this?"

"You used a fake social security number on your job application, and your driver's license is phony too."

"You're the one breaking and entering." She was grappling with him. "How did you get in here?"

"You shouldn't leave your windows unlocked if you don't want company," Lloyd said, his breathing heavy, continuing to stab at her. "Who are you?" he yelled, the needle landing in her right arm.

"Not a pushover," she said, snatching the nearest thing on her nightstand and spraying him in the eyes with room freshener.

He screamed, "My eyes! My eyes!" He rubbed them furiously, flopping back and forth on the bed. She shut herself in the closet. Through the slats, Rory watched the bedroom door splinter after each blow and kick. The last impact caused the door to crash open, bouncing against the wall and creating a hole, sprinkling white plaster dust on the floor.

Rory observed Blondie from the closet as he stomped in, leaving white footprints on the floor. "Where is she?" he asked as he pulled Lloyd from the bed and repeatedly beat him around the face until Lloyd appeared unconscious. Blondie threw Lloyd back on the mattress, got down on his hands and knees, and searched under her bed. He clambered up, ran to the window, opened it and leaned out, looking down and side to side before coming to the closet door.

"Come out, come out, wherever you are," he said in a sing-song voice, sliding the door open and kneeling over her. Rory shrank back as far as she could, squeezing her eyes shut to avoid looking at him, folding one arm around herself and sliding the other under her armpit. She opened her eyes as she felt his breath on her cheek and brought the aerosol can out to fire. "I don't think so," he said, wrestling it out of her hand and throwing it toward the bed. His bleached hair, dry and smelling of gasoline, dragged across her face. "I heard what the man had to say. Runnin' from somethin', honey?"

Rory bounced up and attempted to maneuver around Blondie's massive form, but he blocked her. She'd been the smallest and most disadvantaged kid in school, making her a target and eventually a master of dirty fighting. She pretended to swing at his head but instead delivered a kick to his kneecap. He held one leg and hopped around the room in pain, hunched over. "You'll pay for that, bitch," he threatened.

She ran to her door. "Out of my way," she yelled, glaring at the third man blocking it. This one was smaller, wearing a do-rag and foggy glasses.

"Cool it, Ripley," he said, gripping her arm.

As panicked as she was, she couldn't help but appreciate the reference to *Aliens*. "Game over," she quoted back. She opened her mouth wide and brought her top teeth down on his hand, closing her mouth as hard as she could.

"AHH! She bit me!" he yelled, squeezing her arm tighter still. Rory turned to an old favorite, stomping on the top of his foot. He hunched over in pain, and she kicked him in the groin. He bent in half, emitting wheezing noises, his glasses sliding over his nose and landing on the floor before letting her go.

Rory ran from the bedroom and down the hallway, reaching the living room and throwing the door open. Only a few steps from freedom. With half of her body out, she tasted the late spring night air. The streetlights shone on the wet, black road until a powerful force—boa constrictor-like—grabbed her stomach and pulled her back inside. The door whipped around, closing. She landed on a firm brick belly and wrestled to break free. Wriggling and writhing, their positions reversed. Someone straddled her, cerulean blue eyes and a smirk staring down at her, lit by the streetlights, shining through the transept. "I can't even," she huffed, raising her hips and trying to buck him off.

"You can't even what?" Blondie laughed. "That little kick was nothin', girlie. I agree with your boss, you need to lock your windows. Now, we can do this the hard way or the simple way. I don't mind the hard way." He pressed his groin against her pelvis and gave a twisted grin. "The hard way, I help your boss and call the cops. Tell them I witnessed an assault on the poor guy, and Bossman tells his story about you, and you get locked up. Or the easy way—leave here with me and come hide out at my clubhouse for a while." She couldn't think. Blondie's syrupy sing-song way of talking, and his amputation of any word ending in "ing," was disturbing.

The other man, goofy with taped glasses, wasn't much better. "I took care of the interloper," he said to Blondie. "Shot him up with H and put him in her closet."

Rory's throat closed, air disappearing. The pupils of

the man with glasses transformed into a spider's body, the lashes into spider legs. She giggled and giggled some more. She couldn't stop laughing. *It isn't funny, but then it is. Funny, honey, bunny, money. I'm repeating myself. I can't think. I'm lost. Why is Lloyd in my closet?*

"What's wrong with her?" the man with the glasses asked, kneeling.

"Bossman stuck her with somethin'." Blondie nodded in the direction of her bedroom, "a needle on the floor." Then asked her with a grin, "You gonna come with us, sweetheart? Room and board, even profit sharing. All clothing provided, although not much, 'cause you won't need them with what you'll be doing." He chuckled. "I need an answer."

"Mmph," she mouthed, lips stuck together, her head flopping and mind drifting.

"I'm gonna take that as a yes. You saw her give consent, right, Johnny? I can't believe that other guy, tryin' to beat us to the punch. The nerve of some people. But Bossman's right about one thing—she needs to beef up security. Nice of him to leave the window open for us, though."

Rory smiled. The spiders multiplied. She struggled against the scampering, swarming terror. No longer funny. They touched and traveled across her body and face, overwhelming her with fangs and feelers. It prickled and tickled. Jaws trailed and tugged, sitting on her eyelids, weighing them down. Taking her deeper into darkness. They fought their way into her mouth and choked her, filling her throat, making it impossible to breathe, her stomach a home for a never-ending battalion. Finally, she surrendered to their softness and fell asleep, pregnant with peace. She floated away on an opalescent cloud, blending into blackness.

****

"Fetch the van, Johnny. Bring it out front," Cowboy said, throwing him the keys. "She won't need this." He took the house key from the girl's neck. "Comin' to our house now. Monitor the girl's condition. Nothin' better happen, or you'll pay. And keep your mouth shut about this. If WM asks, she agreed to come. Don't tell him the particulars. Now, get going. Gotta send a text."

He got out his phone and shot off:

Cowboy—*Got her*—

—*Call the dogs off my bro*—

—*1 hap coincidence 4us*—

—*Her Boss showed, wacko*—

—*Accused her of using false ID, drugged her*

—*Handled him2*—

A few seconds later, Cowboy received a message back:

MM—TTYL—

Chapter 2

Good Girls

"If the Man in the Moon was a real man, anything like you, the sun would never come out and shine" ~ Rory Riley

According to Cowboy's text, he was going to be here in fifteen minutes, and that was thirty minutes ago. Our entrance is unlit, no sign, easily missed. The whole four hundred desolate acres are surrounded by barbed wire. Unless a person knew about us, he or she would cruise by…and best that person did, unless he or she had been invited.

Smoke billowed from my last cigarette for the night, or at least that's what I told myself as I watched the gray clouds disappear into blackness. With my eyes, I followed our long driveway twisting into the night, leading to Interstate 15, in Mesquite, Nevada and searched for headlights. It was normally an hour and ten minutes' drive from Las Vegas, if Cowboy believed in speed limits.

I took another drag, reached the filter, held the last inhale, then pushed the smoke out slowly. Gazing at the moon, I noticed its craters, and thought of all the holes in my soul since coming to the Knights of Steel Outlaw Motorcycle Club. I rubbed the cigarette butt on the railing, tobacco remnants blowing across the porch and disappearing as quickly as my old life had six years ago. Trying not to smoke around this bunch was like being on the *Titanic* and refusing to swim. *Whatever*.

I scratched my chin. Hadn't shaved again, practically a goatee, and I needed a haircut too. I didn't recognize myself nowadays. The straitlaced West Point graduate was long gone. No impressionable kid willing to believe anything; instead I was a cynical old man at thirty-two. At the diner this morning, I'd noticed how other men shielded their wives and children from me. Good. I didn't want their world. I lived in a different world now, with a different set of rules, with brothers who shielded me. If I needed shielding, which *I don't*.

Some of my brothers refer to me as the Philosopher among other names, mainly because I don't run my mouth. I learned early in life that if I don't talk much, when I do say something, people listen. But the truth, the best thing a person can do in a place like this is keep their mouth shut and their eyes open. "Prepare yourself, Turk," I said to my companion. "God knows what Cowboy's bringing us."

"Come on, WM. The last one turned out fine, earnings galore," Turk said. Turk was the best prospect out of the new applicants, and assisted me with taking care of the girls. Did whatever I told him, all to earn his patch and become a bona fide member of the Knights of Steel.

"Yeah, but some are drama queens. We don't need more of those. Shitfits over bullshit. No more oxygen suckers either, the ones that talk too much and ask too many questions."

"We got guys in our OMC who do that too, WM,"

Turk chuckled.

"Don't be a wiseass." Then I saw them. Headlights, coming fast. A junker. Didn't have the shocks for an unpaved road. By the time they reached the security fence, Cowboy's heavy metal music was loud enough for us to hear. Cowboy's favorite, "Welcome to the Jungle," thumping bass echoing through the night.

Seconds later, Cowboy skidded the clunker to a screeching stop by the clubhouse, shooting dirt and gravel everywhere. We never parked the Loser Cruiser in front, always in the rear. He jumped out, cursing, and announced, "WM, we got a problem." His face was red and his pupils were large. His eyes were the blue of those morning glories people planted by their mailboxes to provide a welcoming touch. There was nothing welcoming about Cowboy's eyes, though. Everyone who met him described them as crazy; and, for a few men, they were the last thing they ever saw in this world.

Johnny spilled out the back of the vehicle, straggles of hair slipping out from his do-rag, his glasses bent and falling off his face. The open double doors framed a petite girl's body sprawled inside, not moving. "I don't think she's breathing," he said.

"Either she is or she isn't!" Cowboy shouted.

"I…I…I don't know."

I hurried down the walk, scrambled into the back of the van, and circled my hands around her wrists to check for a pulse. Thin, like my mother's. "Weak and slow," I reported. A tiny thing, more a girl than a woman. What was Cowboy thinking? He usually brought the right kind. Women beaten down by life, looking for a family that would treat them right. *And we do.* Even offer a 401(k). Truth. My idea. We don't have a Peyton

Manning in the bunch. Beauty doesn't last forever, and in our business, it disappears even faster. The girls serve five to ten years and done, and 'serve' really is the best word for it.

The overhead lights revealed a couple of needle marks. A junkie? Her color was off too, white-blue skin. I remembered my racing kit. By pushing forward on the gear shift, I could make the car go faster. When my mother's heart stopped, I thought I could start it the same way. "Stop crying," my father had lectured. "If you're going to cry, go downstairs with your grandmother and the other women." The racing kit was my last gift from her. *I loved those cars. I loved her.* "Please don't let her heart slow too much," I choked.

"What did you say?" Cowboy asked.

"Nothing." My face caught in the girl's hair. A scent of burning wood weaved through my nostrils. I performed chest compression and CPR. After several minutes, she was worse than before. Kneeling beside the girl, still holding her hand, I reported to Cowboy, "No pulse."

"I thought you knew what you were doing," Cowboy said. Throwing Johnny against the vehicle and slapping him about the face, he yelled, "I warned you. You'll pay with your hide."

Johnny whined, "I did my best," covering his face with his hands. "Maybe an allergic reaction to whatever the other guy gave her. I dunno."

"You dunno?" Cowboy jeered. "I should've known better than to trust you with anything, especially an asset."

"There's nothing more we can do," I said. *Afghanistan all over again.*

Cowboy stood silently for a minute, clenched his fists, turned away from Johnny, and stared into the night. All my brothers, now on the porch, whispered amongst themselves. "We need to lose the body, brother," he said, glaring inside the vehicle and back at me.

I clambered down and lifted the corpse into my arms. "Where do you want me to bury it?" I wished I could disappear too, but my mission was to make sure she did. *Always stuck with the dirty work.*

"Away from here, for sure," Cowboy muttered, opening his glove box and rifling through it.

"I'm not doing this anymore," I said.

"Got it." Cowboy found a flashlight, turned it on, and pointed it out into the desolate space. The beam of light bounced from side to side and revealed a path for me to follow. We ambled down a trail behind the clubhouse toward the woods. *I couldn't protect them either. Being a Knights of Steel member is all I'm good for.*

Cowboy lifted the flashlight, searching. "Hear that?" He asked. Moving it back and forth, his circle of light framed some juniper trees, then suddenly bounced off yellow eyes, making whatever had been there scatter. The drumming of hooves, pounding soil and striking rocks, reverberated through the night. Mule deer stampeded in and out of trees, appearing and disappearing like ghosts. As we continued our pilgrimage, rows of sage grass blew back and forth gracefully, until we reached a bubbling creek spilling into a pond. My brothers partied here. The remnants—a forgotten keg left rusting, empty and broken liquor bottles, and burnt timber from an old pallet fire—were strewn about. A hawk led the procession until we reached the water's edge, flying close. *Kreeee, kreeee, kreeee.*

Cowboy's light touched the water. "Put her here. It's muddy and there's lots of limbs for the body to hook onto, to keep it under." I looked down at the girl's lifeless body in my arms and over at Cowboy with disgust. Like a sacrifice to Poseidon, I marched into the moon-kissed water until my lower torso was immersed, then lowered the corpse and pushed the body farther and farther from shore. It floated on its watery bed, hovering horizontally in the liquid calm, hair swirling and sailing, resembling Ophelia. I pressed down, submerging the body. It sunk lower and lower, vanishing into the murky depths, except for a few strands of hair drifting upward. *I failed her too.*

Turning, I made the funeral march toward shore. My head was hung low, boots sloshing, mud sticking as I stepped through debris. I'd check every day for a while and make sure the body stayed down.

"WM, over there!" Cowboy yelled, arm outstretched, finger pointing back to the boggy boneyard from where I'd come from. I couldn't believe what I was seeing.

Her body, no longer submerged, floated in my direction. Bubbles strung on a milky thread came from her mouth, and her eyes suddenly fluttered open. Outstretched arms swam towards me. I drew her in and carried my ghostly, shivering treasure to shore.

"You should have let me go," she whimpered, teeth chattering, head curled and pressed against my chest.

My rib cage expanded. "Consider this your baptism. You're born again. You belong to us now. Body, mind, and soul." The reason for my anger—the girl's reprimand. The truth was that I was mad at myself for being a part of something this dark. *How bad am I that she prefers death?*

"Wow, quite a speech, WM," Cowboy chuckled, standing on the shore by broken and bent reeds. I pushed through them and placed her feet back on solid ground. We walked back to the clubhouse, with her stumbling and shivering, the only sounds around us were the crickets, owls, a hawk, and what sounded like a fox screaming.

I found a blanket in the back of the van and wrapped it around her protectively. I got a better look at the girl thanks to the light from the porch. Red hair in disarray, filled with grass, leaves and sticks, with porcelain skin kissed by freckles on her nose and a smattering of mud. She resembled a wood nymph from a fairytale, with lashes that looked fake but turned out not to be, and forest green eyes full of questions. The kind of eyes that brought most men to their knees. *But not me.*

"Ready a room, separate from the others," I whispered to Turk. "I don't want the rest of them putting ideas in her head. Flip the mattress on the rack and make the bed, and don't drag your feet. The sooner she's tucked away, the better, before anything else happens."

"She's shivering. Got goosebumps on her goosebumps," Turk said, peering at the girl. "Anna can make some tea."

"Add something to eat too," I said. "Could be hungry." I removed my wet cut, water drops dripping from it.

"I don't understand how the water revived her," Johnny said. "The cold should have killed her."

"The Lord works in mysterious ways, my jackass," Cowboy preached. "You're lucky she's alive or your ass would be mine. Say amen, close your mouth, and get out of my sight before I crucify you right here." Cowboy's roots were showing. His father had been a pastor—the hell-and-brimstone, rattlesnake-handling kind. He strutted over to my brothers on the porch. "I picked a good one," he boasted.

The girl's eyes gazed left and right, considering her options. "Too early for running," I growled. "You just got here." I grasped her elbow, holding her near.

"WM, take the cover off," a brother from the porch yelled.

"Let's preview the newest member of the family," shouted another. Damp yoga clothing clung to her body and peeked from under the blanket, generating whistles and lewd comments from yet more of them.

She wrapped the blanket around herself even more tightly, but she was still exposed from the thighs down. I walked in front of her, blocking their view. I rarely concerned myself with propriety or became emotionally invested, but for some reason this felt different than usual. *I shouldn't feel anything.* "Remove the jacket and pants, they're wet," I said. "I don't want water dripping on the steps and the cellar floor. Dangerous." A horrified expression appeared on her face, like I'd asked her to streak around the yard naked. "Now. Next time I won't ask."

Holding the cover with one hand and trying to maneuver the wet pants off with the other proved impossible. "Um...please," the girl said, stumbling and struggling. "Could you hold it?" She asked, her shoulders slumping.

I took the blanket and shielded the girl from my brothers while she removed her clothing. For a small girl, she was solid and muscular. She wore plain white cotton panties, the good-girl kind. *Why did Cowboy bring a good girl here?* Her legs, white too. She hadn't seen the sun in a long time. The kind of skin tone I like. Would mark nicely. Dreaming already about getting black rope around them and imagining some—

"Boys, quiet down and behave yourselves," Cowboy said, interrupting my thoughts as the members continued their catcalling. He was never the chivalrous type. *What gives?*

I handed the cover back, and she hugged it to her body. "This way," I said, shuttling her towards the cellar steps, my wet shoes emitting unseemly squeaks. "You can't enter the clubhouse through the front door. Only men have the right." Part of the spiel I gave the new recruits. Rules and regulations were vital if one wanted to keep problems to a minimum.

My foot suddenly slipped, tossing me forward. The girl grabbed my arm, keeping me from falling, saving me. "Worry about yourself instead," I said, hiding my embarrassment by shoving her hand away. *She better not think I owe her. Righting me. An impossible task, little one. Too far gone.*

I pushed her by the shoulder down the corridor and through a gated door. "Your room," I announced, noticing a black cord circling her wrist, with multiple silver angel wings attached. Light reflected off the etched wings. My body shook. All the scents of death flooding in, the smell of burning flesh and shit, overwhelmed me. The wings were like Chet's feather, the one he had worn around his neck under his uniform, every day until…

"Hand over the bracelet," I ordered. Midway she

froze. I captured her wrist, brought it closer, and forced the finery from her fingers. "You can't have jewelry until you earn that right." I stuffed the silver into the darkness of my pocket, relieved not to look at it further. "Give me the watch too," I said, staring at her other hand.

"How will I know the time?" she asked.

"Seriously? You have somewhere you need to be?" I gave her a sideways glance.

"Ah…no…but I thought—"

"Now there's your problem. Don't think. Do what I tell you."

"But I might need to know—"

I interrupted. "You only need to know what I decide. No reason to concern yourself with time or anything else. I'll tell you when it's time to do things. Hand it over." I wasn't used to explaining myself, and I don't with the others. It's easier to control a new girl if I take everything away that provided past comfort. Makes her dependent on me. After she's trained and proven herself, I'll let up. Kind of like the first few weeks of school when a person had a new teacher. The teacher acted like a hardass with lots of rules and regulations, and then after order was established, they were all peaches and cream. This was the same. Anyway, she should know time was nothing but an illusion. Here in the cellar, it's Whoremaster's Theory of Relativity; everything moves relative to what I want. I was her master, and the sooner she bought into that, the better.

She handed over the watch reluctantly, forcing me to grasp onto her wrist again and take it from her. With all the fuss she made, I'd expected a luxury watch, not a Swatch, although it was certainly colorful like her, the band striped, red, pink and purple. I put it in the front pocket of my T, next to my heart. That is, if I had one. I'm like the Tin Man.

"Put the shirt on and put the blanket on the bed," I ordered, crossing my arms and leaning against the wall. The girl trembled and changed into the shirt under the blanket (or 'green girl,' terminology from my military days), all bashful, before folding it. She folded a perfect rectangle, managing minor creases in something threadbare. Disappointment welled inside me, knowing she knew the right way without me getting the chance to teach her. The girls constantly gossiped about my OCD tendencies and discussed how I must be 'on the spectrum.' The first part was true. There's a right way to do things, and I enjoyed showing it to them. But the second part was false, or at least I thought so. My father, a lifer who eventually reached colonel, would have never admitted to it anyway. If he had, there would have been no West Point for me.

Then my eyes traveled across the bed. Uh-oh. The sheets and blanket were in disarray. I called Turk on my cell and said, "Get down here. Yeah, the new one." I spun my ring on my finger while the girl stared at me. *I'll need to change that. Obviously not submissive if she doesn't know to avert her eyes.*

"You need me, boss?" Turk asked breathlessly, shirt partially unbuttoned and jeans unzipped.

"Remake the bed."

"What's wrong with it?" he asked. I directed my eyes to Turk's zipper, and he looked down. "Oh, sorry," he said and quickly adjusted his pants.

"Can't you tell?"

Turk stared at it. "Not really. Looks ready to go."

That was when the girl stepped up. "The corners

25

need to be tucked and—"

I interrupted. "Did I ask for your opinion?"

"No, but since I'm the one who has to sleep on it, I should be able to give one. I'll make it if you like." She moved towards the bed.

"Don't touch it. His fuck-up. He'll learn by fixing it." I turned back to Turk. "Do things the right way or don't do them at all. Remember, the dull side of the top sheet goes up, then fold the top part back and use hospital corners."

"Got it," Turk said, his lips turned down.

I watched the girl shiver. Some of the other women called it drafty too. If a person was from Michigan, like me, it was nothing. Winters back home lasted nine months of the year. Nevada was a paradise in comparison. My thinking—if it made the women eager to leave their rooms and go to work, it was a reason not to change it. "Turk, bring another blanket," I said. Until the girl recovered from her ordeal, it seemed wise to consider her health.

"May I please use the restroom?" the girl whispered. Polite to a fault—'please' and 'thank you' already. Not like the others when they first arrived. The girl shouldn't be like this yet, with manners.

"You can address me as Sir, WM, Master or Whoremaster, your choice. The toilet's there." I pointed to a portable one in the back corner of her room and slammed the gate shut, taking just a few steps down the passageway before her voice rang out.

"What's going to happen to me now?"

What's going to happen? Why doesn't she know? I didn't provide any information, but kept walking. I stopped Anna as she came down the stairs. "Don't talk to her, and take Turk with you anytime you need to go in the room. Got it?"

Anna nodded her head affirmatively.

Past her expiration date, she served as a housemother now. I didn't want Anna to be motherly with the new girl, or bum-rushed by her either. Something wasn't quite right about her. I didn't want anyone close to the new one. In my playbook, it was time to make the girl dependent on me.

****

I stopped in the kitchen where Cowboy was holding court. I needed to find out more about this one. "A space cadet?" I asked him. "Why not our usual? A buxom bad kitty?"

Cowboy held up his hand to stop me. "You got it wrong, WM. A girl-next-door type. She's not a junkie. Some guy shot her up with something. Teaches yoga. I'm diversifying with the red hair, is all."

"What happened to your nose?" I asked, surveying Cowboy's swollen nose and developing black eye.

"A physical girl. Lively, plays hard to get, but nothing for you to worry about."

"More like Buffy-next-door with mixed martial arts training, if you ask me."

"Yogis aren't into fighting. Peace lovin' people. Don't you know that?"

"Yogis are too spiritual for our line of work, and our clients prefer blondes, last time I checked. Plus, redheads feel pain more than others. Scientific studies prove it."

"The carpets might not match the drapes," Cowboy argued. "And even if they do and her hair is legit, we can build tolerance. By and by, she'll crave pain like the others. We can buy hair dye if the clients don't dig red."

"Got it all figured out, do you?" I asked. "She's not our usual. More the kind you take home to meet you mother, if you had one. She doesn't belong here."

Cowboy fashioned his hand and fingers into a gun, then aimed it at my forehead, reminding me and everyone else at the table that he was the boss. "Neither of us have mothers," he said, losing his smile. "Do your job. Turn her out. Two months at most. Her yoga mat and purse are there." He kicked them with his boot. "She can dance at Kitties to start. Then in a couple of weeks, she can go to Vegas with the others."

"You're in charge of the training now?" I asked. I opened the purse and found her phone. It came alive in my hand, opening without a password.

"I thought I left that thing on the ground when it fell out of her purse," Cowboy said. "I guess not. Shouldn't have brought it here."

"Wow, no password. Stupid." Not stupid, just innocent about how guys like me worked. Would strip or rip away everything she held dear and use it against her.

"Destroy it after you're done snooping. They could trace the signal to the closest tower," Cowboy said.

"Why's that an issue? Her phone helps me."

"Just in case, Sherlock. What can you tell me?" He peered down at my hand.

"Her boss is all over this. Text and phone messages, putting the pressure on."

"Yeah, that's how I got her to come." Cowboy smiled. "To get away from the mutt."

"Most women would have reported him. Hard to believe this one wants to become a sex worker. Seems strange." Cowboy was shrewd and practical. There had to be a reason he'd recruited her, beyond her willingness.

"Are you thinking her yoga background is going to be useful for our special clients?"

Cowboy's chest puffed up. "I saved her. She's lookin' for protection and a place to hide. Diversifying, like I said. Who knows about the yoga?" His shoulders went up and down.

"Superman, are you?"

"That's right. Ain't I like him? Muscles of steel, a square jaw, even the dimples. You know red and blue are my favorite colors." Cowboy flexed his biceps and chuckled.

"Still…A yogi needs to be mindful, aware of themselves, their environment and others. I suppose it could translate to becoming a submissive. I can still use her on Vegas runs if she doesn't work out with the other."

"How about in our films? She's eye-catching enough," Cowboy said, sipping his beer.

"I'm concerned about her youthful look. We don't need the law snooping around, asking her age." Like most motorcycle clubs, if she was just a woman and not someone's old lady, she was expected to contribute. In our case, women performed all sexual services for club members, visitors, and the escort service we ran. Then there were the X-rated films we made and sold on the internet. The big money, though, came from entertaining our special high-end clients in our dungeon. Not all our girls were cut out for that.

"She's gotta be at least twenty-one. Had a job, her own apartment. No parents on the premises. You'll figure her out. *But*, I want her as a submissive," Cowboy said, taking a cigarette out.

"You can't fit a square peg into a round hole. She

doesn't seem all that submissive to me."

"It's conditioning. Teach her up and she'll acclimate. When in Rome…"

"You know there's more to it than that. Some are easier than others because they're wired that way. If she's not interested, it doesn't matter what—"

"Don't give me excuses. Do your job and get her done," Cowboy said. His eyes grew darker.

Chapter 3

Garden of Eden

"What if she changes her mind and wants to go home?" I asked.

Cowboy lit his cigarette, the light casting a rosy flame, painting his face red and transforming him into the devil he was. He crowed, "Change it. You're good at talking people into things, WM. That's your forte."

"Could be hard work talking this one into anything, if your black eye is an indicator. Let's hope she's eager to baddify and go to the wild side."

"I'm sure she will. What girl doesn't like a bad boy?"

A good girl, that's who, I thought.

"I should tell you, we dealt with her boss," Cowboy continued, taking a drag off his cigarette.

"How's that?"

"Johnny gave the mutt something and stuck him in her closet. The guy's bad news. Had zip-ties, hypodermics, knives too. Meant to do her harm. Like I mentioned, he drugged her." Suddenly, a familiar but old song, "I'm Every Woman," blared from her phone. "Where did that come from?" Cowboy asked, throwing the cigarette into the sink.

"Her phone. Incoming call. Weird choice. Before her time. Must mean something." I turned the volume down.

"Yeah, it means she's got weird taste in music," Cowboy said, shaking his head. "Here's hoping she gives me what I need, naturally." He held his beer up for a toast. The song continued to play until the caller, someone named Sarah, gave up.

"Most girls have zillions of pics and selfies galore," I said, scrolling again through the device. "This girl only has a handful. The rest are pictures of DIY projects. Doesn't seem right. My gut tells me something's amiss. A young girl should have an exploding phone. She doesn't. No images of family either. It's suspicious. Nothing on here but hundreds of eBooks."

"So what? I wasn't keen on mine, and you weren't fond of your dad. And so she's into books, like you. They were all over her apartment, too. Spilling from the shelves and piled on the floor. Art, mythology, travel, romance novels too. What's with girls and their romance novels?" He laughed. "She ain't gonna find romance with the Knights, is she, WM? And two copies of *It* by Stephen King. Why two?"

Interesting question. Our club, which specializes in BDSM, was a dream come true if horror was the new girl's thing. If Cowboy, the Chief Motherfucker in Charge, didn't scare the life out of her, nothing and nobody would.

I shut the phone off. *Dump it*, my head told me. Too many unanswered questions, or answers that didn't make sense. I removed the SIM card, snapped it in half, took the pieces out the back door, threw them and the phone in our fire pit. I added some kindling and bigger slabs of wood, sprinkled charcoal fluid on everything, and lit it up. *Woosh*—the flames forced me back. Then I remembered the watch and flung it in, too. The colorful band melted and turned into black goo, and a chemical smell permeated the air. *Now I don't have to worry.*

But I realized I was lying to myself. No pictures of parents or boyfriends? Something was off. A yoga teacher wanting to come here? Didn't smell right. But when the prez told me something, I tried to believe.

Cowboy stepped out of the kitchen door, carrying two beers, and crossed over to the bonfire. "Gonna start with her in the morning?" he asked, handing me a beer.

"Yeah. I know you don't want to hear this, but she's not like the others." I took a sip. "We usually give them better lives. Get them off of drugs, eating three meals a day, getting eight hours of sleep a night. This one already had a life. Plus, her confidence is a problem." I used my bottle to point at Cowboy's nose. "Tried to tell me how to make a bed too. You believe that? I can't recall the others ever telling me how to do anything. She looked me in the eyes, and *didn't look away.*"

"She's different, I agree." Cowboy nodded his head up and down. "But she'll learn. Why can't we ride a winner for once? It'll be fun, having a girl who's more of a challenge."

"I don't require fun," I said, taking another sip.

"Yeah, you'd have to take that stick out of your ass," Cowboy teased. "As I said, she agreed to come. Peace, love, harmony and all that." He chuckled.

"And if she doesn't work out?" I asked.

Cowboy smiled down at the embers in the fire pit and then across the desert into darkness. "You know, like our thing—no quitting, no going back until she puts in the time. Our mini crematorium will handle her." He pointed at the fire pit, then chugged the remainder of his beer, threw the bottle into the trash, and left me alone with my thoughts and my drink. Not a thing I enjoyed. My thoughts, that is.

I returned to the clubhouse, grabbed the girl's yoga mat and purse from the kitchen floor, and went to my room. I climbed up the three flights, remembering what one of our girls had once said about Cowboy: 'He's like a mango they tricked you into buying at the grocery store, pretty on the outside but tough inside.' My experience with Cowboy up to now had been up and down, but one thing I knew for sure—once Cowboy decided on something, there was no way around it. Whatever I thought was wrong with the new asset had to be dealt with. Step one, get rid of all of the yoga mumbo-jumbo in her head, scrub her mind clean, and squeeze my stuff in there somewhere. She'd fight me. They all did. *So much easier if she's a snotty bitch.*

****

It angered Rory when the man called WM had demanded her bracelet. Covered with angel wings, it was a talisman that had given her the will to fly away from her past. By taking it, he'd figuratively clipped her wings. He had stared into space with watery brown-gold eyes, the color of the tiger's eye stone in her mother's ring. His lips had been frozen in a straight line, not smiling. She wondered if he even could. Her mother never smiled at her either. The thing she had noticed most about him, though, was his fear, cloaked in cockiness. *'I'll do the thinking and you'll do what I tell you to do'* indeed.

Rory rubbed her hands together and wrapped her arms around herself, shivering, placing a blanket over her feet and another one on her lap. She should have gone to the police after being attacked on the street, but they would have asked for ID, and hers might've raised questions. At her apartment, the hypodermic Lloyd had shot her with had left her confused, and after Blondie had threatened to call the police, leaving Vegas suddenly became a priority. She admitted to herself that she was also intimidated by Blondie. Ballooned arms, a body coated with ink, and a fake smile that never reached his eyes. *A mistake, coming here.*

The room was similar in size to the one in Rory's mother's trailer. A prison. Concrete cinder block walls, a twin bed, a toilet, a stool, and a small table, all of it dimly lit. A wood door with a barred gate on the top portion, leading to a hallway of other doors, contributed to its coldness. Some rooms had been occupied with women when she'd passed, others empty, their doors open and unlocked. The back wall of her room offered a window with a view. She crawled from the bed, stood on her tiptoes, and peeked out. She saw a lit parking lot filled with bikes and an oversized garage, the moon shining down. Still there, high in the sky, pale yellow, swollen—her truth moon. The one she sent her wishes to, the one she told her secrets to, the one she prayed to. *I pray things turn out well for me, truth moon.*

A noise in the corridor made Rory turn. A woman who looked like a Modigliani painting come to life entered her room, carrying a tray, while the man from before who made her bed, named Turk, waited outside. "I'm Anemone, but you can call me Anna," she said. Graceful; not a drop of the tea spilled from the over-filled mug. "If you need anything, I'll get it for you. I have to run it by WM, of course, and see if it's all right." Her eyes darted back and forth. "He has certain rules, especially in the beginning. But he's fair as long as you don't give him a hard time." Anna placed the drink and a sandwich on the small table. "Cowboy's different. Be careful." Her red, red lips slid downward. "He's dangerous. The only good thing, one giant explosion and he's done. Welcome to our little Garden of Eden." She chattered nervously and backed out of the room.

"Thank you," Rory said, picking up the teacup and taking a sip, as Turk locked the gate and they walked away. *Chai, my favorite.*

The sandwich had turkey, so it was out of the question and who knew what kind of bread it was. She didn't touch it, instead laid down and played back her 'drug dream.'

Prone on a burial pyre, a black crow's sharp beak touched her lips, parting them, sucking the spiders from her. Emptied, the bird cleaned her as if one of its own. Its eyes shimmered greenish-blue like black pearls, and its beak was dark and shiny like a Tourmaline stone. It spoke in a language unknown to her, but somehow she deciphered its meaning telepathically, only to lose it seconds later. She begged to hear and understand it again. The bird, its feathers silken with shine, ignored her pleas. It released her hair from its talons, flapped its wings, dove and dipped as if waving goodbye, and disappeared. *How does something so dark deliver comfort?*

Later in the water, she had searched for the creature or anything to keep her tethered to this world. Losing herself, she'd sunk deeper into waters of sorrow until reaching a tunnel of bright light. She'd swum toward it, but a man had pulled her back reeling her in like a fish, keeping her in this world. Warm hands had caressed her body and carried her from the water. She had come alive again wrapped in his arms, his eyes like the birds, piercing but wise and knowing. When she'd told him she preferred the weepy, watery world below, he had burst out in anger. Yet he still cared, wrapping her in a blanket.

Now, she drifted in and out of consciousness, waiting for sleep to take her away.

****

I placed the woman's bracelet next to Chet's silver feather in a box on my nightstand, and the yoga mat against the wall. The phone had revealed little about our newest recruit. Would the girl's purse divulge more?

I sat on my bed and ran my fingers across the suede—comfy and supple. Dark gray in color, bucket-shaped, it collapsed in my lap as I opened it. Hopefully the girl would go down this easy, and be as yielding. I pulled out a wallet, my index finger sliding across the embroidered Hello Kitty design decorating the front. It made me smile. "Hello, Kitty," I said. I'd never noticed the missing mouth before. Life would be simpler and more enjoyable if nobody had mouths.

I flipped open the money part of the billfold—empty. The card section held a blood donor card. Her name was Rory Riley, blood type B positive. Other than that, just a couple of grocery store customer cards. No driver's license, no credit cards. Who didn't have formal identification? No lipstick, makeup, mirror or hairbrush inside the purse, either. It would likely affect her earnings if she didn't care about her looks.

The only other thing inside, buried at the bottom, was a small book, *The Yoga Sutras of Patanjali*. I read a few pages. The ten commandments without the moral imperatives. One topic was titled 'Ahimsa'—not judging others. *Forget that. Prepare for judgment from your master, little one.*

I returned everything to the wallet, and then put the wallet and book back in the purse. I squirreled the bag in the back of my closet with the mat. At some point, I needed to dump it. Cowboy wanting to get rid of the phone had raised my suspicions. I wanted no connection to this girl in my possession. *Welcome to your new life, Rory Riley.*

A quartet of nightmares blitzed my sleep that night, each escalating in intensity or absurdity. The new girl fell down the stairs and broke her neck. An assailant left the new girl stabbed and bleeding. The new girl went swimming, got a cramp, sank to the bottom like a heavy stone, and drowned. In the last one, the new girl refused to eat anything, wasted away, turned into a skeleton, and then pursued me with a canister of artificial cheese until I woke up, exhausted. *Invading my dreams—and not in a good way.*

****

The phone vibrated near my pillow, waking me. "That new chick isn't eating," Turk said. "Maybe come check on her."

"Roger that, I'll be down shortly," I said, throwing my cell on the pillow. I looked up at the glass ceiling I'd designed and built myself. The sun was powerful today, the perfect alarm clock. It would've woken me if the phone hadn't. *Not even twenty-four hours and the girl's already a problem.*

My lower back spasmed as I stumbled out of bed. An injury I'd learned how to live with. Luckier than the other guys in the vehicle. They weren't living at all. I dressed, body hunched over, and headed to the kitchen for my drug of choice.

Turk pointed to the uneaten breakfast and another plate with a leftover sandwich. It wasn't a 'call out the hounds' situation yet, but I didn't want to give my nightmare a chance to come to fruition. Chief, one of my club brothers, next in line for coffee, said, "Maybe she's too good for our cuisine," and smiled.

My face twisted. "We'll see about that," I replied. My back pain was contributing to my shitty mood. I picked up the plate of eggs and headed down the steps.

The other women moved toward their open doors when they saw me. Nosy bitches, all. She lay curled in a fetal position and faced the wall. "Rory," I called. I seldom raised my voice beyond a whisper with the others. Didn't need to. They hung on every word. I was their god. It sounded egotistical, but it's the truth. I decided when and where they went, and what they wore. I kept them safe. Even the not-so-bright ones understood it was best to smarten up and listen. Their well-being depended on me.

She lifted her head and turned over. Her skin was still the color of a corpse, white and blue. Strands of hair shot in every direction possible, an explosion on her head. Dark circles under her eyes and a wrinkled shirt completed her fashion statement. Like me, she hadn't fared well through the night.

"Come over here," I ordered. She rolled out of the small bed and approached me. "Why didn't you eat?" I asked, waving the plate back and forth in front of her, vying for her attention. "You're mistaken if you think you're going to get something better."

With a subtle shake of her head and a sigh, Rory returned to her bed, plunked down, and twisted a piece of her hair around her finger. Her face got redder as her eyes avoided mine.

I opened the door and entered her space. "I expect an answer when I ask a question, and you don't move unless I tell you to." She seemed clueless in sensing my displeasure, or if she did, she didn't give a crap. *I kind of like that.*

"I wish I could. I'm hungry," Rory said. Her eyes were wavering and watery, a crease forming above her nose, "But I can't. I have celiac disease. I can't eat wheat. If I do, I'll get sick. I'm a Buddhist too, and we don't hurt sentient life through cruel practices. So meat and eggs are out too. Sorry, bro." She wrung her hands and looked down at the floor.

Bro? Buddhist? I didn't realize someone could speak that fast. The celiac part seemed plausible. Her eyes were fixed on the floor—a good sign. I handed the plate off to Turk and instructed him to locate paper and a pen. "We'll accommodate your medical issues and beliefs," I said, grunting as I parked myself next to her on the bed. "But do not ever address me as 'bro.' Understand? Use 'Sir.'"

She nodded her head up and down.

"A nod is not what I asked you for," I corrected.

She sat there as if in deep thought, then mumbled softly, "Yes, Sir."

My back spasmed and I ignored it. Too busy observing the girl shrink away. As we discussed her condition and dietary needs and made a list of appropriate foods, I noticed Rory's body settling—her breathing slowed, and her hands stopped twitching. I got up to leave when we finished our discussion but discovered my back had seized up and I couldn't. "Ah, crap," I gasped, hobbling on one foot, unable to straighten up.

"Is it your gluteus medius, Sir?" she asked.

"Just a muscle spasm." I limped towards the gate, hunched over.

The girl came at me like a kung fu master, the sides of her hands pointed and stiff. She moved quickly, applying a series of blows on either side of my spine, making it emit sounds—*rack clack crack*. Something gave. I pushed my shoulders back and straightened up, the pain gone. Whatever she'd done worked.

"How's that feel?" she asked, forehead furrowed.

"Better," I acknowledged.

She walked behind me and gently adjusted my shoulders and hips. "Don't hunch," she said. "Keep your shoulders back and your head level. Use all three corners of both feet." She rambled on about the foot, describing it as a triangle. I didn't hang around and left the room quickly, embarrassed.

"Put ice on it for the inflammation, and drink lots of water for the healing," she called out as I walked down the corridor, some of the women staring from their rooms. "Oh, add Arnica gel to the list too. Rub it on your back. It reduces pain." None of the others had ever put their hands on me, especially without permission. The girl had overstepped her bounds. *Why would she help me anyway? Brownie points?*

I ran into Turk in the passageway and handed him the list. "Buy nothing with gluten. Read the labels on everything." Turk's forehead creased, and a long sigh escaped his lips as I passed my credit card over. "It's not all peaches and cream in an OMC. We do what we have to, and this one needs different food. Make sure it reads gluten-free, preferably manufactured in a gluten-free facility. She's a vegetarian and allergic to dairy products too, so purchase fresh or frozen fruits and vegetables, and coconut or almond milk. Get some vegetable-based protein powder if you can find it."

I returned to Rory's room and handed her a towel. "The bathing area is open," I said. "You've got one hour. Come with me."

The nearer we got to our destination, the tighter she wrapped the shirt around her body, and the closer she brought the towel to her chest. Her eyes widened as we reached the room and she soaked in all the activity in the shiny, tiled space.

"Come on, Rory, you're holding up the others," I said. "Remove your shirt, select an empty tub or shower, and jump on it."

Her eyes looked back and forth, then connected with mine. "Nope," she said and bolted down the hall like a runaway horse.

I chased after her and caught her arm, preventing her from entering her room. She leaned backward and dug her heels into the floor, becoming a mule with a poor attitude. "You're going," I said under my breath. Rory's refusal to walk was like carrying a heavy backpack on maneuvers, but I got her there, almost dragging her.

As she lay in a heap in front of me, the other women froze, their eyes and mouths open wide. "Back to your rooms," I said, not wanting to provide an audience for Rory acting out. Water splashed noisily and lapped over the rims of the tubs on the tile floor. Showers turned off in unison as the girls moved out hastily, grabbing towels and robes. Within seconds the place was empty, except for us. I crouched next to Rory, invading her space. She flinched and scooted away on her rump until I seized her hands, holding her in place.

"If you wanted to destroy me," Rory said, her eyes not leaving mine, "you should have let me go last night when I died."

"You're being dramatic. A bath will destroy you?"

"I'm not clueless. I understand what you're doing. Making me undress in front of strangers takes away my dignity and gives me no choices. It mentally breaks me down."

I released Rory's hands and stood over her. "I can't shut down the entire area so that you can bathe privately. If that's a problem, I'll just bring a bucket to your room. Now you have a choice. Happy?" She said nothing. Rory was turning into a challenge to figure out. *One minute a mouse and the next minute a lion.*

I considered her words as I strode down the corridor. How did she know she didn't have a pulse last night? None of the women had ever accused me of 'breaking' them. I realized if I was in her position, I would've acted the same, or probably worse. I chuckled, then stopped. I never identified with the others. It wasn't a good idea to do it with her. I admired the way she stood her ground and called me out, though. No one had done it since my mother.

Chapter 4

Gotcha Pretty One

Rory didn't even change in front of others at the gym she attended five days a week, and now some bossy bad boy was expecting her to parade naked in front of others? *No way!* He was cray if he thought she'd be ordered about like some private in basic training.

The bathing area was devoid of people. The cellar was quiet except for music playing in someone's room. "No," a Meghan Trainor song drifted down the passageway. Rory snooped around, looking for possible weapons, and selected a can off the counter. After putting on some extra clothes she found in a hamper, she glanced down the hall. The rectangular emergency electrical signage attached to the wall cast a red glow and provided light.

She snuck towards the row of three doors at the end, passing empty rooms, until a slurping noise caught her attention. Rory gazed into the room and looked down. A woman was on her knees, nestled between jean-covered legs. Rory followed the jeans up to a man's face partially hidden in shadow.

He turned towards her.

Enough light from a small window revealed his identity—WM. He sat on the bed, his head and back resting against the wall, relaxed, with his hands on his partially opened thighs. The woman's long hair fell on his lap as she moved up and down, taking his cock in her mouth again and again. *George tried to make me do that.*

WM's eyes shifted to hers. He didn't stop the woman. He smiled and winked at Rory instead. He wrapped a bunch of curly, blonde hair in his fist and began pulling, simultaneously murmuring to the woman. He seemed to be directing the woman, changing her position, and timing. *Was WM instructing the woman to go faster or not stop?* Rory froze in place, mesmerized as the woman came down more quickly and WM's thighs flexed, mouth opened as if about to—

Rory bolted, unwilling to watch anymore, running back to the bathing area. She paced back and forth on the checkerboard tile floor. Multiple Rory's appeared and mocked her from the row of mirrors. There was no escaping the reason she was there anymore—*I'm going to have to do that and more.* She heaved the can of hairspray at her many selves. Shattered glass fragments shot everywhere, with other pieces staying attached to the wall, jagged and broken. *Just like me*, she thought. She picked up the cannister where it had landed. *I need to leave. But where? And how? I don't even know where I am, exactly...It doesn't matter. I can't give up.*

Rory ran, making a beeline for the last door on the left, opening to a set of stairs. Her eyes followed them up as they disappeared into the darkness. She placed her hand on wrought iron, cold radiating through her body. The way the metal twisted against her fingers reminded her of the railing she had touched last night. She took a step, then another, then closed the door behind her, the walls closed in around her.

She cocked her head, listening, wiping her toes

loose of fragments as she climbed. "Yuck," she whispered. Dust and other debris she couldn't identify in pitch blackness clung to them. When she reached a larger landing, a stabbing sensation shot through the sole of her foot. She bit down on her bottom lip to keep from crying out. Blackness surrounded her, making it impractical to check her wound, but the liquid pooling under her foot must have been blood.

She kept climbing until she reached the slivers of light at the sides, bottom and top of a doorway. She pressed her ear to the wood, listening. Nothing, just the rhythm of her heartbeat echoing in her head. *Is this the door to the kitchen?*

Rory's fingers danced around the knob and stopped. Her jaw tensed and her fingers trembled. Dizziness forced her to take a step backward as she gripped it tighter.

Hands sweaty, fingers itchy, she took a deep breath. "Open it. Stop being a baby," she whispered. She turned it as hard as she could and pushed.

Nothing, it didn't budge. She tried again. The door refused to open. *Locked?*

She let go, arms relaxed at her side, contemplating her next move, when there was a sudden movement. Air blew across her body, and an orb of shocking yellow light blinded her. Rory closed her eyes and stepped away, wobbling and stumbling backward. Her hands reached and clawed for something to hold onto to keep her from falling, making her drop the canister. Large, powerful hands latched on, grasping her shoulders, bringing her into a protective bear hug. WM's firm voice rang out. "Gotcha, pretty one."

The canister hit each step, *clunk, clunk, clunk,* until

reaching its ultimate resting place, the cellar floor. The aerosol nozzle made a dying declaration and a critique of Rory's breakout attempt—*hiss, hiss, hiss*.

"You weren't going to hurt me with that, were you?" WM asked. *His arms are radiating heat everywhere*, she thought. *I mean everywhere. Yikes, don't be an idiot. He's probably a felon wanted in three states. Shut up, I'm wanted too. Someday soon I might appear on America's Most Wanted.*

****

The best part of Ivy's blowjob today—the new girl spying on me and the expression of shock she wore. I didn't know what to think when Rory's eyes filled with fear, other than I better keep an eye on her. I hadn't expected she'd be afraid. If I had, I would have stopped and made her leave.

I viewed the entire video again on my phone, including her meltdown in the shower area when she broke the mirror. *I should probably punish her for that.*

As Rory tried to pull herself together in the showers, I used the stairs in the dungeon to bring me upstairs. I had a feeling she might run. I waited in the kitchen, listening. One of the steps creaked. I'd tried climbing them myself and found it impossible not to make noise. I hadn't replaced them for exactly that reason. If any of the girls tried sneaking out to meet a boyfriend at night, or some meathead male tried to go downstairs uninvited, I'd hear. Of course, Rory's on the small end of size, an advantage.

The latch jiggled and I waited. She must have thought it locked, but I was merely holding it in place. I could almost feel her panic surging through the brass into my hand. I thought about releasing my hold but changed my mind in case she lost her balance. I waited until the knob stopped moving, then opened the door, scooping her up as she fell backwards.

"Gotcha, pretty one. Now we're even," I said as I brought her close, head pressed against my chest. The scent of a Creamsicle—

"Let go," she said. Body tensing, struggling to push me away, unable to do so, she turned her face up to me. "Why do you think we're even?" she asked, her eyes filled with curiosity.

"On the stairs the other night, I slipped and you helped me. Today I returned the favor," I said.

Her green eyes grew darker and her pupils enormous. "If you believe in checks and balances, help me get out of here."

"Now why would I do that? I thought you wanted to come here." I grinned, enjoying the banter. None of the others dared argue.

"I thought maybe I did, but—"

"I expect you to keep your commitment," I said in a more serious tone. "It may take a day or two to adjust. If longer, I may need to do something extra. We lock these upper-level doors for your safety, to keep the men out."

Rory continued pushing me away. "If you expect me to go along with everything you say, you've taken the wrong girl."

I tightened my grip until she stopped. "Actually, I do expect that. So I guess we both have our work cut out for us. Go." I spun her around to face the steps, holding on to one arm to keep her from falling, and escorted her back down and into the corridor. She entered the room of her own volition, and that's when I noticed blood—a trail of it on the floor and back down the hallway. "What happened?" I asked, pointing at the stain by her foot.

"Nothing," she said.

"Hand over the pants and hoodie. You only wear clothes I give you, and you haven't earned those."

In a huff, Rory removed them begrudgingly, throwing them in a heap outside the gate in the hallway.

"Next time fold them properly and pass them to me." I used my boot to kick them to the wall. No way would I pick up her clothes. *I'm a Dom.*

Rory ignored me, returning to her bed, still wearing the dirty white shirt. I could see the bottom of her feet as they hung off the edge. One bled.

"I'll send Turk down with something for your foot. Don't break mirrors and you won't cut yourself." She refused to respond.

I needed to address the way she ignored me and moved without direction, but before I could, she piped up with, "Why am I here, Mr. Whoremaster?" She climbed up off the bed and faced me.

It was all I could do to contain myself. *Mr. Whoremaster?* "That's not how I asked to be addressed. Try again."

"Why am I here, WM?" Rory asked.

What the hell? I removed my shades, meeting her eyes. "Cowboy said you agreed to come here."

"I did, kind of, but he didn't provide any details. What's my function?"

"You're an intelligent young woman. I think after watching me with your next-door neighbor Ivy, you can figure it out," I said, holding my laughter back.

Rory's face turned a glorious shade of crimson. "In that case, I imagine I'm to…" She took two deep breaths before proceeding, shifting her gaze back to my eyes accusingly. "To perform sexual favors?"

I read her eyes and knew what she thought. That I was a heartless shit. And no doubt about it, I was headed in that direction. "Correct. I'll give you the details and teach you what you need to learn, like I did with Ivy, when the time comes." I winked at her. "For now, no more hanging around the steps." She said nothing, but her face turned even redder. She looked away. "At least you have one thing going for you," I continued. "You know when to keep your mouth shut."

"Maybe you should try it as well, WM," she said smoothly, strutting back to the bed and standing in front of it with arms crossed, staring me down.

"I enjoy the verbal sparring, Rory. But I suggest you be smart about it. Doing it at the wrong time could be trouble. Be careful around Cowboy, for example. He's not likely to put up with talking back. Like I said earlier, part of my job is keeping you safe. You've already gotten away with something most women around here don't. I don't think Cowboy will let anything more go."

Rory flopped back on the bed and lay down. She threw her arm back so the top of her hand was covering her forehead, as if ready to faint. "Right," she said, her voice weary. "He's obviously not as accommodating as you."

After heading down the hall, I stopped in the bathing area. As I swept up the broken glass, I smiled. Strange, how I had to lay the job duties out for her. Leave it to Cowboy to skip the details. Climbing the stairs to the kitchen, I replayed the scene on the steps when I held her in my arms. She felt good nestled there, and her lips looked so soft and pretty. I'd like to feel her lips on my—

Soon, I told myself.

I was relieved Rory hadn't fallen and broken her neck, like in my dream. A cut foot I could deal with. Another part of my nightmare averted. She had me jazzed, and I was standing at attention just from having held her a little earlier.

An old chrome motorcycle wheel converted into a ceiling lamp hovered over the kitchen table, like a flying saucer with aliens, searching for intelligent human life. I wondered if I'd meet their requirements. My ex always accused me of being less than human.

Turk handed me the credit card and grocery-store receipt. "Two hundred and fifty dollars?" I asked.

"Yeah. That hippie shit's expensive."

"Another thing, Turk. You need to be careful to lock the doors leading to the kitchen and outside until she settles down. She tried to leave."

"Really?" Turk's eyes opened wide. "Never happened before with the others."

"Yeah. This one's different. Inform the rest of the guys, too. She's a rainbow, a recruit. Hopefully in a few days she'll settle down, and we can go back to normal and leave the door unlocked during daytime hours."

"Sounds good."

"When you take her lunch down, check her foot. She cut it. Clean and cover it with a bandage and find her a clean shirt. Also, as soon as possible, mop the floor in the bathing area. A mirror broke. I swept up all the broken glass, but smaller pieces could still be about."

Turk returned to the kitchen a short while later with an empty plate and a Cheshire Cat smile that revealed his teeth. "Just a splinter. I yanked it right out." He held it out for me to examine. "She didn't cry a bit and thanked me for my efforts. Asked my name too."

"Don't get chummy. I need her dependent on me, not you. If you can't do what I'm requesting, I'll find someone else."

Turk lost his smile. "I understand. I won't talk to her, I promise."

Not a glamour girl, but Rory turned men's heads effortlessly. According to Johnny, Cowboy wanted her and no other. Getting kicked in the nose did nothing to dampen his enthusiasm. Then Cowboy developed a case of amnesia and transformed into a proper English gentleman when he brought her in and shushed all his club brothers, not wanting to scare 'his poor little lamb.'

I wasn't immune either. Usually, I ran a tight ship and kept things the same for all the women. This morning I let her shower alone and gave her choices. On top of that, I didn't punish her for breaking the mirror. I have little confidence in Turk's commitment to not talking to her. None.

I needed to get my head straight. Show her exactly how things worked here. *Tonight.*

****

Church, the first Thursday of the month, was always held in the hall. The club's monthly bitchfest usually started quietly enough, but by the end of the meeting it almost always turned into a wild free-for-all. No reason this one would be any different.

I didn't enjoy clutter of any kind, and that's what the room was full of. The first thing a person noticed was an enormous sign, dead center, hanging in front of the room. KNIGHTS OF STEEL it read, in a strong serif font, all caps in black. Underneath, our center patch, a sea of blood, in red of course, with a knight's helmet in gold, our other color. In a smaller writing, our motto: *We Take*

Care of Our Own. Truth. Hopefully it wouldn't turn out badly, like a bullet in the head. The rest of the wood-paneled walls were covered with club memorabilia celebrating our club member's misdeeds, mischief, and misdemeanors through the years. Much of it should never have been photographed in my opinion—too easily used as evidence.

Loyalty was an essential requirement in a club like ours. Still, loyalty changed, depending on who was in power and who wanted to be. After six years of watching the jealousy and greed of some of my brothers, the honeymoon was long over. The good thing about the Knights was that we'd been lucky compared to other MCs. Our presidents all came from one family for the last seventeen years which provided some stability, but insurrection was always lurking. Luckily Cowboy was a paranoid motherfucker, and had no problem mounting a defense against anyone he thought a threat, perceived or imagined. The sea of blood in our center patch made perfect sense, considering Cowboy's involvement.

The Knights of Steel was the oldest OMC in Nevada. Before Cowboy was club president, his brother Whiskey had held the reins. That was until he was shipped off to the federal penitentiary in Lompoc for the manufacture and distribution of methamphetamine. Illegal shit. My idea was to expand our involvement in prostitution, specialize in BDSM, create our own dungeon, and use internet-style marketing to promote our X-rated films, taking us in our current direction. Slightly legal. Since then, no arrests and the money was flowing in. Sex, it seemed, sells.

My favorite thing about the room was elevated on a stand in the corner: an original Indian Chief motorcycle from 1953, the year the club was founded. I had spent hours resurrecting the old bike I'd found in pieces when I was a prospect, only for it to become a bone of contention. Some members wanted to keep it to celebrate the club's past, and others wanted to sell it for the money it could bring at auction. I attached more importance to this motorcycle than any past lover, and would sooner part with a kidney. I enjoyed finding something others ignored or considered a mess, and turning it into something valuable and coveted.

The treasurer's report was the first thing on the agenda. Of course, the expenditure on Rory's food bill created questions. "Why does the broad eat so many lemons and limes?" one member asked. I ignored the question. She'd explained the anti-inflammatory benefits of citrus fruits this morning, and I wasn't about to open that can of worms with my brothers.

"How come she can't eat what the others do?" another member inquired. I'd printed materials from the Web on celiac disease. They had gotten that all right. But the meat thing, most members wanted her to have a hamburger and be quiet about it.

The big issue, though, was the brothers had never met a Buddhist before. "A Buddhist hooker?" one asked. "How's that gonna play out? Will she meditate before each client, then bang a gong when he cums?" The members hooted and shared high-fives.

"Bring the new one up here," Cowboy said, annoyed. When Turk looked at him with confusion, Cowboy threw his hands in the air and added, "Yeah, now."

A few minutes passed before the door sprung open, and Turk guided Rory in. It didn't take long for things to go wrong.

She took a long look around and said, "This isn't a church." The whole place went nuts, the guys laughing, stomping their feet and clapping.

I got out of my seat and went to her side. "Calm down, you're only visiting," I said.

"I'm not dressed for visiting," she retorted, eyes angry. She still wore a man's white shirt, but at least it appeared clean. It hung down past her thighs, doing nothing to show off her body. I thought other things more enticing. Her hair pulled back in a ponytail, for instance, showed off her cheekbones, enormous eyes, and luscious lips. I knew some of the muscle heads would appreciate her first-rate legs and well-developed calves, too.

Louie, Cowboy's sergeant-at-arms, bounced from his chair and approached her. "Let's see what we're working with," he said.

She flinched away from him, her torso twisting away as she said in a nasty tone, "Stop touching me, you pervert." My hands slid down my face as hysterical laughter echoed through the space. Rory raising her voice to a member was a sure-fire way to rack up punishment. I wasn't fond of Louie putting hands on her, but he was a brother and Cowboy's right-hand man.

The next thing I knew, Louie had started fumbling and wrestling with the buttons on her shirt, while Turk held Rory's shoulders. "You thought I was a pervert before? Wait until I get these undone, honey."

Rory struggled as Louie cackled and buttons popped. There was nowhere for her to go with two hundred and thirty pounds of Turk behind her. Once the shirt opened and exposed her bra, it got eerily quiet. She had everyone's complete attention. Cowboy wasn't wrong about this girl—she was stunning—but this whole thing seemed wrong. We'd had other women up here, and it had never gone down like this.

I moved closer. I couldn't leave her unprotected, as the guys got out of their chairs and walked up to get a better look. "Back up," I said as they ogled her up and down and bobbed their heads in approval. A couple of "ooh's" and "ahh's" were let loose. Fit and toned, she didn't have those fake boobs like so many of the girls we recruited. She had cut muscles, too, and a six-pack. A six-pack on a girl, damn sexy. The piercing above her belly button was another thing they liked. I had thought better of removing that particular jewelry.

Rory's eyes transformed as she stood on display, getting slitty as she looked around the room, challenging each member to make them look away. Jinks, an old-timer, said, "WM, you need to work with her. She shouldn't be sayin' nothing or lookin' us in the eye."

"It's only her first full day. I haven't worked with her at all." That got a laugh out of Jinks and two other guys.

Rory elbowed me, her face red. "Why are they laughing at me?"

"They're not. They're laughing at me."

Chief, one of the longest-standing members, got out of his chair and, before I could stop him, came behind Rory and grabbed hold of her scrunchy. She pulled away, making her hair come loose, curls floating down her back like a model in a photoshoot.

"What color is her hair? Reddish blonde or auburn?" Chief asked. "Hard to tell in this light."

"All those colors," Worm said.

"Is it natural?" Phil asked.

"Can't get all those different shades by dying it," Worm answered.

The entire room fell quiet, hypnotized, when Chief lifted the back of her blouse. Her ass was heart-shaped, tight, and creamy white. A perfect canvas. Framed by a hot-pink, lacy thong—it was spectacular.

Chief broke the spell when he pronounced, "The most magnificent moon ever." Truth. The place went wild in agreement, whooping, clapping, and stomping. Rory's face turned red in embarrassment, and she dropped her head to the floor.

Phil, the treasurer who'd been complaining about the cost of her food, walked up, dazzled by the diamond piercing in her belly button. "Enough. Don't touch," I said, pushing Phil away. Other men were also out of their seats and fast approaching, crowding in, and a few who had been standing on their chairs now jumped down. I placed myself in front of her to offer protection.

Cowboy whistled with his fingers to get everyone's attention, then said, "We've got twenty-four experienced women downstairs you can feel up. Let this one go. We'll have a coming-out celebration when she's ready." The men stomped their feet and went wild, whistling and howling like dogs.

I signaled to Turk, pointing at the door. "Move her out of here. Now!" I yelled. The howls, grunts, and whistles grew louder, my brothers crowding closer. Exploding inside with anger and frustration, my throat closing up, men in my way, I couldn't reach her.

Rory stumbled and went down, sprawled on her stomach against the floor. She lifted her head. "Help me," she begged in a quiet voice, her arms reaching up through a multitude of men's legs towards me.

Chapter 5

Just a Creeper

I lifted Rory from the floor, the men running after her. She clung to me, her face white and eyes pleading as I shoved and beat my brothers away. With Turk leading the way for us, we reached the hallway.

"Wow, that was weird. I didn't expect it to get that wild," Turk said.

"Escort Rory back to her room and give her a snack," I said. "Women are right, men are pigs sometimes."

Rory came at me like a demon possessed. "You're the pig. How dare you treat me like that?" She jabbed a finger at my face. "What kind of man are you? It's going to take more than stale cookies to buy me off." Her voice was low and angry and her teeth were barred.

I slid my sunglasses down off my head and over my face. "We'll discuss it later," I said. I loved her cookie comment, taking the edge off my anxiety about the meeting.

Rory transformed into a bull set to charge, her bare feet slapping the floor, stamping up and down. "I want to discuss it now. And stop hiding behind your shades." Her jaw was tense, as Turk held her arm.

"You keep doing that, you're going to hurt yourself," I said. "You've got one bad foot already. You don't want two. I can tell you're upset, but nothing happened. Maybe you're embarrassed, or you're worried about what may happen, but truthfully nothing occurred tonight, and if it did, learn to control your—"

"I'm not controlling my feelings to make things easier for you and your band of hooligans. You don't get a free pass to act like animals. Not happening. I'm through." And then she slapped my arm.

"You're correct. You're through." I turned to Turk. "Take Rory to her room and skip the cookies since she prefers not to have them."

Then I added in whisper to Turk, "Make her some special tea." He'd know what to do. We placed a sedative in a girl's drink when she had a traumatic event with a john or something similar. I could tell that the 'coming out party' comment was circulating in her brain, and her almost getting trampled didn't help matters. Plus, I wanted her to get some rest after not getting much last night. Another night of missing sleep would set back her training.

"Move," I said, turning back to Rory, pointing the way.

"You're delusional! Controlling! A narcissist! You allowed your friends to humiliate me. They undid my clothing and almost killed me. You can forget me providing sexual favors. You can't make me. Not happening." Rory squeezed my arm and glared at me.

"You're untouched for the most part. And you're correct, I can't make you do anything you don't want to do, so settle down."

She pointed her finger at me again, "You're not a gentleman, just a creeper."

"You're right. I'm no gentleman." I should have

talked Cowboy out of bringing her up. I wished she hadn't come upstairs and I do hide behind my shades. But *creeper*?

"You'll pay. Karmic retribution," Rory seethed, her head turning back.

"How do you think I ended up here, sweetheart?" I professed under my breath, not finding the right words to say back. Nothing but karmic retribution since my mother died. This one seemed to know how to push my buttons. Turk would control the situation when he got Rory back to the room. Eventually, the girl would figure out that throwing fits wouldn't lead anywhere. *I like the fire in her eyes, though.*

The last thing I caught sight of was her backside, hoisted over Turk's shoulder—it looked beautiful, too—and her parting words, "Put me down, lunkhead," fading off as I stepped back into the hall.

The members' consensus was that the new asset was an exciting addition. They liked the way she yelled at Louie and stared them all down, even if I didn't. She earned even more street cred having given Cowboy bruises. Some members respected Cowboy, but quite a few only tolerated him because of his brother, Whiskey, who they held in high regard because he accepted a twenty-year plea deal rather than let any other club member do time. Another fourteen years to go, or less with good behavior.

The barkeeper Hammer, a member and ex-boxer, winked at me. "I like any girl that can give a fella a black eye. Damn impressive."

"We should put them all on vegetarian diets, if they can look like her," Chief said. The room thundered with laughter, and members wanted to know how long until she'd be ready to ride.

I swallowed and felt something hurt in the pit of my stomach. "Too early to predict," I said. Truth. The idea of anyone laying a hand on her filled me with uneasiness.

*****

An eerie hush settled as I descended into darkness. The reposado, tequila from our bar had left my mouth burning, my belly warm and fuzziness filling my head. I had needed those shots after Rory's words had made me reflect, something I'd avoided since walking out on the red, white, and blue and becoming a member of the Knights of Steel Outlaw Motorcycle Club. Is this what I was meant for—tearing girls down and building them into something we could use?

All the rooms were empty except the last one; the other women were upstairs entertaining my brothers. Rory was one of the lucky ones tonight. I peered through the bars, observing. She looked A-okay sleeping. Curled in a ball, hands positioned underneath one cheek, doll-like, lips pursed, kissable.

I wish I could stop my brain from working. I'd like to go in there and take her in every way I knew. And I knew a lot of ways. But I couldn't, not yet. What kind of man would I be if I stayed here a few more years? Had I always been such an asshole?

My eyes traveled around her room. Crap. Writings and drawings were scattered around the bed. How had she gotten her hands on paper and a pen? Subs had to earn those, and she hadn't. No keys on me. A mop leaning against the opposite wall in the corridor could help. After one try, I swept them up.

Two poems seemed about recent events. One read:
They all saw

But didn't see
Me
He tried to touch
Me
I imagined his hand rough
On my nipple
But he couldn't
Touch the real
Me
Buried deep inside.

That one was dark. Cowboy shouldn't have put her on display. *Why did she come here?*

The other one read:

I soared free through the heavens
Saw everything below
Understood everything and everyone
Love was everywhere
Suddenly
A potent force pulled me back
It was cold and dark
A man held me there
I wanted to go back
He wouldn't let go
There is no heaven
Only hell from here

I knew what that one was about. The other night when I saved her life. Only a day and the girl had concluded she'd gone to purgatory. I felt that way myself…about this place. How would she feel in a week, a month? One reason I didn't allow subs writing materials was that their focus should be on me, not on what was in their head. But in this case, it provided—

"Give them back. Those belong to me," a shrill voice rang out. Rory stood before me like some kind of auburn-haired witch, eyes burning, shaking her finger at me again. Whatever Turk had given her hadn't done a darn thing. Good thing the gate was between us when she had sprang up. I hadn't been prepared. *Losing my edge*.

"You own nothing I didn't give you," I replied, coming back at her. "I own you, little one, and since that's the case, I suggest you lose the attitude."

"I need them back." Her eyes softened and shone with wetness. "Those words are my inner thoughts."

"Like I said, I own you and your inner thoughts. See?" I shuffled the papers slowly in front of her.

"It's the only way I can keep going," she whined, shoulders slumping and a couple of tears breaking loose.

"You can do better than that. Try again," I said.

"I'm sorry. Please, may I have them, sir? I promise I'll try harder." She bit her lip, her tilted head looking up at me with her voice softening like a song.

"That's more like it. You apologized, said please and sir, and made the sweet pledge. Now you can have them." I offered the papers through the bars of the gate.

Rory grasped them and I seized her hand, pulling her closer to the bars and me. "Stop fighting me and I'll meet your needs," I said. Her eyes opened wide, lips the deep red-pink shade of cherries, and as I tasted them I decided they were even sweeter.

For a brief instant, she went along with me, her eyes closed—into it, until she wasn't. Her eyes popped open as if surprised. She tried to jerk away, struggling, and then stopping. We stared at one another, her green eyes shifting back and forth. Cornered prey.

"Changed your mind?" I asked, my thumb and fingers circling her wrist, holding tight.

"No...ah...yes, you said you'd meet my needs," Rory said, glancing around the room as if searching for answers. "I need something to read. Books."

"You're catching on...*Quid pro quo*. That's how it works. You'll get something when you do something for me," I said, our eyes dueling.

"You already got something. You touched and kissed me," Rory challenged, her chin held high. "You owe me books."

"I owe you nothing," I replied, letting go of her hand. "A kiss and holding my hand doesn't bring reading material, but you're on the right track, and it's a start for not being locked up like an animal. To earn books, you'll be expected to do much more. Tomorrow, I'll tell you exactly what. I suggest you get some sleep."

****

I left her and headed down the corridor. Rory's tears didn't bother me. Girls sometimes cried—but her shoulders were another story. My mother's slumped after tough conversations with my father, so many times. He had destroyed everyone around him, but I got away.

It was shrewd, the way her tactics changed. I shouldn't have returned the papers. She didn't get away scot-free, I did steal a kiss from her, or maybe she gave it. She hadn't fought me right away, a step in the right direction. Too early for books. I didn't need anything taking her attention off of me and what I want her to learn.

Don't trust anyone, especially a woman. It hurt me when I discovered my fiancée screwed other men, almost as much as it hurt losing my friend Chet. Now I kept all the women in my life on a short leash and under my complete control. Most women in the outside world were too intimidated by me and wanted someone they could manipulate—that wouldn't be me. I had made myself unapproachable. Women had a term for my kind—alpha assholes. I was, no doubt. I was at the wheel and if a woman didn't like it, she shouldn't climb aboard. Truth. What was the point of dating anyone anyway? I could have any of the women here, anytime I wanted, with no obligation. The new asset seemed like a straight shooter.

Don't be a chump. My orders were to turn her out. She couldn't belong to me.

"Checkin' on the girl?" Cowboy asked, coming down the cellar stairs, beer in hand.

"Yeah, the meeting unnerved her. Still awake," I said.

"Aren't you a gent? Gonna check on her too. Doin' another kind of checkin'. My dipstick needs greasin'."

"Too early, Cowboy. Couldn't even handle church. Too much touching."

"Come on. Gonna be more than groping comin' her way. I'm surprised by you. Don't fail. Nothin' at the end of the line."

"For her or me?"

Cowboy patted my shoulder and walked down the passageway towards her room.

****

"I was forced to wait until your other visitor left," Cowboy said, staring at her through the barred gate, teeth shining. "WM doesn't know about you. Still thinks you're a Disney princess. We know better, don't we?"

Her body tensed. She clenched her fists behind her back

"Impressive show tonight." He laughed. "Gave Louie a run for his money, for sure, and WM too. Be careful, you're going to end up with a sore bottom, although I sure like the looks of yours." He curled his lips and ran the tip of his tongue across them. *Disgusting.* "Quiet with me? Nothin' to say? Come over here…I'm waiting, and if you make me wait any longer, I'm coming in there."

She bit her lips and drew in a slow, steady breath and walked over to him.

"That's better, up close and personal. Don't pull away. You gotta get used to touchin', according to WM." Cowboy snickered. "I enjoy seeing your breathing change when I talk to you. Your eyes change too, you know that? Your pupils grow bigger, darker. Work on that if you're going to hide things. Found your license— Jersey girl. Funny, you don't appear twenty-three. I'm thinkin' fake. The article all folded up in tiny squares in your wallet is interestin'. People don't save things unless they mean somethin'. Am I right? I'm going to have my man Worm work on it, unless you want to save me the trouble."

She avoided eye contact, fantasizing something bad happening to Cowboy, him falling from a plane without a parachute. She put on a false smile.

"Nothing to say, huh?"

"Who styles your hair?" Rory asked, batting her eyes.

"Ha. Funny. Found your legs, did ya? Keep your secrets." He winked at her. "Be a good girl, do what WM says. You make problems, and he'll come down hard and then I'll make trouble for you, too." Cowboy turned his finger and thumb into a gun and pointed. "Plenty of ammunition, it seems." He walked away.

"Out of my gourd to agree to come here," Rory mumbled as Cowboy walked away.

****

MM—*How did it go?*—
Cowboy—*Princess made debut*—
—*A scene. Princess :'(but Bros <3 her*—
MM—*I bet*—
Cowboy—*?beef w/princess*—
MM—*Just do job*—
—*Put pressure on*—
—*She feels hurt or ur brother will*—
—*I want to C or hear her pain soon*—

****

Two burly, unshaven men hovered above her. "Move," one said right in Rory's face, adding, "Eat your breakfast," slamming a tray down on her table, making her jump. She looked down. Gluten-free toast and water, sparse but a start. This meal was prepared with more care than her supposed family gave. Her mother wouldn't have bought the proper non-dairy milk, and her stepfather had taken delight in sneaking flour into recipes, giving Rory perpetual stomachaches.

The other man placed a metal bucket and an old towel on the floor, the water sloshing. "Clean yourself. WM's working with you," the bucket guy said. "He don't wait, ever." They banged the gate closed and moved down the passageway.

She brushed the tangled hair away from her face and tossed the blanket on the bed. She noticed her poetry and drawings scattered all over the floor from the previous night, like stepping stones.

Hurriedly she collected and concealed them under

the mattress and suppressed a smile, remembering yesterday's success in stealing the pen from WM's pocket and persuading Turk to provide her some paper. Last night she succeeded in the recoup of her journal pages, the cherry on top, even though she had been forced to grovel.

The kiss was something else. WM not letting go, trapping her in his darkness, tasting her—set her imagination on fire. Who would have thought a hardass like him would have lips so soft? He had said to stop fighting. Well, possibly for another smooch. Blushing, she envisioned it. No kiss before had been anything like his. *Whenever he touches me, I can't think straight. It's different with him. I'm not nervous. I should be.*

Cowboy's visit to her room was another story. It was foolish of her to have kept the article.

Rory scrubbed the areas where the men had groped her last night. She wished she could clean the memory away as quickly. She had been a bug ready for dissection at their stupid meeting. How could WM not understand how it crushed her? Or maybe he did and didn't care? At least he'd stood by her side, protecting her, and when she had fallen down, rescuing her. She thought about the stairs yesterday when he had wrapped his arms around her and kept her from—

"Put these on," Turk said, interrupting her thoughts, shoving a brown paper lunch bag through the bars.

She poured the contents onto the bed, revealing a thong and something that looked like a cocktail server's uniform. Rory had never worn this style of underwear before arriving here. Before dressing, she waited for Turk to disappear, then tugged them on and adjusted, attempting to make them comfortable. Impossible. "I hate these things," she said under her breath. Stuck in all the wrong places.

No footwear? They probably figured she'd book it if she got them. She imagined herself streaking down the road in stilettos and a thong as she pulled the tiny shorts over them. Heels would be fabulous. *I could use them as a weapon. Poke Cowboy's eye out.*

Rory slipped on the camisole, and a hush fell over the corridor. She peeked through the opening to determine why and glimpsed WM, Cowboy, and Turk coming. Turk unlocked her door and WM and Cowboy strode in, both dressed in black.

WM didn't wish her a good morning, ask if she slept well, or offer any other courteous conversation. Even her crazy parents had taught her manners. Now here he was again, hiding his eyes behind those ridiculous sunglasses. Fancied himself some movie star. *I don't think so! And Cowboy and his riding crop, who's he supposed to be? Master of the Hounds? Master of Dunces, more like it. Fool.*

"I'm going to go over the rules today," WM said. "Remember them. Obey them. First, you must stand and await further instructions when any man enters a room."

Rory did what WM directed, thinking it would make him stop. It didn't.

"Never look a man in the eye," WM said. "Keep your eyes on the ground, except if instructed otherwise." He paused, waiting for her to glance down.

The reason I'm looking down, fellas, is because there's nothing worth looking at up here. She smirked to herself.

He proceeded when she complied. "Very good. You do things the right way, and you'll earn the kinds of things you like to eat and wear. For instance, today you got toast and water. You do things correctly and tomorrow morning you'll have sunflower butter, and if you do something well the following day, a protein shake. Every day you do something positive, I'll add a reward, something you like."

"Swell," she said, rolling her eyes.

"That brings us to the next rule. Don't speak unless I ask a question and then respond with 'yes' or 'no,' followed by 'Master' or 'Sir,' nothing else."

The idea of calling either of these men her master seemed utterly absurd. A giggle slipped out.

Cowboy invaded her space. "What are you cackling at?" His breath smelled. *Who ate garlic in the morning?* She mistakenly glanced into his blue eyes and wrinkled her nose. "What are you gawking at, bitch?" Then he spun around and started ranting at WM. "Did you see the face she made?"

WM slid his sunglasses off, staring her down. It was better than hearing Cowboy's hollering. At home with her parents, Rory had squirreled away in her closet to escape the screaming. "Repeat the three rules, Rory," WM ordered.

"I'm never to look any man in the eye. I'm to keep my eyes on the ground unless told otherwise. I'm not to speak except when I'm asked a question and then only reply with a 'yes' or 'no' answer, nothing else, *Sir*." At the ashram, her teacher and spiritual advisor had mentioned that children who lived in abusive situations would do whatever they could to avoid confrontation, acting as docile people-pleasers. Her instructor must have been partially correct, because relief flooded her when WM's mouth curved upward with a sly smile.

"She's listening," WM said to Cowboy. "We can attribute her laughter at certain things to immaturity. She's most likely younger than the others."

Pompous ass. "What can I attribute your unacceptable behavior to?" Rory asked. "I can't blame it on your age because you're old enough to know better. It must be unfortunate life events or poor upbringing."

"She's talking back and insulting us?" Cowboy slapped his crop against his thigh, spinning around to face WM. "This girl demands correction. She should pay for the abuse to my nose the other night, too." He moved towards her, waving the crop over his head. *Whoosh, whoosh, whoosh.*

"Stop. I haven't discussed the Dom-sub relationship, and she hasn't agreed to punishment," WM said.

"Got a shiner because of her. We can bend her over your knee and spank her," Cowboy offered. "After a spanking, she'll be new and improved." He continued to bring the crop down on his leg, the leather popper bouncing off his jeans. *Whop, whop.*

"You touched me without my permission. I fought back,'' Rory said. "You got what you deserved for picking on me."

Cowboy charged. Large, calloused hands encased her neck and lifted her from the floor. He pressed her hard against the cinder block wall, leaving her feet dangling. His eyes mutated into snakelike slits. A twisted, turned up lip revealed sharp teeth, and saliva on wet lips suggested he hungered for flesh and blood. *Mine?*

Rory kicked her legs, reached for his hands, took hold of one of his fingers and twisted it back. He didn't loosen his grip. His nose was so close it appeared bulbous and shook as he spoke. "You can't hurt me. You may be queen bee in your world, but you're nothin' in mine, just another bitch requiring re-education."

She turned her head to the side, trying to escape his rancid breath. WM grasped Cowboy's arm, attempting to pull him off her, "You'll crush her larynx. Let her go."

Cowboy pressed harder still. Rory gouged her nails into the flesh between his thumb and index finger, but he ignored that assault as well. "You need to do better than that," Cowboy sneered. Rory kicked out wildly, but she couldn't reach him. She was nothing but a puppet controlled by a malicious marionette. Her air supply dwindling; Cowboy's face was fading. Everything was turning gray.

Abruptly he quit pressing, allowing his disturbing face to come back into focus and his words to roar back. "I run the show, not you. I don't give a rat's ass what you think. Keep your mouth shut or catch more of this." He pressed down on her throat again. "You're in my house now."

"Put her down," WM said, slapping at Cowboy's arm, but he pushed her harder against the wall. Her face must have turned white and WM tackled Cowboy instead. Cowboy fell to the ground. Rory shook loose and slid down the wall.

Rory gasped for air, inhaled deeply several times, and staggered to her feet. Her eyes darted between them both. She charged Cowboy. "How dare you touch me, you chauvinist creep." She backhanded Cowboy, leaving a mark on his cheek.

He was speechless at first, then seconds later he turned to WM, mouthing, "What the fuck?"

But Rory didn't stand around waiting for them to make their next move. She launched herself out the unfastened door, crashing it closed behind her shocked captors, leaving them the captured ones.

Chapter 6

Bullies & Bullets

"The stars don't stop shining in the sky because it's dark. Why should I get down when things appear so?" ~ Rory Riley

Rory careened down the hall as the other women stood by their doors and egged her on, calling, "Go, Rory, go!" She ran up the cellar steps, the ones that led directly outside. She threw the door open wide and stood there several seconds, half-closing her eyes as the sun licked her face.

I did it.

I'm free.

She bolted across the empty parking lot, racing in and out of parked bikes. She spied none with keys in them, and the van that brought her was also nowhere in sight.

The gravel path to her left seemed to lead back to the highway. She'd be too visible if she chose it. Rory ran to the right, toward the desert with rock formations and twisted trees, the jagged mountains hazy in the distance.

She went across the playa, a dried-up area of land. *How long can I keep going with pieces of rock piercing my feet?* The temperature had already reached over ninety degrees and it couldn't have been later than noon. She was thankful now for her minimal outfit. *Nothing to weigh me down.*

She focused on her yoga training—live in the present. Her breathing became manageable, her running stride evened out, and she emptied her mind of all worries and concerns. Rory was no longer thinking about anything, not even her feet. Mind empty, doing a running meditation, she repeated her mantra silently: *Ohm Shanti forty-nine, Ohm Shanti fifty,* and on and on until she reached *Ohm Shanti one-hundred*, starting again with *Ohm Shanti one*.

****

She didn't appear on either set of steps.

"Damn." I viewed the older tape from the camera aimed at the parking area and saw the door pop open and Rory darting in and out of parked choppers. "She's loose," I said, and shoved the phone back into my pocket.

"How?" Cowboy asked.

"The door leading to the lot was left unlocked. I told you the girl wasn't right for us. She's FTA, as we said in the Army. Failure to adapt."

"A slow learner," Cowboy seethed, slamming his hand against the cinder blocks.

"How many girls have come here?" I asked, not waiting for Cowboy to answer. "A couple cried for a day or two, but *none* ever asked to leave. Or ran away."

"You shouldn't have interfered," Cowboy said. He picked up the steel bedframe, heaving it against the wall, the mattress sliding and hitting the floor, causing the girl's writings to shake loose, a couple flying. He seized a page as it floated and scanned it. "A poet in our midst? She really will be a suffering artist when I'm through with her." He took the paper in his fist, wadded it into a ball, and threw it.

"You know my policies about physically hurting women." My stomach grew queasy, contemplating what Cowboy would do to Rory if he got her back. Then I thought about the ramifications of not finding her, and what would happen to us if she ran to the cops and complained. Hopefully, the girl would be like the paper ball and go nowhere.

I changed my mind when Cowboy slammed his boot down, turning the ball into a pancake. He picked up the flattened paper, put it in his mouth and chewed. His eyes lit up and foaming, chewed-up scraps of poems seeped out of the corners of his mouth. Mysteriously the letter R stuck to the edge of Cowboy's lip. Was this some kind of coincidence or warning?

Her Buddhist background seemed to give the girl a solid moral code, and inner strength too. A dangerous combination in a place like ours. The Knights code was not a moral one. We lived by one thing, loyalty to each other, and everything else was inconsequential. She wasn't like the other women, malleable and easy to control. She was fearless—or had a death wish—going head-to-head with Cowboy. Not afraid to stand up for herself, either. Compulsive and a risk-taker. Too much like Cowboy. Whatever her problems or inclinations, they were now mine. I had to get control of her.

I accepted blame, and not because I knocked my boss down. She could have died if I hadn't done that. Someone in my crew hadn't secured the cellar door. I should have double-checked. It's standard operating procedure for a reason. Plus, I should have had keys to her room. I was still in denial. It bothered me to lock her room when I had never locked the others.

The silver bed bashed against the wall again—*bang*—bringing me out of my thoughts. Shit, I needed a cigarette.

Cowboy beat the bars with his fists, veins popping out of his neck, and rammed his shoulders into them. Bellowing and snorting, he transformed into a deranged bull, "I'm going to kill this bitch."

I leaned against the back wall and imagined Cowboy as a little boy, crying for his mother. That was how it had all begun, according to Cowboy's older brother, Whiskey. Their father, a pastor from Oklahoma, employed the 'spare the rod, spoil the child and wife' approach to keeping his family in check and had driven the mother away, deserting her sons. Now Rory was fanning the flames. I didn't enjoy emotional outbursts of any sort. Trained out of me long ago. Suddenly Turk skidded in front of the gate, with terror-filled eyes, holding keys and out of breath, "I got your text."

****

Right before the emergency meeting, Turk leaned over to me and quietly said, "The rumor mill's going nuts over this. I kept my mouth shut. Didn't verify or deny."

"Smart. Cowboy will tear your tongue out if he gets wind of anything." I glanced at him from the corner of my eye. "Spill tea."

"Brothers are saying the newest asset locked Cowboy in a room and slapped him silly, then abducted a prospect to drive her out of here."

"The second part's bogus. I hope."

"All the prospects are present and accounted for," Turk confirmed. "Probably wishful thinking by some. Everyone believes she's incredible." Turk's gaze was dreamy as if he'd just seen Dolly Parton.

"Not everyone." I smirked, looking over at Cowboy.

"Luckily, your name didn't come up."

"I don't care if my name comes up or not. I'm not less of a man because a girl handed me my ass, am I?"

"No, but it makes her one hell of a woman. Impressive, the way she out-maneuvered the both of you. A whole other story, her standing up to Cowboy. Our own members don't even have the balls. Do you think something might be wrong with her?" Turk leaned closer, tilting his head and making strong eye contact with me.

I scratched my chin. "I'm thinking along those lines myself."

We couldn't discuss it further, though, because Cowboy lowered the gavel and called the meeting to order. "Attention, everyone. The new girl is loose. Changed her mind, it seems. We gotta bring her back."

Most members believed Rory would still be on foot. Our clubhouse was one of the few things out here, and our stretch of highway was desolate.

Cowboy called Cookie, the manager at Kitties, a strip joint we owned a few miles down the road. "Keep your eyes peeled," he instructed. "Put her on lockdown if you see her. Of course, there's something in it for you. I'll let you have a turn with her."

No way would Cookie lay a hand on Rory. I'll give him one of the other women if the guy somehow captured her. A few of the women actually liked that cracker.

The meeting ended when Cowboy instructed everyone to meet in front of the clubhouse in five minutes ready to ride. Once outside and ready to ride,

Cowboy crouched down outside the doors and scrutinized the ground. "Ah, here we go, footprints." He followed them away from the porch. "She's runnin' across the desert, it looks like. Won't last long in this heat. Too fragile. No shoes and no water either. The rocks will tear her up." He turned to me. "A cut paw, right?"

"Yes." *But fragile? I didn't think so.*

"Mount up. According to WM, the girl's foot is injured," Cowboy bellowed to those waiting outside. "Should make her easy to hunt." Cowboy leapt onto his motorcycle and fired the four-stroke engine. With a giant puff of dirt and noise, he took off, with the rest of the OMC following. *Game on.*

****

"What a dump," Cowboy said to me after reaching a deserted cabin surrounded by several large Joshua trees, desert shrubs, and Pinyon pine. The place had windows with peeling paint, shattered glass, torn screens, and a faded green dented metal roof. A ripped-off front door propped on its side against the porch welcomed us.

Cowboy ordered the two prospects to check it out. They vaulted over the missing steps with enthusiasm and entered the house, returning minutes later to report only trash inside.

Cowboy scouted the ground near the house for tracks and followed them to a well with damp soil. "Shit." He paced back and forth. "She's found sneakers, and now she's got water too. See the tread prints and the marks from the containers she filled?"

I secretly applauded her resourcefulness. *One man's trash is another woman's treasure.*

Cowboy trailed her tracks, leading us deeper into a chiseled red stone canyon full of vegetation. Not one of our members dared to complain as the terrain got rougher and the brush grew denser, the branches scratching them. After he bumped a decayed stump, Cowboy ordered everyone to abandon their bikes and go on foot. Long faces and heavy sighs said it all. It was not their choice on an early summer afternoon to bird-dog some runaway girl through the thicket, when they'd much prefer an air-conditioned space to nurse their hangovers and prepare for another day of drinking, drugging, and fucking. Not geniuses by any means, but the men knew what could happen. The club would go down if she reported us, and we'd all go to jail for a myriad of charges.

"Lookee, over there." Cowboy pointed at a clump of pine trees in the distance. "There she is."

Likely a mirage.

Then I saw a glimpse too. Sun bouncing on copper hair until she disappeared behind a group of trees.

Cowboy summoned Rat, a rodent-like prospect with beady yellow eyes. Overjoyed with his handle, Rat had tattooed one on his forearm, long tail and all. "Hustle ahead along the tree line where the route is clear," Cowboy said. "You'll end up being in front of her. Corral her when she reaches you, and by that time we'll have caught up. Take Jolly with you. If you two fuck this up, you're both out of the Knights, and you can expect a beatdown." The two prospects took off, running as fast as they could toward the clearing, and Cowboy smiled. "That should motivate them,"

But I didn't want them too eager. They might hurt her.

****

Truth Moon

An odor of spice overpowered the smell of pine. Rory looked back and saw them. She remembered reading in her yoga book, "Everyone has to go through the woodland and meet the Big Bad Wolf to arrive at Grandma's house." Hopefully, she'd find Grandma's house soon, or someone like her. Cowboy was her wolf.

Rory walked briskly and dropped one water jug. The other container Rory wore crossbody, using rope from the cabin. She'd discovered lots of good stuff in there, sneakers and a T-shirt too. People left a lot of surprising things behind. *When I left my parents' home, I left nothing. And left them nothing too.*

Cowboy's bleached hair gleamed against the blue sky. Shivers of fear radiated down her spine, and her leg muscles tightened.

She didn't know anything about motorcycle clubs, but she knew this much—in Cowboy's world, striking him was unforgivable. Cowboy would do something about it for sure. Physical retaliation wasn't even in keeping with her yoga studies. But she didn't understand turning the other cheek. Rory believed in fighting back. She'd lost count of the number of times she'd gotten sent to the principal's office in elementary and middle school, forced to justify why she'd been in another fight with an unruly classmate. Her stepfather, George, was a bully too. Her mother had warned, "Anything that happens in our family stays in our family. You don't go to others." *I never did.*

A red-haired, pimple-faced man-boy with yellow eyes blocked both her thoughts and the trail ahead. The word 'PROSPECT' in block letters, emblazoned on his black leather vest, stood out like a billboard. She picked a large branch off the ground as the yellow-eyed man ran forward and seized her hands. Rory's sweat made them slide. She noticed a tattooed rat circled up and down one of his arms as he grappled with her.

Another shorter, bulkier man, also leather-clad, joined the fight too.

Crouching low, with the yellow-eyed prospect still holding on, she aimed the branch at the new shorter attacker's knee and struck him, causing the man to stumble. She was still wrestling with the yellow-eyed one, when the bulkier man climbed to his feet. She struck the bulky man again, poking his genitals with the stick.

"God almighty, help me, Rat! My nuts! It hurts so bad!" The man squealed in a high-pitched voice, falling to the ground causing the yellow-eyed man to release her hands as he went to his friend's aid.

Rory swallowed her laugh and ran the opposite way, dropping and leaving the branch behind. She froze, as she came face-to-face with all the other Knights.

She backed up, turning to return to the path blocked by the other two Knights she'd fought, but Cowboy stopped her, snagging a sleeve of her T-shirt.

Startled, with nowhere to flee, she tilted her face to the heavens. Sturdy tree limbs beckoned and promised refuge.

She pulled away, making Cowboy lose his grip, and she grabbed hold of a tree limb. Hoisting herself up, she started climbing.

"Get back here," Cowboy shouted, motivating her to move faster and farther. The plastic water container strapped around her body slapped against her hip not slowing her down, but the spines on the leaves that pricked her skin made her gasp, pull her hands back and cry out. "Keep going," she repeated to herself.

She didn't go to the top of tree. This one was over fifty feet easily. Well above the uproar, she placed her back against the broad trunk and thanked the graceful tree and God for guiding her to it. Out of breath, she took sips from her jug and gazed at the whole vast vista, the view of the canyon, other pine trees, mountains, the forest, and the clouds above—sublime. But not a building in sight, no one to run to. *No Grandma*.

****

Cowboy shouted, "Lookee! She's way up there. That tree's got to be old, maybe four or five thousand years. You don't see bristlecone pines that big."

Rory performed feats of strength, like some superheroine out of a comic book. She didn't fly, but she came close. The entire event was comical, a young girl outmaneuvering a bunch of one-percenters at every turn. I kept my smile in check. Cowboy would wipe it off my face if he got wind of it.

"How are we going to capture her?" Cowboy kicked the ground in frustration, spraying dirt in all directions. "None of these lower limbs are going to hold us. I have my gun," he said, patting his cut. "I can fire a couple of warning shots, shake her up. I could try to wing her if she doesn't come down."

My face dropped. "Shoot her?" He couldn't be serious. With Cowboy, everything discussed in simplistic terms worked best. I shook my head no.

"Probably not," Cowboy said. "I don't think I can fire off a good enough shot. Those branches are thick, and she's way up there. A bullet could land on one of us."

"Yes, too risky," I said. If Cowboy took his weapon out, I'd tackle him again.

"What do you think, WM?"

"The best solution? Send everyone back, you included. We'll talk Rory down. She trusts Turk and me. We haven't touched her. You—"

"Are you saying that I shouldn't have corrected her?" Cowboy asked.

"I've told you before, you can get what you want from the girls without putting your hands on them. Subtle manipulation and persuasion can get women to consent to most things."

I made each woman who worked for the Knights feel special. I kept mental notes of their birthdays and other important events they mentioned and fed it back. People needed to be heard and believed that they mattered. I kept a careful eye on the women's moods, and if I observed one of them depressed, I'd buy something small but meaningful, book a massage or a day at the salon for her. My actions surprised the women under my charge, because I don't come off as a very caring individual. This bit of comfort awakened loyalty and devotion. A necessary thing when I needed a girl to complete a task not included in her original assignment. They almost never said no, and if one did, she had a good reason. I seldom had to get rough or lower the boom. I noticed this myself when I was at West Point. I tried hard to please my lieutenant, commander, or anyone else in authority, if they remembered me personally.

"I…I think—" Cowboy stammered, trying to force his words out.

"She's got to believe we're on her side," I said. "No retribution later if I talk her down today. Agreed?"

"Done." Cowboy waved his hand for the men to follow, walking away.

****

"Not punishing her?" Louie asked, talking behind his hand.

"Don't be nuts," Cowboy said. "She embarrassed me and wasted a day of our lives."

"WM won't be happy when you double-cross him," Louie said.

"He'll get over it, but she won't." Cowboy snorted. "She'll remember and never fuck with me again. Slow down, don't walk so fast. I gotta send a message."

"Who to?" Louie asked.

"None of your business."

Cowboy—*Found bitch*—

MM—*Punish her*—

Cowboy—*Covered*—

MM—*How?*—

Cowboy—*Beating*—

MM—*No, gangbang*—

Cowboy—*Handler won't go for it*—

—*Members either, we don't do that here*—

—*Trouble w/Rico*—

MM—*If you don't, brother will drop the prison soap*—

Cowboy—*Come on, no rape*—

MM—*Your choice, she gets her due or brother*—

Cowboy—*You win*—

MM—*When?*—

Cowboy—*2night.*—

"Motherfucker. I'm going to kill this guy when I find out who he is," Cowboy said under his breath. Sighing, he stuffed his cell in his cut.

"What did you say?" Louie asked.

"Nothin'."

****

"Rory, Let's work this out. Things will get better." It was emasculating to beg a girl to come down. I was supposed to be a puppet master. *Yeah, right.*

Rory shouted and waved. She looked like Snow White, with those cobalt skies and cotton ball clouds behind her. I kept expecting a bird to land on her shoulder and start singing to her.

"You'll need to come down eventually," I continued.

"Go away. I'm trying to meditate, and you're ruining it for me."

"Shouldn't you be able to block out noise if you're any good?" Most people didn't realize they'd done exactly what I planned. She'd be the same.

"You're right, but I'm distracted. I was thinking about a place I used to eat. So, *gucci.*"

"It's called Gucci?" Keep her talking. I'd pull the strings and she'd dance to my tune soon enough.

"No." She giggled. "The place is called Scoops. They're renowned for their ice cream. 'Gucci' means good. Unfortunately, I can't often go, because of my dairy problem. But when I do, I buy a vanilla ice cream cone with a maraschino cherry on top. The cherries are bad for you because of the dye. But I crave them. One time I bought a whole jar and ate them in one sitting. I got super sick."

All the things we like are bad for us. I bet you're one of those things. "I'll tell you what. You come down and I'll buy some. I'll fix you something delicious for dinner, too. You can use my private bathroom and try the Jacuzzi. You can use my bedroom for a yoga and meditation session. You'll love the ceiling. I designed it. The entire span is glass. You'll see every star in the sky." *I lie in bed every night and think about how I got my friends killed, stare at the moon, and ask why I was still alive.* "Come down now," I added in a quieter tone.

"Oh, come on." She laughed. "Cowboy's a salty dude. He'll punish me for sure. I need receipts. No way will he let me slide for smacking him in the face and running away. He'll make me pay."

"Receipts?"

"You know, proof."

"Cowboy promised. He told me he wouldn't. He'd always kept his word. That's all the proof I can give you." She's wise to ask for confirmation.

"You're right, I can't stay up here forever. I'll come down." Too easy. She trusted me and shouldn't.

"I hope she takes it slow. She's way up there." Turk looked at me with concern. "Should I return to the bikes in case this takes a while?"

"Good idea. There should be a flashlight in my saddlebag. Retrieve it and come back. We'll meet up with you on the path."

"Solid, boss. Catch you later."

Rory took her time climbing down. I thought about seizing her when she was closer but changed my mind, deciding to let her be. She dropped in a pile of pine needles under the tree, right in front of me. "I guess I wasn't frightened enough," she said, grinning. "It took me longer coming down than going up."

"Fear is a powerful motivator," I said.

"Feel free to motivate me another way. A regular pair of underwear, perhaps?" She raised her brows.

What the fuck is wrong with the underwear? I

wondered. I figured I'd offer up some advice, now that she was calm. "You shouldn't provoke Cowboy. He angers easily."

Her smile vanished. "Cowboy shouldn't put his hands on me. He was totally cray, no cap."

"No cap?"

"Yes, no cap. Seriously, he acted cray."

"You're right. You had to defend yourself. I tried to get Cowboy off you. But you saw—once he gets wound up, he's hard to deal with." I nodded my head slightly and tried to get her on my side.

"I appreciate your help," she said, simulating a defiant stance, hands on her hips. "But perhaps everyone should worry instead about angering me. I'm only going to tolerate so much."

"You're a wiseass, aren't you?"

"I prefer the word 'spirited.'" She flashed a Hollywood smile.

She has balls, I'll give her that. "I would tone it down, especially with Cowboy. Don't take so many risks. Think before you act."

"You can't touch the star's if you never leave the earth," she said.

"A quote from Buddha?" I asked.

"No, another great. Me." She smiled. "Truthfully, I see myself as a patient person, but your establishment has more lunkheads per square foot than any place I've experienced."

How much experience could she possibly possess at her age? I got serious. "We're talking truth here. You came to us, and you're going to suffer whatever comes your way." I stood in front of her, blocking the path. "You're not in charge; we are."

"I never signed up for abuse." She walked around me.

I hustled to catch up. She moved lickety-split for being a shorty. "Tell me about yourself, Rory." I waited for her to pick up the bone and bring it back to me. Most people loved to talk about themselves. I needed to figure this chick out and fast.

"I stayed in an ashram in Virginia, pursuing my Buddhist studies, and attended yoga teacher training there too, before I came to Vegas to teach. As far as what happened before, it isn't meaningful or relevant. What about you?" Her eyes glanced over to me.

She handled questioning like a CIA operative and revealed little. When anyone says he or she doesn't want to talk about it, I believe it's something I need to get to the bottom of. "I graduated from West Point, went to Ranger School, served in Afghanistan a few years, came back to the good old USA, and went in a different direction," I said.

She stopped walking. "I think you made a wrong turn somewhere," she said, smirking. "Consider a U-turn. A strange career path from ranger to one-percenter and brothel manager, just sayin'. You're better than that."

No filter. Was Rory socially awkward? Cowboy would wipe the floor with her if she talked to him like this. "Isn't there something in that yoga book of yours about not judging others?" I asked.

"You read my yoga sutra book?" She took a step backward. Her eyes and mouth fell open.

"I know how to read." I stared her down.

"You're right. I apologize. Ahimsa is about nonjudgment. It just seems like you could—"

She couldn't continue. A reverberating rustling sound filled the forest. Thousands of bats flew from the trees, painting the sapphire sky black. We both covered our ears with our hands; the chirping and screeching was deafening. Out of nowhere, a hawk zoomed in and snagged one bat out of the heavens. It dipped away slowly, clutching its prey.

"Did you see that?" Her eyes expanded in disbelief.

"Yeah, impressive flying."

"The poor bat, it didn't have a chance."

"The strong survive, and the weak perish. Life is brutal and unlucky most of the time," I said.

"I disagree. There's room for all creatures. Humanity and beauty exist in the world, too. Maybe I'm not lucky or strong enough if I ended up here, but…"

I lost my smile. "Don't give up," I said, reaching out and squeezing her hand.

"Don't worry, I won't. I'm not keen on perishing, no matter what the big, bad hawk plans on doing to me." She squeezed my hand back and pulled away.

"You seem to be accomplished at running and hiking. Do you camp too?" I needed to get her attention off the unfortunate bat and me, with her attacks on my career and lifestyle choices.

"I did all those things when I was in yoga training. The only activity I didn't enjoy was camping. I don't understand it. When there's a comfortable bed at home or you can go to a nice hotel down the street, what's the point? Are you sure Cowboy won't punish me?"

"He told me he wouldn't." I agreed with the girl. Unless I had no choice, camping made little sense. It could be I'm jaded where camping's concerned, having found myself hunkered down too many times in the past to count, sleeping on the ground with other farting, snoring soldiers. I noticed Rory shivering and took off my colors. "Wear this," I said, handing her my jacket. Rory put it on appreciatively. It came down past her thighs.

The trees closed in on us, and the trail became difficult to keep until I saw a light coming toward us— Turk with the flashlight. He guided us back to the choppers. Once there, he mounted his bike, gave me a quick salute, and took off without us. I didn't even hint to him that I wanted to be alone with her.

"A full moon tonight. Some people believe it symbolizes the truth. I hope I made the right decision coming back." Rory's eyes searched mine.

"You couldn't stay up in the tree. You'd have starved." I took her hand and walked her closer to me. She didn't resist but should have, even though I hadn't lied to her yet. The truth was that I would soon. But who knew what could happen if she kept looking at me like this and talked up the moon?

Chapter 7

One with Nature

Doesn't she know people are untrustworthy and life is meaningless? I'll have to lie to her, tell her how she's my one and only and how someday I'll make her mine, and on and on. Yet...I can't cross the line with her.

"I shouldn't be here," Rory said. My bike shone in the moonlight behind her.

The quiet hung between us. My allegiance was to my brothers, not to a girl I just met, marked for Cowboy and our club. The truth was that I didn't want her to go, not ever.

The moment I realized that, I knew I had a problem. I pushed it out of my mind, walking her away from my bike. I pressed her body against a Pinyon pine, my fingers grazing the rough bark. I took Rory's face in both of my hands, her skin buttery soft, losing myself in those eyes lit by the moon. I moved one hand down her neck, resting it there as I brushed her hair with the other, pulling my fingers through silky strands, nuzzling the back of her ears, and breathing into them. Moving on to her lips, like an arrow flying toward a target, I touched, tasted, and torched them with my own. I penetrated her mouth with the tip of my tongue, velvety, willing, and frothy. *Why did I think her mouth was frothy?* I waited for a signal to give her more.

She inhaled, blinking up at me, giving me a look of wonder. Green, round, glass Christmas balls swam in a sea of white: She hid them away and buried her head in my chest, allowing a tumbling mane to shroud us. Her body joined and blended with mine, yielding.

I brought her chin up gently and this time I kissed her full-on, slipping my tongue in her mouth more deeply and worming my hand inside my jacket, the one that she now wore. The combined smell of her, of me, and of oranges hit hard. She gasped, and a little moan snuck out as our tongues danced and retreated. I enjoyed the sound and wanted more of it.

"May I touch you, Rory?" The only reason I asked was because of her earlier comment. I didn't want to join the lunkhead group. *I'm supposed to control and teach her, and here she is…*

"Yes," she whispered, "please."

Her arms moved up and dangled around my neck, allowing me easier entry. I towered over her, but at that moment she was the powerful one. I slid my hands under her shirt, shifted to her waist, and worked my way up her body. Skin like satin. She didn't stop me.

I continued caressing her, first gently and then like a starving man who couldn't get enough. She gave back, participating, not stopping me. Her hands stroked my hair and moved to my neck. I was electrified.

I was confused for the first time in a long time. Should I pretend something here? Provide instruction? Should I distance myself somehow, like I usually did? Then a moment of clarity. I focused on her. The things I'd done with every other woman before Rory were meaningless. I couldn't remember the last time I was fully present with someone. Who was I kidding? I was never this way.

Adrift in her kisses, I longed to take her further, but she stopped, her entire body resting against mine. The beat of her heart thumped against my gut, reminding me of a day my father took me deer hunting, and I watched a doe die after my father brought it to the ground with one shot. The heartbeat went so fast and then drifted away, the eyes once so bright and alive now glazed over. Gone just like that.

I needed to get us out of here. The forest floor, pine needles, and the rich sienna dirt would become her resting place, her bed, if I didn't. Yogi girl might be one with nature, but things would get complicated fast in my world. It was necessary to think this through. I always thought matters through before I acted. Things were moving too quickly. It wasn't my time. Cowboy always took a girl first. That was the way it worked in our world.

"We need to go," I said. Her eyes were questioning, confused, and then touched with relief. I couldn't look at her. I enveloped her small hand inside my own and guided her toward my chopper. I took my helmet and placed it on Rory's head, tucking her hair inside of it carefully. I balanced the bike with my legs and motioned for her. She threw her leg over and climbed on behind me. I took one last look at the woods and breathed in deeply before starting the engine. I wanted to hold on to the scent, to remind me of what we'd shared.

"Hold on tight, Rory," I said, taking her hands and wrapping them around my waist. I couldn't remember the last time I had a rider. Usually, I rode alone and disliked having a back warmer. This was different. I was riding with someone I wanted to share with. *Lose that thought and do it now. I didn't deserve to share anything with anybody.*

"I love this. Go faster!" Rory said in my ear as I accelerated, shrieking with delight when I let the bike loose. I used to go on rollercoasters with my mother. She loved speed too, screaming with joy in the turns and twists, her eyes wide, gazing up to the sky.

I hit some rough terrain and turned quickly to avoid some rock formations. Rory leaned into me, along with the bike, demonstrating her excellent balance. She must have ridden before. A moment later, she confided, "I'm a virgin."

"What!" I said, swerving and then straightening the bike.

"I meant to say, I'm a virgin rider." She giggled. "I scared you, didn't I?" She had. There were enough things about her that were troubling. I didn't need another one.

I didn't want the ride to end as I reached the security gate and drove through it. Impending doom overwhelmed me. I parked in the back of the club. The screen door banged as I assisted Rory off the bike. Cowboy's eyes were all over her and landed on me, a thin smile appearing. I pointed Rory toward the cellar, attempting to extract her from Cowboy's line of vision. A crow flew overhead as I opened the cellar door. The image of the hawk with its prey in its talons crept back into my head. I hoped it wasn't an omen of things to come. I shook it off and escorted her down the passageway.

****

Cowboy's eyes crawled up Rory's body, holding her hostage. The hair on her neck stood until she was out from his sight. This room was a different one from before. Exhausted, she collapsed on the bed, but not before WM placed new bedding down. Her heavy limbs surrendered to the mattress, her eyes drifting upward. He knelt beside her and his lips brushed her cheek. "I'll be back," he said. The scent of pine trees followed him as he walked away.

The ceiling became a screen for her movie as she replayed the ride back. Moon and stars had lit the way as they sped in and out of silhouetted trees, nature's obstacle course. All concerns had been blown away by the speed of the bike. Hair had transformed to flails from a vicious whip as it had flown from under her helmet and around her. Pressing her body closer, she felt WM's power in front of her and the vibration beneath her. Wrapped in his jacket, she'd found peace in WM's presence. Surrounded by her dark prince and his scent— leather, tobacco smoke and pine. *It took me years to break free of my monster. A new master, now.*

She had whispered in his ear, "I wish I could do this forever." She remembered how she had pressed her lips against his neck, standing on the pegs of his bike. The short hairs from his jaw scratched hers. Smiling, she had kept cautioning herself she wasn't on a date. It hadn't worked.

Her asana practice had never given her this kind of exhilaration. If only he'd passed the entrance to the Knights and kept going. The glow from the lit windows of the clubhouse ahead, warm and inviting, camouflaged the reality of what happened inside.

WM was not like the other men Rory had gone out with. Maybe she could tell him the truth. He would understand, know what to do. Show her things. She'd never felt the emptiness inside of her, the longing to be filled, until this moment. Rory imagined what might be possible, her body heating until shrouded by sleep.

Sounds of fabric ripping and cries broke through her dreams. A bad one? Shocked to find Cowboy grabbing at her, she screamed. Hands in balled fists, she struck out at him. Cowboy straddled her torso, weighing her down. More hands attached to ham hock arms snared her wrists from the head of the bed. "Keep her hands pinned, Louie," he ordered.

"God, she's a wild one. And strong, considering she's an itty-bitty thing," Louie said.

"I'll handle her bottom half and you take care of the top and we can get this done," Cowboy said to Louie. "Stop fighting, Rory. I'm going to hit you back if you don't." Cowboy forced her legs apart, denim rubbing her stomach and thighs, his pants already unzipped. The aroma of gasoline permeated her nostrils. A carnival freak show, two sets of eyes—one set upside-down—peered down at her. "You gotta be punished. Runnin' your mouth, runnin' off. I'm gonna do you and then Louie is, too."

"No. Please. Don't. I—"

Platinum hair dragged across her face. "I'm fast-trackin' two other high-rankin' friends down here. After we're done, you'll never make the same mistake again." A twisted smile appeared on Cowboy's face. Rory struggled against them, panting, out of breath. How could this happen? Where was WM? "No ifs, ands, or buts," he said in a sing-song way. "Punishment is due."

"Leave me alone," Rory cried, rotating and lifting her hips, fighting to get Cowboy off.

"The sooner you stop struggling, the quicker this will end. Make it easy on yourself." Cowboy's eyes met hers. "I'll make it as good as I can, if you go along."

"No," she said, looking away and then back at him.

"Have it your way." Cowboy's eyes burned brighter.

No matter which way she moved or how hard she fought, she couldn't buck Cowboy away. Her body weakened. She remembered the butterflies her stepfather had collected, frozen permanently in a framed box. Now it was her…pushed flat on tangled sheets, a specimen for enjoyment, arms like fragile wings, hands held firm by Louie, instead of pins. *WM's right. Life is brutal.*

Clang. The gate bounced open. A blur of movement. "Get off her," WM's voice boomed.

Surprised, Louie fell against the wall, having lost his footing. Limbs now loose, Rory's fist connected with Cowboy's face.

"She popped me again," Cowboy yelped, stumbling backward, blood dripping down his face. Louie led Cowboy, still blubbering and holding his nose, out of the room.

There was a splatter of blood on the sheet from Cowboy's wound . The color red obliterated everything. Sucked free of her physical self, she floated in space, directionless. WM's calming words echoed: "You're safe, I'm here." She swam toward his voice, swallowed by a full palette of colors, but everything was distorted, disjointed. His fingers stroked her shoulder. "Rory, Rory…" he sang her name. "It's okay." He lured her back, his welcoming eyes her landing field. Rory wrapped her arms around herself and rocked.

"Come on. I'm getting you out of here," WM said. "We're going to my room upstairs." He took her hands, pulled her to her feet, and swaddled her in his jacket once again. *He came back for me. There is humanity in the world.*

"I can't walk through the club." Rory jerked away. "I don't want everyone knowing."

"We won't. We'll go another way," WM said. "We stopped him. Nothing happened." WM escorted her up the basement steps to the door. He fumbled and searched through his pockets for keys. When he found them, he cast her a smile, unlocked it, and threw the door open. This time there was no sun, no light, just darkness. *I should never have come back here.*

"You're in no condition to run," WM said, taking her hand and guiding her behind the club, up several flights of stairs to a different world, leaving the dark one behind. This world was magical, like the Garden of Eden. A variety of greenery in rainbow-colored pots were scattered about on the third-floor landing.

"I can't believe these are yours," she whispered.

"I'm not one-dimensional. I do other things besides torture women."

Rory astonished herself by letting a laugh escape. Her therapist had told her she might react in unusual ways to stress and trauma because of past abuse. Maybe this was one of those times. Her eyes landed on all that was beautiful, transported to a different place. Chinese paper lanterns in different colors hung along the overhang. Tiny twinkle-colored lights traced the doorway and windows, flickering. A hot tub, lounge chairs, and a fire pit beckoned. WM held one of the French doors for her to enter. Out of politeness? Or did he want to make sure she wouldn't run?

It got even more impressive inside. A ceiling of steel and glass shot up at least fifteen feet. WM hadn't lied. Shelves along one wall were stacked with books and ceramics. In the center of the room was an Asian-style rug of beige, red, mustard brown and turquoise. Music played throughout the room, but she couldn't identify the artist. "Who is this?" she asked, lost in awe. "I've never heard this song before."

"Christone Kingfish Ingram," WM said. "A prodigy from Mississippi. A singer and guitarist. They say he's the future of the blues. I saw him at Rosa's when I visited Chicago."

Her eyes traveled around his room, taking it in—a four-poster bed placed against one wall, the headboard tall, carved, ornate. It appeared handmade. On either side of the wall, sconces provided intimate lighting. Over his headboard, he'd hung crucifixes in various sizes. Some wood, others paper-mâché, tin and mosaic tiles. *Is WM a Christian?*

There were art prints and sculpture reproductions throughout the room too. She recognized them because they were her favorites too—Gustav Klimt, Richard Diebenkorn, Fairfield Porter, Marlene Dumas, Odd Nerdrum and Lucien Freud. *Does WM bring other women here? Ivy? What a dumb question. Of course he does.*

In the distance was the sound of water running, getting louder when he slid the pocket door open. Streams of water trickled down a gigantic slab of slate, a wall fountain. Her stepfather, George, used to mock her when she said, "Water is my element, a healing force," but she had always found comfort in it. There had been a creek near the trailer, and whenever times had been rough with her parents, she had walked there and listened to the water as it spilled over the rocks, and dreamed about her future life. She'd believed someday it would be better; and it had been, until Lloyd. And this.

In the washroom was an enormous tub with a Jacuzzi and a walk-in shower. This was the nicest bathroom she'd ever seen. The one in her apartment had walls of robin's egg blue and white woodwork, and she had paid to have the old iron clawfoot tub resurfaced by babysitting some of her yoga clients' children. Everyone at work had teased her. Lloyd had said, "Making improvements in places you rent is foolish." She thought it a small price to pay to make something better she used every day. *And now I've lost it all.*

"You'll find shampoo and anything else you need in the vanities." WM handed her a washcloth and towels. "You can turn on the Jacuzzi or take a shower, your choice. Use the robe on the back of the door. Take as long as you need." He turned to leave.

"Do you believe in God, WM?" Rory's voice cracked.

"I think there's a higher power, if that's what you're asking, although sometimes it's difficult with all the shit happening in the world."

"Did you know Cowboy was going to do that?"

"Do you think I would allow Cowboy to rape you?" His face grew dark.

She squeezed her eyes shut. "I didn't think you would." Tears escaped anyway.

WM came to her, knotted his fingers in her hair, tilted her head up, and caressed her throat. With each stroke, her agitation melted away. "I'd never do that to you. Or to any woman. Ever." He brought her even closer and embraced her.

The sound of trickling water, the music wafting in from the other room, and the smell of his sweat enveloped her. Their breathing was in sync. *I've never felt as protected and cared for. Yet, I'm in the arms of one of them.*

"I don't know why Cowboy broke his promise, but I'm glad I prevented it in time. I'm going to do something about it. I vow I'll take care of this." He took her hands, still holding her close. "Life is hard, and it will get harder. It doesn't stop. When you're feeling sorrow, rub the vein around your arm and press your palm. See the blood inside? This is your life flowing. Something my friend Chet said, and it's gotten me through a lot of challenging times. You're strong and tenacious. I can see it. You're a survivor. You'll get through this."

"Sorry, I…" She choked on her words.

"Don't apologize. You have nothing to apologize for. You do what you have to, and if crying makes you feel better, do it. Take the bath." He moved his hands to her shoulders. "I'm going to finish up the dinner I made, like I promised, and then I'll be back." He extracted himself and closed the door.

Rory sank to the cold tile. Cowboy didn't rely on fake gifts, persuasion, and stealth visits like her stepfather had. She pushed her thoughts away. *Persevere, get through it, move on.* She used the tub to pull herself up from the floor, got the water as hot as she dared, and found a bar of lemon and lavender soap in the vanity. She held it to her nose, inhaling—like springtime in Virginia at the ashram. It was one of the happiest and most carefree times of her life.

She tossed it in and watched it sink, the heat and water releasing its essence. She fired up the jets, the bar quickly melting and changing into bubbles. Rory touched her foot to the scalding water and then plunged it in, joining the soap as she submerged her entire tired and sore body, ignoring the pain.

She sat in the water, wanting to burn their touch away, rocking, tugging at her fingers, soothing herself. She turned off the jets and stared in the cloudy water, searching for answers and inspiration. *I used to think nothing would hold me back from having the life I desire. I wonder…have I met a force that can?*

****

My ex complained about my OCD tendencies, among other things. Truth. The shiny black quartz countertops with silver flecks, a clean sink and counter, and the brightly lit kitchen buoyed me.

I made some special tea for Rory and contemplated making some for myself. Insurance to get some sleep.

The song "Shit List" by L7 announced an incoming call, and caller ID flashed Cowboy's shit-eating grin. He qualified for my shit list today. I pressed the answer button and turned down the volume. Even though I didn't want to talk to him after he'd lied to me, I needed to get the conversation over with.

"You got the girl?" Cowboy asked.

"Yeah, she's in my room getting cleaned up."

"Too early." Cowboy snickered. "I'm not done. Louie and I have plans."

"I don't understand your logic. You want this girl, yet you're doing everything in your power to make her want to leave."

Cowboy waited a couple of seconds before responding, "You should have stayed clear. I'm gonna come for her."

"No."

Cowboy's voiced went up several notches. "Don't

you understand what the bitch did? She disrespected me and wasted our time. She's gotta pay."

"We had an agreement, no punishment. What you're doing is wrong," I said. "It's not in keeping with the tenets of a good Dom-sub relationship, either. Rory never agreed to this. She's finished for tonight."

"You've got to be kidding. Is this how you're going to play this?"

"It's the only way I can. I need to safeguard the girl, for the good of the club. This type of punishment needs their approval. Her actions don't warrant abuse of this type. She's an investment, and a losing one if you continue on with your behavior. We can discuss this tomorrow. Tonight, we need rest." I cut the bastard off, ending the call and giving Cowboy no chance to argue.

****

Rory jumped at the clatter when I returned. "Your dinner's here," I said, placing the tray on my desk. I sat on the side of my bed and watched as Rory pushed the food around. I had failed to protect her. The last time I had fallen short, men had lost their lives. My father used to say, "If you plan well and make the right decisions, you won't be defeated."

"This is delicious. Thank you, but I can't eat." Rory's hands shook. "Please forgive me." She took a few deep breaths, tears welling up, then collected herself and poured from the teapot. She palmed the cup in both hands and brought it under her nose, eyes sealed, inhaling, as a peaceful expression appeared. "Chai is my favorite. Can I sit on your deck and study the stars while I drink it?"

The idea of saying no and hurting her further made my throat start to close. "Stay where I can see you," I answered.

She sank into one of the lounge chairs and sipped the tea, eyes cast toward the heavens with a wondrous expression. I sat at my desk and checked my email, keeping a careful eye out as she dropped more deeply into the chaise, eyes closing, chin dipping lower toward her chest until there was no movement at all. I crept from the chair and inspected the bathroom. There was nothing to straighten. The floor had been dried, towels hung, the tub rinsed out, and the sink counters wiped down. The perfect guest.

I went to the deck and found the empty teacup cocooned in her lap, her eyes closed. I called her name and touched her shoulder. She didn't respond. I glanced around and up to the sky. I spotted the Milky Way. Magnificent. I used to be like her, sitting out and watching the heavens at night.

I went back inside, pulled back the covers on my bed, and returned to fetch her. She still didn't stir, even after I lifted and delivered her to my bed. I placed Rory down like she was a Faberge egg, an irreplaceable object of beauty that the slightest bump could damage. I scolded myself for my sentimentality and silently laughed. She wasn't a priceless egg, but I was an egghead for sure.

I freed her from her robe and deposited it at the end of the bed. I smelled lemons and rosemary. I toured her body, enjoying the voyage—the terrain, mountains and valleys. A natural wonder for sure. She was right. *There is beauty in the world.*

I realized her shoulders and arms were sunburned, and noticed scratches on her legs from running in the brush. I took some aloe lotion and dabbed it on. The bottoms of her feet had minor cuts on them too. I returned to the bathroom and retrieved some antibiotic ointment, applying it to her wounds. Her wrists were red too, but by tomorrow there'd be no sign of the struggle she'd endured.

Unfortunately, the emotional damage would take longer to heal. It occurred to me that there would be more to come, and I pushed the thought away like all the other things I didn't want to think about. How does a person prepare for a six-year-old suicide bomber? One small sandal had lain in the street in Kabul, the other sandal blown into me. The orthopedic surgeon informed me I'd never father children.

I covered her carefully with the sheet and cover, then put another blanket on the floor. Before I could stop myself, I kissed her forehead, something my mother did for me until she passed. *No going back if you keep on this road.*

Chapter 8

Like Falling Off a Horse

An enormous black bird peered through the transparent ceiling, hitting the glass with its beak—*tap, tap, tap*. Eyes covered with sleepy sand, her mind was filled with slippery, silver thoughts, like swimming carp. Then a solid one. *I shouldn't have come here.*

Before Rory could compare it to the bird in her dream or its eyes to WM's eyes, the bird flew away. She didn't remember preparing for bed last night. Did WM undress her? Her body heated as she thought about it. *Did I do anything? What would WM feel like sliding inside of me?*

She bolted up, her face flushed, and searched for something to wear, noticing the robe at the end of the mattress. She reached out, but her arms weren't long enough. She stood to grasp it, almost tripping over WM stretched out on the floor below. He didn't look away. She gasped and grabbed the garment, throwing it on while sprinting into the bathroom, slamming the door behind her. She was mortified and blushing in shame. WM chuckled and shuffled outside the door. *He saw me naked. OMG.*

"I'm going downstairs for coffee and to score clothes. I'm locking the door. Don't open it." She pressed her ear to the bathroom door. She heard dishes rattling, fading footsteps, and finally the bedroom door closing. Why hadn't WM looked away? He must have seen her last night too. God must have a plan if he'd allowed her to end up in this testosterone-infused place. What did WM look like without his pants? Her eyes danced in the mirror, as she tried to imagine. Finally, she decided WM was well-endowed, and giggled. *I'm dotty*.

She cracked the bathroom door and peeked out. *My prince of darkness, gone. Why did I think that?* A square, multi-colored, silk brocade box with a lotus flower motif beckoned on his nightstand. She opened it slowly and jumped up and down, happiness surging—her angel wings bracelet. She ran her fingers over the different feather shapes as the light bounced off the etched silver textures.

Rory remembered the day she had received it. She had just turned sixteen. "Your father left this in his will," her mother had said, placing it in her palm with lustful eyes. Rory had loosened the cord just enough to hurriedly squeeze her hand in, before her mother could change her mind and take it back. At the time, it had symbolized her future. To her mother, it was something to pawn.

She wasn't stealing. Rory told herself she was taking back what was hers. She removed it from WM's box and stuffed it deep into the robe's terrycloth pocket. She returned the box with another piece, a single feather on a silver chain, to WM's nightstand.

Across the room, she noted his laptop had been left out. Was it a test or an accident? She didn't care and viewed it as an opportunity. She flipped up the cover and pressed the return key. The screen flooded with color, and an unexpected image appeared. *He could have chosen a better picture of me.*

The cursor blinked, waiting for a password. Still stunned over discovering an image of herself, Rory keyed in "Whoremaster" and then tried "KNIGHTS." Neither worked. Her third attempt, "99999," locked her out, and she banged the lid closed, frustrated that she was unable to email Sarah.

Does WM like me? She shook her head trying to focus.

Gaining access to his computer was as tricky as getting into the man's head. Mission impossible. She blushed and wrapped her arms around herself, satisfied anyway. *I'm his screensaver.*

His bookshelf called to her as she left the laptop behind. She was curious to know his tastes and interests. *The Social Construction of Reality* by Berger & Luckmann. *The Art of War* by Sun Tzu. *SM101* by Jay Wiseman. *The Brainwashing Manual* by Barry Bastards. She'd already read *The Art of War*; skip.

She selected *The Brainwashing Manual*, hoping to learn what she was up against and how to manipulate him. She scanned the words on a random page: "If you want an individual to do you a favor the best approach is to request they do something insignificant for you, first." Before she could continue, the handle jiggled, and pounding on the door followed.

****

A Goddess. She transformed into Venus, right out of Botticelli's painting, as she stood above with hair and hands floating around her body to cover herself. It touched me, the way Rory had slipped the robe on all girly-like. I admit it. I liked her ways.

I had seen the real painting at the Uffizi when

visiting Florence, Italy on leave. Rory didn't have the elongated body of the model. Still, she had the hair and the angelic face, and captured the spirit of the work. What had gotten to me was the way she'd blushed and hidden in the bathroom. I wasn't used to girls acting like that, at least not around here.

I preferred the clubhouse like this, quiet. The only sound, water dripping into the coffeemaker. The scent of fresh coffee brewing spread throughout the space. Cinnamon and nutmeg in the oatmeal contributed to the aromas. Almost perfect, until I detected a few grounds floating in the coffee. Shit. I made it over. The second batch was fine. I picked an apple and two oranges from the fruit bowl and held an orange to my nose, inhaling deeply to remind myself of her scent. Girls and their different smells. Ivy has an overwhelming scent, like I'm being buried in roses.

I put everything on the tray, heading toward the stairs. Discovering a basket of clean clothes, I selected several pieces and tucked them under my arm.

****

A roommate at West Point once said, "Always expect trouble and you won't be disappointed." Truth. Outside my room, Cowboy's hand was on my doorknob. Hunched over and disheveled, with his shirt and belt were missing, jeans hanging low.

When Cowboy saw me, his expression changed from angry to "Aw shucks, you caught me."

"What's going on?" I said casually.

"I didn't like how things ended on the phone last night. You've never gone against me in anything before. I stopped by to work things out."

"It might be better if we discuss our business after I

return Rory to her room, but you're the boss."

"Makes sense. I'm glad you still see me as the man in charge. How did it go with her?" Cowboy leered. "Did you get any?"

I eyed Cowboy incredulously. "You know I don't take women against their will, and you left Rory as an emotional wreck." I squeezed behind him. "I'll meet you in your office later," I said, unlocking my bedroom door, closing it abruptly behind me, and locking it.

Rory was standing by the door, almost blocking it. Her pupils were enormous, arms hugging herself. "He's gone," I said. "Come, I have your breakfast and clothes too." Rory looked back at the door and followed me reluctantly, hesitating.

"Come on, ignore him. He's not coming in." I placed the tray on the desk, and she acted like it wasn't there, whisking the garments out of my hands and sprinting into the bathroom.

As I waited for her, my eyes traveled the room. The bed was made, corners crisp, pillows puffed, and my blanket folded neatly at the end of the bed. Perfect…until my eyes landed on the bookcase. Something didn't appear correct, and I approached to take a closer look. Some of the books had spines sticking out from the shelves, like they'd been pulled out then placed back haphazardly, and they were no longer in alphabetical order either. One of them, my favorite, the one on control and manipulation had been put back upside down. *Seems I'm failing in that department with this one, if she's snooping.*

After she returned, her appearance demanded my attention. The top fit perfectly, but the bottoms were too large. "Which book did you like best?" I asked, pointing to my bookshelf.

"Uh, what?" Her face turned red and she looked away.

"I asked you a question."

"I didn't have time to read them," she said, not smiling.

I put my books back in the proper order as she wolfed down her breakfast. I let go of the nightmare: Rory turning into a skeleton wouldn't happen soon. She played with the oranges, tossing them up and down in the air and eventually juggling them.

"You're pretty good. How did you learn to do that?" I asked.

"A library book and practice. You can find out how to do almost anything from reading about it or YouTube. I'm glad you're not like them, WM," she said. "You told Cowboy you don't take women against—"

I interrupted her. "Makes you trust me more, is that it?" I asked.

"Something like that."

"I'm going to give you some advice. You'd be wise not to trust any man, especially based on something he says."

"Jane Austen said something similar in *Sense and Sensibility*. 'It isn't what we say or think that defines us, but what we do.'"

"Exactly. And next time, don't touch my things. If you want to learn how to be a proper sub, I'll be glad to teach you and provide appropriate reading material."

She didn't return my smile or meet my eyes. "That's okay," she murmured, looking at the floor.

"Don't listen to conversations not meant for you, either."

"Are you accusing me of spying?"

"Weren't you?"

"Someone was trying to get in. I went over to the door to find out who, and—"

"Don't argue. Finish eating. You're going back to your original room. Cowboy destroyed it. I want you to clean it. Better than the second room where Cowboy almost raped you. Am I right?"

My words caused her to miss and drop an orange. It rolled under my bed. Her face turned pink; even her neck flushed. I tossed that hand grenade to distance myself. If I didn't keep my mind on business, her ashes would end up blowing across the desert. And I'd be responsible for another death.

She got on her hands and knees, searching for the orange, retrieving it seconds later. "I'm ready," she said, taking a step with the oranges held high over her head, apparently thinking she was leading a platoon into battle, starting with me.

"We go when I say. Sit and leave the fruit here." Bringing my leadership skills to sex workers was something I was good at. At least I used to be.

She plopped down with a sigh, placing the oranges on my desk, the citrus scent stronger. She tore a cuticle from her fingernail, waiting. Why did it seem more daunting every day to establish my dominance? It had never been this difficult with the other women. How would she last five minutes without Cowboy coming down on her with both feet? How could she work in our dungeon? Also, I needed to prevent the mutilation of fingernail number two. "Time to go," I finally said.

She meandered toward the door, suddenly making a U-turn. "I should use the bathroom first." Attempting to delay her departure? Vying for control?

"Stop stalling. You can go to your room now." I pushed her out the door into the hall.

I guided her toward the steps. I noted a layer of dust as Rory grabbed hold of the railing. I'd add it to my to-do list. Suddenly her head snapped up, her descent slowed, and then she stopped moving altogether. Her eyes were glued to Cowboy at the bottom of the landing. Turning back to look at me and lowering her voice, she pleaded, "Please don't make me walk by him."

"Pull those big girl panties up," I said. "Like falling off a horse, climb right back on. Remember the rules. Keep your eyes down and just keep moving."

"Don't be condescending. I want my big girl panties back. I'm tired of these damn thongs giving me perpetual wedgies. It's nothing like falling off a horse." Her eyes flashed. "I've ridden horses. Fallen off a couple of times, and I was never afraid to remount. A stupid analogy unless you're telling me Cowboy's a jackass, which might be the truth."

"Stop talking back and complaining about your skivvies. Keep your head down and go," I whispered, suppressing my laughter, concerning Cowboy. She was going to get us killed.

"Good morning, girlfriend." Cowboy's voice tinged with sarcasm. "You kept me waiting. Were you afraid to come down here?" He never took his eyes off her, scanning her body like she was a prize filly at auction. "I'm sorry we got interrupted last night. We can play catch-up today." *SMACK*. His hand slapped her rear end as she went by.

Rory walked faster. When we arrived in the cellar, I heard some women catcall from their rooms, "Welcome back, Rory." Ivy sang a few lines from "Like a Virgin" by Madonna. I decided right then Ivy was going to learn to mind her own business. I added 'take Ivy down a peg or two' to my to-do list, too.

Rory's eyes flew around the ruined room, taking in the devastation as she stood in the corridor. I provided a gentle nudge to encourage her to enter. She righted the bed frame and dragged the mattress to it. She gathered her torn poetry and slumped down on her stool, clutching the papers in her hand, elbows on knees, hunched over, hands covering her eyes.

"Ignore them. They're a bunch of catty bitches, and you can fix the room. All temporary," I said.

I turned back once after leaving. She hadn't moved from her place on the stool, but I couldn't go back. I couldn't give special attention to one girl, even if I wanted to. It would be the death of me as whoremaster.

And I did want to.

****

WM's right. My situation's temporary. Things change, and a person must change with them. Rory put a pillow on the floor, sat in the lotus position, and placed her hands in the Dyana Mudra. She counted each cycle, breathing in through her nose and exhaling long breaths through her mouth, until she reached one hundred. She took note of everything in her body. Her left nostril itched and was stuffed up, and her left kneecap ached.

Distracted, she was aware of other things too, footsteps and heavy breathing from the hallway. She ignored them, bringing her attention back to her body, but the breathing got louder. Whoever it was must suffer from emphysema, perhaps, or needed a new lung. Unable to resist, she opened her eyes. The person initially outside was now standing inside the room. She followed the snakeskin boots up to black jeans, a fancy silver-buckled belt, a white button-down shirt, and then finally to—Cowboy's face.

"Aren't you supposed to stand when a man enters your room?" Cowboy asked in a throaty voice.

She pulled her eyes away, looking down at the floor instead, and got up as fast as she could.

Cowboy circled her, his body brushing against hers, all the while reprimanding, "You're not answering me, Rory. Don't you know the rules yet?"

"I didn't know anyone was here. Once I did, I stood," Rory responded.

"Brief answers," Cowboy's voice was low and threatening. "Yes and no, remember?"

"Yes," she said, eyes glued to the floor.

"Yes, what?"

"Yes, Cowboy, Sir?"

"There's my girl. You're doing much better. You try to do what I want, and I won't hurt you. I promise."

He promised once before and then tried to rape me.

Cowboy put his enormous hands on her shoulders, pressing her against the cold wall, and placed his body on top of hers. Heat radiated from him. She couldn't move. His scent overwhelmed her, fresh-cut hay and gasoline. Her body stiffened. He kissed her neck, then nipped it and chuckled when she tried to move away. He shifted his attention to her lips, forcefully sticking his tongue in her mouth, probing. He wanted her tongue in exchange, and bit her lip when she didn't give it.

She cried out, tasting blood. Hers. Salty.

"You need to be more responsive," Cowboy said. He tilted his head sideways and sighed. "It's simple. To get along, go along. An old expression, but a true one." His hands, rough and calloused, moved under her shirt, traveling to her breasts. Then he slid his hands under her bra, rubbing her nipples and pinching them. She held her breath, wishing she'd lose consciousness. "Hmm, you feel good. If you behave yourself, we'll get along just fine. Remember, I know about you. Soon, we're going to understand each other even better." He took his leg and put it between hers, the bulge in his pants swelling as he ground into her.

Her mouth was dry, her heart raced, and her stomach heaved. She exhaled, "Please don't…"

Suddenly she rose skyward, leaving her body behind, floating. *Like before with George…I'm up here alone.*

Clang. The gate closed.

She was drawn back into her body. The sounds of the metal toe plates on Cowboy's boots faded away, but the kiss lingered. Rory rubbed her lips frantically. She didn't cry. Not this time. The smell of gasoline remained. *If only I could burn this place to the ground too. Where is WM?*

She took her bracelet out of its hiding place and held it, running her fingers over the textured silver feathers. *He's gone. I'm safe.* She turned the wings over and examined the numbers again. What meaning did they hold?

****

Ring, ring.

Walking down the corridor, Cowboy answered his phone. "I thought we agreed, no phone calls. Keep it short, I'm not in my office."

Pause.

"I'm leaving her room right now."

Pause.

"What do you want from me? You got everything I could get. I couldn't film it all. Ever try fighting someone holding a phone?"

Pause.

"I don't have any fuckin' selfie stick. I sent you somethin' else just now. Look at it. See what a good little sub she's turnin' into? She'll be perfect in a few weeks. My man can do it with my help."

Pause.

"What are you talkin' about? What bracelet? Didn't have anything like that. Yeah, I'm sure."

Pause.

"You wanna see her? I don't know…she ain't ready for company. I'll think about it. What's so unique about this girl that you gotta have her?"

Click.

"Don't worry, motherfucker," Cowboy mumbled into the now dead line. "One of these days I'm going to find out who you are, and then you're gonna pay."

****

I couldn't stand the mess and clutter. Spilled drinks, peanut shells, and old lottery tickets decorated the floor of the bar. Cowboy was late, as usual. The decor—a mishmash of neon beer signs, biker memorabilia, and Nevada state tourism collectibles—hung throughout the smoke-stained space. It needed a sweeping, and the sticky tables needed to be sponged off as well. The neon signs gave the room an unearthly glow.

The sound of Cowboy's boots announced his arrival. He glided to the table, adjusted his seat, planted his feet firmly on the floor, and held on to the chair arms with his hands, as if blasting off into space. A beer-shaped neon light cast a green pallor over the table, changing us into visitors from another planet. I often felt like an alien. Truth.

Within minutes, our meeting went to hell in a handbasket. I took Cowboy to task for his deception. "You promised no punishment. You destroyed her trust in us. You're making it difficult for me to justify why she should stay here or submit to me. There's no upside to this."

"She survived, that's the upside. But you're right about some of it. Before we discuss Rory, though, good news. I got a new prospect I'm sending your way to help downstairs. An Irish guy, right off the boat. Got an accent and everything. His name's Mike."

"Always nice to have some extra hands. Had no idea we recruited abroad."

"Funny, me either. I admit, I made a mistake, going against my decision not to punish Rory and not listening to your concerns. We've got options." A smile spread from his puffed cheeks. "I know a couple of guys that take girls in a van and drive to truck stops all over the country. They might be interested in taking her off our hands. Then there's the other option, the one we originally discussed when she first arrived."

Cowboy had lost his mind if he thought I was going along with either of his 'options.' "Why can't we just send her back home if it doesn't work out? Chalk it up to an experiment gone wrong," I suggested. "She hasn't been here long."

"Don't be stupid. Have we ever let any of the others go without doing their time? It doesn't work that way."

"Let me do my job, then. I'll turn this around if you keep out of things. What happened last night was bloodlust. What did you achieve, other than revenge?"

"I don't agree. Even though I didn't complete the job, her attitude this morning is vastly improved. She's a wild pony who needs the right rider, is all. A whip occasionally, and a kick with the some spurs when she needs it. You're the right rider, brother, and I can be the whip and spurs." Cowboy chuckled.

"In my opinion, positive reinforcement garners better results in training anyone on anything," I said.

"That's why I told Rory she's improving, and caressed and kissed her too. It's like—"

"What? When did this happen?" Most Doms are regular guys, and any more unwanted attention from Cowboy could ruin Rory as a submissive.

"This morning before the meeting, in her room. Like I was sayin', when I train my dogs, I reward them. Girls aren't that much different. Dogs like to be pet. Why not girls?"

"How did she react?"

"Just fine and dandy. Calm as could be when I left."

I bet. "Philosophically, I agree with some of it," getting up from my seat. "But here in the real world, don't touch her unless I'm present, or we've agreed to it." I left the room.

****

"What ya think?" Louie asked.

"I think I need that new prospect to monitor WM and report back to me. He's losing his balls, holding back with her. I don't get it. He's never been like this before. Plus, last night, him threatening to snitch to the membership rather than doing what I ordered?

Unacceptable, and again, he's never done that before neither. He needs a reminder that I drive this train."

"How ya going to do that?"

"A surprise. We'll see about not touchin' the bitch without his permission." Cowboy lit up a smoke and winked at Louie.

Chapter 9

Ms. Manners

I shook hands with Cowboy before leaving our meeting, but nothing was resolved. Rory had experienced more sexual harassment this morning from the idiot. My failing this girl had become a daily occurrence. Cowboy's analogy of comparing dogs with girls was asinine. Girls and dogs are nothing alike. A dog's mind is a simple thing, while a girl's mind is complex. Dogs don't hold grudges, and girls did. The list could go on and on. It was like saying men are like horses because a few of them can sleep standing up.

I handed Rory the yoga mat and a journal I purchased for her poetry. "Yaaaaasss!" she called out and then pretended she hadn't, shoving the notebook under her mattress and the yoga mat under her bed. When I had discovered Rory had violated my laptop, I'd hesitated to reward her with the journal gift. Still, with more unwanted attention from Cowboy, I needed to do something for her, and the journal would keep loose pieces of paper from accumulating all over the room. I needed to secure my laptop better if I left her alone again. After checking the security manager software on the computer, I saw that one password she'd entered had come damn close. She could have hacking skills for all I knew, and I couldn't underestimate her and allow that to happen.

"Keep your hands off my laptop, if you're ever in my room again," I warned.

Her eyes curious, she replied, "Why?"

"I said so. That's why. You don't touch people's things without asking."

"I wanted to communicate with my friend Sarah, is all."

I narrowed my eyes, didn't blink, flashed a look that usually scared the other girls, and purposefully deepened my voice. "You speak to no one. Is that clear enough? Also, when I ask a question, answer with yes or no responses, that's all. Understand?"

"Yes, WM."

"You can now add the word 'Master,' or omit our names altogether and use 'Master' alone." Seconds passed. "Response, Rory?"

"I can't call you Master. There's only one master in my world, God. And why is my picture your screensaver?"

I'd forgotten about the photo. "Not your concern." The image of Rory meditating relaxed me, or at least it used to. The real girl in front of me now made my blood hot. She's a religious nut too? "Say my name, followed by 'yes, WM' or 'yes, Sir,' 'no, WM' or 'no. Sir,' or just 'Sir.' Got it?"

"Yes, WM, Sir," she said.

Problem solved. "Next, I want to discuss our relationship. We went over why you're here the other day. Our club specializes in BDSM. The men who use our services consider themselves dominants. Their primary interest is submissive women. Our female employees follow certain protocols. Our relationship will be based on this as well. It's all about mutual respect. Give me your respect, and as your Dom I'll give you mine. There'll be more peace and harmony between us and less chaos if you do this and follow my rules. I'm sure with your yoga and Buddhist background, this is something you can get behind. Am I correct?" Once she accepted my dominance over her, things would become easier. Giving her a reason to do so by making the premise acceptable and preferable was step one in the process.

"I respect people who respect me," Rory said, wetting her lips before proceeding. "But I can't honor someone who abuses me and doesn't consider my opinions." She glanced around uneasily and backed up from me.

"I didn't do that, did I?" I asked while moving closer, talking in a firm voice. "I'm dealing with the fallout. You came here willingly. Your job is to do all you can to please me. If you do, I'll reward you." I crossed my arms in front of my chest and stared her down, trying to diffuse the situation and shifted through my memories for any other instances where a sub had countered with her own opinion.

Her eyes lit up and her mouth parted suddenly, choking sounds spilling out. "Hilarious. I don't think so. You should take responsibility for what's happening to me. You could make the correct choice," Rory's shoulders were now pushed back, and her chest and chin jutted out. "Or do you just follow every order that bleached, inked freak gives you?"

"Whoa, little girl. Maybe those panties are too tight, or maybe it's code red, that time of the month. Regardless, once again, stop talking back," I steadied and lowered my voice. "Didn't you learn anything last night?"

"Yes, I learned I'm in a hellhole," she said, fidgeting with her hands. "Cowboy's the devil and it's not safe here."

"What's wrong with your hands?" I asked.

"I suffer from hives when I'm upset, and thinking about all this is stressful."

"Stop thinking," I made a hard smile. "Like I told you before, you don't need to. I'm the Dom and I'll do all the heavy lifting in the partnership. I'll make all the decisions." I deliberately raised my eyebrows. "Any orders I get from my boss are my concern, not yours. All you need to do is obey and please me." I rocked back on my heels knowing I had the upper hand. I'm the Dom and she's here to learn and follow me.

"Why should I obey you?" She asked, her voice soft and her head tilted to one side.

"Think about where you are. Do you believe you can survive here without my help?" I asked, moving closer to her.

Rory's face changed again. Her eyes lost their twinkle, her smile faded and her shoulders now slumped. "I'm not sure—"

"Rory, I'm going to provide the answer. You can't, not without my assistance. Therefore, you need to please me. I'll keep it simple and short. Memorize it, treat it like a prayer. We'll call it the submissive prayer. I have my beliefs, too." I gave her a sly smile. Rory returned a flat expression, but it was better than her talking back. "Listen carefully. Your single purpose is to please me. You can achieve this by submitting to me and obeying my orders. Repeat the prayer: 'My single purpose is to please you. I accept your domination, submit to you, and will obey your orders without hesitation.' Questions about this?"

After what seemed like an excessive amount of time, she shook her head. "Sounds more like an oath than a prayer to me."

My voice lowered as I took another step closer, my eyes almost closed as I squinted down at her. "Opinions are fine, but don't share them with me."

"What do you mean by domination?"

"Like I said domination means you'll submit to me and obey my orders, as if I control you, and if you think about it, I already do. Are you ready to submit?" The space between my eyes had begun to throb. She was giving me a headache. I attempted to rein in my frustration with her questions and non-compliance by telling myself to calm down. *Remember, you're the one in control.*

Rory furrowed her brow, and under her breath she said, "No," before responding in a louder voice to me, "I can't put myself in that position if I don't trust you. And how can I trust someone associated with a gang of thugs?"

I took another step closer. Crap, if I get any closer, I'll be on top of her. I was leaning over her until only a breath separated us. "I'm worthy of your trust. I've saved your life three times already. I'm all that's standing between Cowboy and the rest of those, in your words, 'thugs,' upstairs. You agreed to come here, didn't you?"

Rory's said, "I did, but I never knew—"

"Did you think Cowboy was Prince Charming? Did he promise you a glass slipper, a castle, and a pretty pink coach?"

Her eyes went down, and she twisted a piece of her hair around her finger. "I guess I'm gullible. I'm trying to explain that I was—"

"I'm not interested in your explanations. You came here. Now that you're here it's my job to train you. Your single purpose is to please me. You can achieve this by submitting to me and obeying my orders. Do you agree?"

A standoff, both of us glaring. Seconds seemed like hours, with neither of us breaking eye contact nor saying anything.

"Yes," she finally barked, letting go of her hair and bringing her hand away from her face, one hand pulling on the fingers of the other hand.

"Yes, what?"

Rory rolled her eyes. "Yes, WM, Sir."

I corrected her. "I don't like eye-rolling. Part of submitting and obeying is accepting correction and punishment if warranted. Are you? Stop playing with your hands."

"What kind of correction, exactly?" She placed her hands on her lap. "Ahh, like what Cowboy, tried?" she stuttered, her pupils growing larger, her mouth open.

"No. In most cases, a spanking, like you'd give a child. Nothing more serious, I promise you. Do you agree to punishment if it's deemed, Rory?"

"I don't know…I guess it would be okay if you spanked me—*if* I did something dangerous. But I don't believe in spanking children ever."

"That's not how you accept. Do it over." My mother hadn't thought spanking children appropriate either. My father, on the other hand—

"Yes, I accept punishment if you deem it necessary, Sir," she said.

I nodded at her, satisfied with her compliance in answering the correct way. "I suggest you take the journal and copy the prayer. I expect you to memorize it and repeat it back to me tomorrow, word for word."

"I don't need to copy it." Rory's face was getting red. "I only need to hear or see things once and I remember. No matter how stupid it is. I have a photographic memory."

I chuckled. "Yeah, right. Watch your choice of words and tone when speaking to me."

"You're insulting and humiliating me," she said. "You expect me not to freak out?"

"You can feel things all you want, but I don't want to see any of it." Rory was a compulsive hothead, something that had gotten her in trouble already. Fun stuff for a Dom like me. The dilemma was I wasn't sure I wanted to play these games with her, but she wouldn't survive here if I didn't. "I don't think there is such a thing as a photographic memory but tell me about your superior memory."

"I seldom studied in school. I just listened in class or read the book one time, and I knew the information. I won the county spelling bee three times. For instance, I can spell the word 'nescience,' and I only saw it in the dictionary once. Do you know what 'nescience' means?"

I deliberately clapped slowly in response. "Bravo. I'd be careful. Say nothing that will lead to discipline. Ignorant I'm not. Save the word for someone who is." I glanced at the time. "We should get along. I'm not the patient sort." Rory becoming a submissive would benefit her. Intelligent women have a hard time turning their brains off. "Part of pleasing my desires involves contributing to the welfare of the club. We own another bar up the road, Kitties, and they need servers. You're eating our food and sleeping here, so you have to contribute to—"

"Excuse me, WM, like I was trying to explain earlier, I didn't want—"

I gave her an icy stare. "Rory, don't interrupt me when I'm speaking, ever."

"WM, etiquette dictates that when you interrupt someone, you say 'excuse me,' which I did," Rory defended. "You said nothing when you interrupted me, which means I was polite and you weren't."

"Really?" I fumed. "Well, Miss Manners, *I'm* here to correct *you*, not the other way around. You're here for our pleasure. Your wishes are of no consequence." There'd be fireworks if Rory acted like this with my brothers.

"But I was trying to explain—"

"I don't want your explanations. You're going to work at the bar, serve drinks, dance, and sit on the laps of the members or any other patrons who frequent it. Eventually, if I want you to do more, you'll do it, since we've covered why you're here." I flashed her a dark smile. "And you've agreed to my dominance."

Her mouth opened in surprise, then closed and slid downward. "I don't want to sit on anyone's lap, WM, Sir," she said, eyes wandering around her room.

"I didn't ask what you wanted, did I?" My voice was low and menacing, attempting to intimidate. Another member or Cowboy would straighten her out if I didn't.

"No, Sir, but I can't be near men in that way. I meant to tell you yesterday. I can't be someone I'm not, just to please someone else. I can't go against my beliefs." Her voice wavered.

"On your knees," I ordered. Rory's eyes didn't leave mine. She hesitated. "Do it." She clambered down, peering up, eyes wavering back and forth and then halting. I commanded, "Eyes down," to rid myself of her pleading gaze. I knew where her mind had traveled—back to Ivy's room and the blowjob. "Why can't you be close to men?" I sat on the bed, my arms folded across my chest as Rory kneeled before me, face paling and body trembling.

Like bursts out an M4A1 carbine weapon, words shot out. "One precept of Buddhism deals with sexual misconduct. Sitting on men's laps and letting them touch my body is something I can't do. Therefore, I won't. You also said something outside the meeting hall about not being forced to do anything I didn't want to do." She lifted her head and stared up at me.

"Eyes down," I repeated. *Fuck me.* All the girls in the world, and Cowboy got starry-eyed over a Buddhist. I prayed she didn't talk about this Buddhist bullshit when serving drinks, or profits would plummet. "Anything else I need to become aware of concerning you?"

"One of the other precepts of Buddhism is abstaining from fermented drink. I don't partake," she stammered.

I squeezed my eyes shut, holding the corners of them with one hand, pausing a couple of seconds to gather my thoughts. Was I so morally corrupt that I'd force Rory to fuck men and get drunk against her will?

"Look at me." I forced a fake smile, hopefully not scaring her. Nothing worse than a bad guy trying to act friendly. "Forget fraternizing with or drinking with men for now. We'll talk about that part later. I'm more concerned with whether you can prepare and deliver a beer with a smile, collect the money, and get it in the register. Can you do that?" *Please say yes.* Her New Age bullshit and a steel-trap memory was more than I could bear right now. Did Cowboy know about any of this?

"Yes, Sir."

Hallelujah!

****

I escorted her upstairs before she changed her mind. My favorite part of the room is the ornate, carved wood front of the bar, original to the clubhouse, running floor to ceiling along one wall. It held spirits, assorted glassware, and souvenirs from our 'runs.' The only downside was dust tended to gather on it. A gilded mirror hung dead center, reflecting the patrons' actions, a relic from another age when taprooms couldn't possess enough glitz and bling. No Mid-Century Modern understated elegance was represented here, nor desired. The club's founders had purchased it from an auction house in Vegas for peanuts. The owners, scared shitless of the Knights, did everything possible to send the Knights on their way as quickly as they could.

Rory sat on a stool while I located the black and white old-school sneakers from her escape attempt, still by the club's back door. Most likely too small for anyone else. As she put them on, I appreciated how sexy she looked in the old-school black sneakers. *Get your mind back on business,* I told myself.

I saw the full-time bartender, Hammer, changing out a keg. Hammer had sponsored my Knights membership. I'd first met him first when he was a boxer. He didn't fight in the ring anymore; he did it metaphorically now, during conversations with others. The girls loathed him and referred to him as Mr. Knock-Out. They avoided working with him at all costs. In his day, the ladies had loved and celebrated what he carried between his legs, but not what was between his ears. Getting hit in the head too often at the end of his career hadn't helped him in that department. I dreaded introducing Hammer to Rory, anticipating fireworks, but I needed to get it over with.

"Hammer, this is Rory. She's going to assist you for a while and learn how to bartend until I send her to Kitties."

Hammer lifted his head and glanced at Rory. "Are you going to steal from the register? Drink up all the profits? Flirt with anyone with a dick and not be of any help, like all the others?"

Rory didn't react like I thought she would. "I don't take things that don't belong to me, I don't drink alcohol, and I'm not interested in flirting with anyone," she said, flashing Hammer a winning smile. "I won't be much use in the beginning. But if you're a patient teacher, I'm a fast learner, and I can help you."

Hammer turned to me and asked, "Is this the gal that gave Cowboy the black eye, locked you both in her room and escaped?"

I smiled tightly. "Yeah."

Hammer turned to Rory. "I like you already. Don't look the same as you did during Church. Must be the clothes." He winked and handed her an apron. "Come with me."

I settled against the bar and watched as Hammer gave Rory a quick tour and discussed the beers they carried on tap and bottle. He explained the glassware for different drinks and demonstrated how to make common cocktails like a screwdriver, a bloody Mary, a gin and tonic, and a whiskey sour. Then he moved on to shots like blowjobs, kamikazes, mind erasers, snake bites and slippery nipples that some girls favored for enticing customers. "We keep a book under the bar, or you can ask me if anyone asks for anything you can't make," Hammer said.

"I can take the book back to my room and memorize all the recipes." She looked up at Hammer, her eyes questioning.

"Most of our guys stick to beer, I wouldn't bother," Hammer said.

"Too bad. Making cocktails is the interesting part. More like cooking, and I love to cook."

"As Hammer said," I spoke up, "you won't be doing too much of that. Besides pouring liquor and serving, monitor the clientele."

"What do you mean exactly?"

"Notice if any patrons are trying to rip you off. Saying they gave you a twenty-dollar bill when they only handed you a ten, or skipping out without paying. If anyone tries that, inform Cowboy or Louie."

"What will they do?"

"Handle them," I said roughly.

Rory's face turned white, and she sucked in a deep breath. I should have kept my mouth shut.

"Hardly ever happens," Hammer said. "Our members aren't going to try anything, and the bikers from other clubs know better than to come in here and start anything. Serve 'em and don't worry about nothing else."

A few more guys filtered in, including Worm, who kept to himself most of the time. He selected a table near a wall outlet and plugged in his laptop. I have never seen him without a screen in front of him. Rory went over to take his order. "What can I bring you today?" she asked.

I couldn't help myself and walked closer, anticipating what smartass response Worm would provide. His eyes opened wide, examining her up and down. A thin smile spread across his lips, clearly recognizing her from the meeting. "What ya got?"

Rory's face turned red, stammering, "All that and beer, sir," pointing to the liquor on display.

Worm smirked and asked, "What do you recommend?"

Hard to believe her face could turn redder, but it did. "Orange juice," she said.

"Sounds good. Add Tito's, thanks," Worm said, returning to his keyboard.

She returned to the shelves of bottles on display, examining them until Hammer asked what she was looking for.

"Tito's."

"On the top shelf," Hammer said. "Vodka made from corn. It's high up, so I'll grab it for you."

I leaned back against the wall between the bar and Worm, watching as Rory selected a highball glass, poured a jigger of Tito's, and added the ice and juice. She stirred it with a mixer stick and garnished it with a slice of orange and one of her beloved maraschino cherries. She stole one for herself, too, popping the red orb into her mouth, becoming more beautiful as she savored it. I should buy the jar of cherries like I promised. I want to watch her consume more of them.

As Rory went to deliver Worm's order, the closer she got, the more the tray rocked back and forth. Half the glass had spilled on it by the time she reached the table. Worm kept his eye on her and held the laptop up in the air, avoiding a major part of the spillage. "I'm so sorry, Sir," she said. "I'll clean this up and make a new drink."

I pushed off the bar and went to see if something on the computer had caused the reaction and casually looked over Worm's shoulder. Two shapely woman's legs were spread east and west across the screen, with a man's head smacked between them. I laughed. "Hard at work, I see?"

"Yep, editing one of our films, until Red thought I needed a shower. Someone has to do the heavy lifting." Worm guffawed.

"Maybe she thought you needed cooling off. I'll leave you to it. I don't want to keep you from your duties."

"Why you got this new girl working here, anyway? Isn't she supposed to be an escort?"

"She's got a couple issues."

"Obviously. Can't seem to keep from spilling things. Could be more trouble than she's worth. I might be able to use her in a movie. We got one about a cheerleader coming up. Got the right look. Bring her to my room, I'll give her an audition. No delivering drinks involved," Worm winked.

"I'll think about it," I said, passing Rory who was carrying a mop and multiple paper towels, followed by Hammer holding a new screwdriver. I moved back to a table and pulled out my newspaper I had been reading earlier. Worm was wrong. The most worthwhile things in life were usually more challenging. She had the cheerleader look, all right—but the other stuff required to act in this kind of movie, I didn't think so.

Later, Hammer plunked down at my table. "You can bring Rory back anytime," he said. "I like her. Once she gets the nerves under control, she'll be a winner. She can take the Jose end, and I'll work my spot. Makes a pretty drink too. I only need to show her things once. Smart." He tapped his forehead with his finger.

Hammer seldom spoke enthusiastically about anyone. It meant something. Either Hammer was getting soft, the 'It Factor' was doing its thing again, or Hammer had been hit one too many times. The more significant issue was how the sexy image on Worm's laptop had affected her. What would Rory do when Cowboy let things get wild in the bar, and he brought out his whips and chains?

Chapter 10

Let's Make a Deal

WM was right about one thing—Rory needed him to survive here. She wanted to trust him; if he'd only stop trying to flex and show off, then she would. This whole Dominant-submissive thing was not that different from her Buddhist studies at the ashram. All about the subjugation of self. After kneeling before him, her mind had raced back to the first day, when she had watched him with Ivy. *Is WM going to teach me how to…?No way am I consenting to that.*

She used her Buddhist precepts and WM's own words against him. *It would be all over if he knew I liked him. I can't tell him the truth. The only man who doesn't cause me panic attacks when he touches me…is WM.*

What was it about WM she found so appealing? She wished she knew, so she could come to her senses. Not what he wears. He dressed in the same kind of thing every day, almost like a uniform. A plain T-shirt, white or black with black close-fitting jeans, either with buttons or zippered, topped off with his cut or colors and simple black combat boots, always cleaned and polished. She tried not to stare at him but constantly did so. WM had muscles but wasn't bulked out like Cowboy. WM's body was lean. He was okay looking, she supposed. Rory's stomach fluttered and she ran her hand down her own thigh before catching herself. *Liar. You like his looks. Admit it, you think he's hot.*

Rory had read about Stockholm Syndrome once. *I don't need another affliction.* She had enough of them already. PTSD, celiac disease, lactose intolerance, allergies to wool, cedar trees, mold, and dust. Her hands started to itch just thinking about it. Could she be attracted to his mind? He was smart enough. If only he wasn't so cocky. A sinking feeling in the pit of her stomach replaced the fluttering.

It was a relief when WM, instead of asking for other things from her, took her upstairs, away from the cellar. Her attention could travel somewhere else, allowing her body to cool off and her mind to rest.

The best thing about the saloon was the front door, and a window in the bathroom leading to a way out. She snuck a knife used for cutting lemons into her jean shorts, just in case. No one noticed. *When the world gives you lemons, make lemonade.*

Rory liked the regular bartender, Hammer. He teased her like a proper father might, was a patient teacher who explained everything about the bar, and didn't hide what he thought. Working there was fun, and the time passed quickly.

On the way back to the room, when she told WM she enjoyed her job there, he got snarky again. Eyes half-closed, he said, "I don't care if a sub likes something or not, as long as she does what I tell her to. You need to realize your role here, what my expectations are, and meet them." WM folded the newspaper in half, held it, and looked down at her like she was a puppy needing correction.

"I understand perfectly," she said, her face getting

hot.

"As I said before, my job is to help you survive and even thrive here. I'm so sure you eventually will, that I'm going to offer you a deal."

"What kind of deal, Sir?" Her mind raced.

"Cooperate, submit, no more trying to leave, and *if* in two months, *if* you still want to go home, I'll take you myself. How does that sound?"

"Sound's good if it's true. I've been here, what, a couple of weeks?"

WM laughed. "No, four days. Granted, it feels longer to me too."

"I feel like Alice in Wonderland. My sense of time is distorted. I've fallen down the rabbit hole, I guess. What about Cowboy?"

"I'm not taking Cowboy home. He's from Oklahoma," he joked, "unless he's the Mad Hatter and you're attending his tea party."

"Ha, funny," she said. "Cowboy's more like The Queen of Hearts."

"Don't tell him that. Better pick a male character, or he'll have your head. Who would I be?" WM asked.

"Let me think…hmm, probably the Cheshire Cat or maybe the March Hare?"

"Why the cat and why the hare?" he asked.

"The cat because you appear and disappear at will, you're detached, and you think logically. The hare because you take delight in frustrating me."

WM laughed, and then his smile disappeared. "It's important not to discuss this arrangement with anyone else. I'm making a deal with *you*. You know I'll keep my word. Do we have an understanding, Rory?"

"Are you going to be truthful about when the two

months are up? Since you took my watch and there's no calendar I—"

"No problem," WM said, "But you do things my way. No talking back. Submit."

"Deal." Rory understood what 'my way' meant. The Knights wanted a doormat. For now, she could be one, but if things got any worse and an opportunity came her way, she'd leave. If no other option became available, in two months WM would take her home.

Clang! The gate closed.

"WM, can I ask you for a favor?"

"What?" He looked at her suspiciously.

"Could I borrow your newspaper? I'd like to read it while eating dinner."

"I suppose just once." He handed her the paper.

Jammy. She thought back to what The Manipulation Manual said, 'start with a small favor first.' It worked.

****

My hand pounced on my cell, vibrating on my nightstand. Good news seldom arrived at two in the morning. The caller ID said, Michael.

"Howya? Mic here. Rory's been brutal, bawlin' on and off for two hours. Gawking at me, telling me to feck off. I tried talking to her, but all I'm getting is the puss. I didn't call Cowboy 'cause he'd eat the head off her, I'm thinking."

"On my way, be there in five." I ended the call and threw on a T-shirt and jeans. I pondered what could have happened since leaving her. Was it her loss of self and time? It needed to happen to turn her.

A disturbing sound like a mewing kitten sound pierced my ears as I walked down the passageway. She looked a mess, sitting cross-legged on the bed in a too-large shirt and a pair of shorts, hunched over, head bent and her hair going every which way. The *Sun* newspaper was in her lap, tears streaked down her cheeks, and a red halo surrounded her head from the emergency sign hanging on the wall.

"What gives, Rory? You're going to wake everyone," I said, entering her room.

Between sobs, she read from the paper. "*Lloyd Landry, owner of Soul Yoga, dead from drug overdose. Yoga instructor wanted for questioning.*"

"Stop," I said, tearing the paper from her hands, exiting, and walking down the corridor. Wait until Cowboy learned about this. Or did he know the guy was dead already?

"Please, please, don't go," Rory bawled. I ignored her and threw the paper in the bin. Her cries grew louder. At this rate, she'd wake the few girls still in their rooms. I'd screwed up, by granting the favor and letting her read it.

"They killed him," she cried when I returned.

"According to Cowboy, the guy tried to kill you. Maybe this is the karmic retribution you mentioned."

"I never wanted him dead," she moaned.

I gripped her shoulder. "It's not about what you want. You should know that by now. No sense worrying about something you can't change. There's nothing to be done about it." I stared into her eyes. "Tell me why you're here, Rory."

"Because you brought me here," she said, her chest heaving.

Her response shouldn't have bothered me, but it did. "You know I didn't. You came with Cowboy because you wanted to. Tell me why you're here."

Rory got a crazy glint in her eye. It clicked. "To please you, to serve you," she said.

I nodded my head affirmatively. "Correct. And how are you going to do it?"

"By accepting your domination, submitting to you and obeying your orders," Rory replied slowly between deep breaths and tears.

In a calm but firm voice, I said, "Correct. What pleases me is for you to stop blubbering and settle down." Her crying ceased, but the sparkle in her eye disappeared too. "Remove your clothing and climb into bed. Do it now."

Rory removed her shirt, folded it neatly, and placed it on her small table. She continued with each article of clothing until she stood naked before me. Her performance shocked me, but I pretended otherwise.

"Lay down," I instructed. When Rory did, I covered her with the sheet and blanket, knelt beside her, and brushed the hair away from her eyes with my fingers. As I gazed into them, they no longer appeared bright and alive but dark and lifeless. "Everything's going to turn out like it's supposed to," I told her. "Whatever happened is out of your control and mine too. Go to sleep. I don't want to get any more calls."

"Yes, WM, Sir," she said, her voice flat.

I stroked her head and kissed her forehead, but her eyes did nothing but focus straight ahead. It was like a piece of her soul was missing. I didn't like it, or the news from the article either. *Cowboy and Johnny smoked a guy.*

Before departing, I looked out her small window, the moon non-existent, hidden behind clouds. Darkness surrounded us.

****

I needed to see her this morning. Her submission during her meltdown…those empty eyes, huddling under the sheet, not moving, concerned me, and I wanted to make sure the other Rory was back.

A mass of untamed hair caught my attention. Rory was lying on her side, staring into space. Then her eyes captured mine, coming alive again.

"I brought you breakfast in bed," I announced.

"My first time." Her lips turned upward.

"Never? No sleepovers?" I asked, bringing a cup of coffee to her lips to taste.

"No," she answered as her lips slid downward. "What is this? It's delicious."

"Cuban coffee. I'll bring it again if you're a good girl," I teased. "Breakfast in my bed, too."

She turned red. "Turk's coffee if I'm bad?"

I laughed. "Turk's coffee's poor?" I asked.

"I'm not talking negatively against Turk. Not when he waits on me hand and foot. That wouldn't be wise."

"Smart girl," I said.

"Thank you for the coffee. You keep doing this and I'll consider you boyfriend material," she smiled.

"Wonderful, because I'm having feelings for you too." I was surprised words like this were coming out of my mouth, and I meant them. I followed them up by reaching over and kissing her forehead. I must have just been relieved that the other Rory was back. Even though I wanted submission, I didn't want to lose what innately made her Rory.

"No one brought me a bucket or towels this morning. I thought I was working in the bar," she said, her eyes questioning.

"You are, but you're cleaning up with the others today."

"I'd rather stay here, Sir. I have a situation."

"Remember, no talking back."

She gazed at me with no smile. "Like I said, hmm…using your phrase—code red…Sir."

"I see. All things relating to the 'situation' are in the shower area. Best I take you there," I said, keeping my emotions in check.

"Yes."

"Try again."

"Yes, Sir."

"Good girl." A small step. More like she'd agreed to wear my collar instead of taking a simple shower with the others.

After Rory entered the space, the girls exchanged glances, expecting significant fireworks. But the only fireworks were from my groin after she threw her wrap aside. I tried not to stare but couldn't stop myself. *I'll need that shower, a cold one, if I don't get out of here.*

****

Rory dried off and got back into the same shirt. WM had disappeared. She went to the line of mirrors, picking up a hairbrush and one of the dryers. She saw Ivy reflected behind her shoulder with eyes narrowed, lips pursed, watching.

Suddenly she flew towards Rory and yanked the cord out of the wall, turning the space quiet. "We need to talk," she said. The other girls' eyes were on Ivy and her.

"What's on your mind?" Rory replied.

"You have something that belongs to me, and I want

it back."

"What?" Rory had never talked to Ivy before or borrowed anything either.

"WM's attention and interest, that's what. He hasn't given me the time of day since you've arrived. What makes you so special?"

"I don't have the answer. Speak with WM. Everyone is unique in their own way."

Ivy stormed out of the room, leaving an uncomfortable silence behind until another woman stepped forward. "Don't mind her, hon. Ivy gets snotty sometimes. Has a thing for WM. She doesn't know any better. Rule number one, never get emotionally involved with any of the bosses. Or the clients, for that matter. My name's Rose. Rory, right?"

"Yes. Nice to meet you, Rose." Rose was a gorgeous blonde, tall like a model out of a fashion magazine. Rory felt like a troll standing beside her. "Where do you keep the supplies for Auntie Flow?" she blushed, not able to look up at Rose.

****

I viewed the video from the kitchen. Ivy and Rory's interaction was disturbing. A catfight brewing? I better nip that in the bud and straighten out Ivy. I cringed when Rory started teaching yoga to the others. I didn't want Rory filling their heads with New Age mumbo jumbo. All her philosophical ideas scared me. Her concerns should be on shopping, shoes, lingerie, and how to please a man like the others. I laughed when Rory instructed the girls to set an intention. I had an intention, all right, to get Rory to take her first client as soon as—

I didn't complete the thought. A call from Cowboy interrupted. He wanted me in his office for a meeting, preventing me from putting a stop to Rory's yoga demonstration and returning her to her room.

Cowboy's door was open and his office empty when I arrived. I surveyed his desk. My eyes landed on one of the taller piles. Rory's picture was staring back at me. I got closer and picked it up—a New Jersey driver's license. There was something off about it. Fake? Any yo-yo could make a counterfeit license. All a person needed was a computer, a color printer and a laminator, and they were in business. Age twenty-three, it read. A lie for sure. Her city, Cherry Hill. Was that true or made-up too? A creased newspaper article, with the headline "ARSON IN TRAILER PARK," lay underneath it. I skimmed it. The police were looking for a suspect, the daughter of two of the residents, George, and Angela Woods. I returned the documents to the desk, sat in a chair and waited. I pondered why Cowboy had kept Rory's license. Was Rory the missing suspect? What else was Cowboy hiding from me?

A couple of minutes later, Cowboy and Louie entered. "You wanted to see me?" I asked, keeping my eyes on Cowboy and away from his desk.

"Yeah. Want a cigarette?" Cowboy asked, holding one out for me.

"No, thanks. I'm quitting."

"You're not livin' forever, WM. You know how you said you didn't want me touchin' the new girl?" He took a drag off his cigarette, boots up on the desk. The bastard's eyes were glistening and happy. Meant only one thing; he was about to spring a trap.

"I said I wanted to be around if you do," I corrected.

"Hmm. I got an idea, mentioned it earlier when she got here. To make Rory's transition manageable and get

146

her used to the touchin', we send her to Kitties. Rory can dance. Ivy will show her the ropes, or rather the poles." Cowboy chuckled. "And teach her how to take her clothes off pretty."

"She's just started working *here*, helping Hammer work the counter," I stressed. "In a couple of weeks, if all goes well, she can go to Kitties. Tend bar there and then move to the dancing."

"This gal's turnin' into a real project, ain't she?"

"She's different. We have to go slow. Did you realize she was a Buddhist and had some moral issues when you asked her to come here?"

"Is *she* different, or are you just treatin' her different?" Cowboy asked.

"I've done this job without your help, and you never questioned or complained before," I said. "Now you want to tell me how to do it?"

"Don't go girlie. You're reverting. Like you used to be when you first joined us. Weak. Toughen up. I'm trying to save a life here."

"I don't need saving."

"I'm not talking about you. Doesn't matter where Rory's from or who she is. We treat them all the same. She's got an expiration date. I can tattoo it on her ass if it helps you. I said two months max for a reason. Our yearly gathering, all the chapters making a run, capping it off with a big party, a barbecue. Our place this year. We need all the girls ready to entertain our guests. Her included. Fire up our mini crematorium if she isn't. We're done. Louie, you can leave too. I got business to take care of," he tacked on, taking out his cell."

****

Cowboy—*Figured a way 4 u 2 c princess—*

—Own a strip club—
—She'll dance there—
MM—*Good thing or ur brother willdance—*
—When?—
Cowboy—*I'll let u know—*
MM—*R things progressng?—*
Cowboy—*Slow—*
—Not ezy—
MM—*4sure—*
—I'll say hello2Whiskey4U.—

****

Rory sat with her tailbone hitting the edge of the pillow, her spine straight, each foot crossed on the opposite thigh, and her hands with palms open on her knees, in lotus position. Sunlight from her small window streamed in and warmed her. A bird fluttered and thumped against the glass, trying to get in. *Funny, I want out.*

She couldn't focus and found it difficult to meditate, her mind wandered and drifted back to this morning. WM's face had winced when Rory asked for a bucket instead of going to the bathing area. His lips pressed tight and turned down in disappointment. When she had agreed, WM's lips curled upward. He grabbed her arm and escorted her to the showers like an excited groom. *Yeah, right, Rory, this is a real fairytale wedding.*

The best part of her time in the showers had been making friends with the other women and teaching them yoga. Rory realized how much she missed her students. It was too bad Ivy hadn't hung around. Maybe Rory could have patched things up. She was full of unrest and 'want' today. She wanted the other women to like her, decent underwear, a softer mattress, more blankets, and

148

a brain that wasn't racing. *I need to be more like Buddha and appreciate what I have.*

"The goal of yoga is adaptability, not flexibility." Rory had heard the quote more than once from her yoga instructors. Her thoughts shifted back again to WM. *Why do I care what he thinks? I don't love him. I don't even like him most of the time. Tell the truth. I can't stop thinking about him.*

More sounds were coming from the hall, the sound of metal scraping. She opened her eyes. "Anna's here to do a few spring-cleaning chores in your room," Turk said, unlocking the door, dragging a ladder and setting it up by the window with Anna following. "I'll be back to lock up when you're done," Turk said.

Anna's long black hair had come loose out of her hair tie, and her eyes looked smaller, with lines at the outside corners. She wrestled with the large pail of water and a bag of other supplies. "I can take that," Rory said, carrying the bucket over by her window.

"Thank you. WM ordered me to clean all the windows in the cellar," Anna said, throwing the towels on the floor and wiping her brow.

"I can handle this one. You take a break," Rory said, scooping the sponge out of the suds, squeezing it out and climbing the ladder, scrubbing the glass, then taking the squeegee and removing the foam. *He's right. They are dirty.* She came down the ladder and selected a soft cloth from the bag, going up once more and rubbing the watermarks away. "Unfortunate that I can't clear away all my problems this easily," she said.

"Is it that bad for you here?" Anna asked, her eyes wavering back and forth and head tilted up, listening.

Rory shrugged. "One of the other girls is mad at me.

I don't know if I can fix it."

"Which one?" Anna asked. "Wait a minute, let me think." She rubbed her index finger on her temple and closed her eyes. "I guess Ivy."

"How did you know?" Surprised, Rory took the sponge, wiped off the sill, and climbed higher on the ladder to brush the cobwebs off the ceiling.

"She likes WM, and he's been spending a lot of time with you," Anna said. "Ivy doesn't seem to understand that everything WM does has one goal, to make sure we do our jobs to the best of our ability. She'll recover."

Not meeting Anna's eyes, Rory said, "I have another problem. I think I like him too, even though I wish I didn't." She climbed down from the ladder.

"When's your birthday?"

"June twenty-fourth. I'm a Cancer." Anna's face changed, no longer relaxed, now shocked. "What's wrong?" Rory asked.

"Someone…someone important in my life from long ago had the same birth date," Anna said lowering her eyes and then shaking her head and getting back to the conversation. "The heart wants what the heart wants. Your feelings for WM should give you empathy for Ivy. WM's a cool customer. I've never seen any evidence of a heart inside of him. Sealed in a cage, most likely."

Anna's eyes brightened. "Your relationship with WM could be destiny, since his birth sign is Scorpio and his hearts in a cage and you're the only one he's ever locked in their room." Anna's grin grew broader, and laughter followed.

Pointing to the window, she said, "Now you have a clearer view of things." She gathered the cleaning supplies.

"I do. Thank you for helping me see what I needed to see," Rory said.

Chapter 11

A Clearer View

Rory focused again on counting her breaths until there was no self and she was floating and drifting away...

"Rory. Rory. Rory. Rory," someone called incessantly, forcing her back. Gray surroundings flooded in as her eyes fluttered open. She saw a gate, a shadowy hallway, green-girl blanket, coal-black boots, and a black leather jacket with embroidered patches. WM's intense dark eyes touched hers. Rory concentrated on keeping her eyes on the ground, scrambling off the floor and returning the pillow to her bed.

"I want to discuss a couple of things," WM said. "What happened just now?"

"What do you mean?"

"Try again." WM's eyes bored into her.

"Let me go," Rory whispered.

"I didn't hear you."

"I don't understand, Sir."

"Your response time when I called for you."

"I can't come out of—"

"I don't want excuses. Remember your single purpose is to please me. Your priority is me. Respond immediately as soon as I enter the room. I realize meditation is important to you. My suggestion, rise early or do it in the evening, before bed."

WM lectured like her mother. She found it easier to comply. "From now on, I'll meditate at a time that doesn't interfere with your needs, Sir."

"Good. Besides requiring your attention quickly, I also want to refine it. I want you to kneel and face me if I enter a space."

"Should I throw rose petals at your feet too?" She laughed. "I thought you wanted me to stand when a man enters the room."

"You'll continue to do that with others, but I'm special. I'm your master. You'll kneel before me and place your hands on your thighs, palms down."

"But I don't think—"

"Keep your eyes down and stop talking back. Do you understand?"

"This is a joke, right?" she asked, pressing her lips together and glancing around uneasily.

"No, not a joke," WM said. "I expect you to do it." His tone grew sharper. "Cease the arguing." He held up his hand.

"I find it offensive to kneel. Plus, it makes you look insecure about your manhood."

"Do it and let me worry about my manhood. Remember the prayer? Repeat it."

Rory stared at him, biting her lip to stop herself from saying something she shouldn't. "Get on with it," WM said.

"I accept your domination, submit to you and will obey your orders without hesitation." Her throat felt sore, the words catching, coming out in a whisper.

"Now that we're clear, are you ready to comply?" he asked.

"No. I'm not. I'm not doing anything this ridiculous. Did you know that insecurity leads to attempts to control others? My—"

"I'll give you time to pull yourself together. I realize this is a big step for you. You did some things well this morning. The way you kept your head down when you presented yourself, for instance. But you need to work on some other things, like timeliness and commitment. Like I said before, you can think whatever you want, but don't tell me about it."

"I thought you said the Dom-sub relationship was based on mutual respect. Mutual respect means listening and considering my opinions, not mocking me."

WM ignored her comment and moved on with his never-ending spiel. "We'll get together after lunch to practice. Lastly, when I leave the room, I want you on your knees unless I say otherwise." WM finally left after he realized she wasn't going to comply.

Whenever she started to trust him, he'd do something to change her opinion of him and herself. He wasn't meeting her criteria for being a human being. No empathy or respect. *I failed at pleasing him. I never pleased my mother either. She's right. I'll never amount to anything.*

****

A tough session with Rory. She'd balked at everything. She was good at presenting logical arguments for not doing what I wanted.

I lit my cigarette, blowing the smoke into perfect rings that drifted and dissolved in the sky. What made what I wanted from Rory right? *It will keep her alive, idiot.*

I'd never asked myself that question before. I always

assumed everything I did was what I should be doing. Not this afternoon. Was it Rory or the weather making me sweat? It would get even hotter for both of us if I didn't force her to do what she was supposed to. *Do your job.*

I stomped the cigarette butt into the dirt. Rory submitted the night she was out of control. All I needed to do was get her in the right frame of mind again.

I walked across the parking lot toward the garage. Pieces of old, departed bikes were stacked high inside the open door. I remembered how I had put the Indian back together when no one thought I could. I'd made a pile of discarded items into something everyone coveted. This situation was no different. I needed to strip her down, take out the things that didn't work, and make her usable. A professional does their job without making excuses.

I kicked the carburetor. My toe stung. It was harder than I thought. I didn't want to feel anything. I hadn't with the others. I wouldn't need to come down so hard if Rory would stop fighting. Why couldn't she cooperate?

All these pieces, once working, were now worthless pieces of junk until someone used them and made them into something. I turned away from it all in disgust.

****

Rory's guru had said there were always reasons people behaved in specific ways. She tried to think of things from all sides like she'd been taught to do at the ashram. Her mind was as dull as the sink full of dirty dishwater at the school, like the sink full she helped clean after meals as part of her service. Now her thoughts were just as murky. She couldn't trust herself anymore or her instincts, when she was so mentally drained. She needed to look beneath the surface. Maybe WM was trying to make her stronger. *Don't rationalize his behavior. He's a jerk.*

Her gate swung open.

Clang, clang. Her gate swung open. "Why the long face, lassie?" the prospect asked as he placed her lunch tray on the small stool. A green apple caught her attention. Most often they were sour, and she didn't care for them. *Like her life now.*

"WM was rough on me today. He seems to have this deep desire to dominate me." The prospect chuckled. "Why are you laughing at me?"

"That's what they're into here. Once the scene's over, you're back to being yourself again." His eyes cut towards Rory. "By the way, my name's Michael, Mic or Mike, in case you don't remember from the other night."

Rory shot up and paced. "Nice to meet you again, Mike. And yes, I know about the Dominant-sub thing. But it's not just role-playing." She shook her head. "WM said I need to kneel if he enters the room. I could never do that, especially in front of others." She'd pushed her ego down in teacher training, but this was something else entirely.

"Why not?"

"Could you?"

"No, but I'm a man. And Irish."

"What's that have to do with it?"

"The Irish bow to no one. Women submit to men in our country. The law of nature. Women are born submissive. It's only because of conditioning that you've turned into something unnatural."

"I bet Irish women would tell me something different." Rory grumbled. "What kind of conditioning?"

"Societal pressures. Women go out in the world now and have jobs instead of staying home, keeping house, and raising children. Destroys their sexuality in the bedroom. It replaces their natural instincts with something that isn't. They're not true females anymore."

"Ridiculous," Rory laughed. "Women can want one thing out in the world, enjoy something else in the home, and still desire another thing with her lover. I don't understand why a woman can't have it all."

"Don't say any of that in front of WM." Mike's forehead furrowed.

"WM's ideas are rigid. People want different things, and it's not just about gender. Some men may want to submit, and some women may enjoy dominating."

"A woman should do what a man tells her. She'll be happier."

"I wouldn't believe everything WM has to say about women. We're all different. Do you think if I do what WM wants, I'll be happier?" Rory asked.

Mike frowned. "I think everyone needs to be true to themselves, whatever that may mean. But it isn't a bad thing to step out of your comfort zone. Now, I'm going to plan tonight's dinner." He turned to leave. "Believe me, your dietary needs are out of mine." He chuckled. "Don't get worked up. You're giving it all more worry than you need to." He left, closing the gate behind him.

Rory took the lunch bag from the tray. Hopefully, there was something she liked inside. The brown bag felt heavier than normal and crinkled. Her fingers wrapped around something cold and heavy. She lifted it out and turned it in her hand first before resting the piece on her lap. A gun. Black with a gray handle. Carefully, she slipped it underneath her pillow while she searched for another place to hide it. Did Michael provide her the weapon? If not him, who?

Finally, she rolled the gun inside her yoga mat and slid the whole thing under her bed. *What do I know about guns? Nothing. And I don't have a book or YouTube to figure it out, either. Should I keep this or tell someone?*

****

"Rory, what's wrong?" I asked, looking over at her tray. It sat untouched, and her face was flushed as she lay on her bed.

"I'm not well," she said, her voice sounding hoarse.

Now was not time to correct her for the missing 'Sir.' I let it go. "You didn't eat your lunch."

"My throat hurts…"

"I'm calling Johnny."

I paced in the room after he arrived, cracking my knuckles as Johnny examined Rory. "Her temperature's one-hundred and two, low blood pressure, a rash on her arms and legs," he reported. "Her lymph glands seem swollen too," he added, touching the front of her neck. "Could be a bacterial infection of some sort. Two other girls were sick last month. A fever, sore throat, and real tired a day or two, and then they bounced back. Have her drink plenty of fluids—water, ginger ale and the like. Put a cold cloth on her head and give her some ibuprofen to bring down her temperature."

"I don't do pharmaceuticals, only herbal remedies," Rory said.

I ignored her and walked up the steps with Johnny. "Keep an eye on her," Johnny instructed me. "Don't let her fever get higher. It doesn't matter what she wants. Maybe her body can fight it off, but it might be a good

158

idea to get some antibiotics, just in case. Amoxicillin oral suspension is better since she balks at taking capsules."

"My friend has access. Turk can monitor her condition until I return." Thunderclaps boomed in the distance as I closed and locked the door to the cellar.

****

The sound of rain and clashes of thunder reverberated down the corridor, interrupted by Rory's cries and mutterings.

"What's going on here?" I asked Turk as he stood inside of Rory's room.

"You mean the leak by the window or Rory?"

"Don't be a moron, Turk. I'm asking about Rory."

"She's been crazed since you left," Turk said. "I contacted Johnny, but he's not answerin'. She's been talking trash the last hour, yelling at some guy called George, said, 'You're not my father, leave me alone,' A stepfather she said."

"Who took her clothes off?" I eyed Turk suspiciously.

"Don't look at me. *She* did. Ripped her shirt and shorts off right in front of me. Hot, I guess." Turk scratched his head.

I patted Rory's shoulder and said her name to catch her attention. She swung at me, screaming, "Don't touch me, George! Leave me alone! Don't take my picture! I'll tell Mom!" Her skin was burning up, and she had a splotchy rash all over. Her face was as red as a beet and puffy. Her eyes, when open, were dilated, and her hair was damp with sweat.

"Calm down. I won't." I pretended to go along with what she was saying. I didn't have time to play shrink.

I turned to Turk. "Keep the lights down and apply

cold compresses. I'm going to find Johnny."

****

Club members, friends, misfits, and malcontents had overrun the bar, but no Johnny. I scoped out the front porch and the yard. He wasn't there. I headed toward Johnny's room on the second floor. After some heavy knocks, Jillian answered. Jillian served the old-timers and brothers who didn't want to pay the going rate. She'd been hired well before my time, and retired before my time too. An independent now—a good thing. I was sure she was stealing from members. She'd go down hard if Cowboy learned of it.

"Where's Johnny?" I didn't wait for an answer, walking into the room. Johnny looked like Jesus on the cross, spread out on his bed. He might end up in the pose permanently if he kept screwing up. I pulled Johnny's skinny body into a standing position. "Wake up. We have a patient downstairs." I slapped his glasses on him and dragged his limp, pantsless body down the stairs and through the clubhouse, his dick and balls jumping and jangling and my brothers loving it, clapping and making all kinds of lewd comments.

We stopped in the cellar's bathing area before heading to Rory's room. I opened the locked cabinet and got a syringe and the ibuprofen in drop form. Johnny's eyes were no longer squinty, and his body stood straighter. He wrapped a large bath towel around himself, rubbed his eyes, shook his head back and forth, and followed me to the room.

I looked on as Turk played nurse to the patient from hell. "I got oral amoxicillin and capsules too," I said to Johnny. "My friend said it could be strep."

"We'll never know for sure without a test," Johnny

said. "We can administer the ibuprofen and the amoxicillin. Squirt it in her mouth." She flopped around on the bed restlessly and Johnny added, "Hold on to her, Turk."

"Not so easy," Turk panted, hands sliding on her twisting, sweating body, punching and pulling away from the collective five hundred and sixty-five pounds of all of us.

As Johnny squirted the ibuprofen in her mouth, Rory flew off the bed, striking out like an MMA fighter, spitting out the contents. My white T-shirt was now a Jackson Pollock painting. We pinned her to the bed again, and this time Johnny got it down her throat. She became a person possessed and in need of an exorcism, fighting and screaming nonsense. Johnny repeated the process, this time with the amoxicillin. With no priest handy, I improvised, doing something my mother did when I was sick. I sang.

Turk commented, "I didn't know you could sing like that. What's the song, WM?"

"'An Irish Lullaby.'"

"You must have trained," Johnny remarked.

I stopped singing, giving them both my deadliest stare. "Keep your mouths shut, understand? Never mention this to anyone."

Turk nodded. "Our secret, boss."

Johnny added, "I don't need problems with you, WM. Whatever you want."

I kept singing while wiping her chest and head with a damp rag. At first, she didn't want anything to do with dreams or hugging or any of the other words from the song, but slowly she settled into it. When I got to the nonsensical part of it, she relaxed and stopped struggling.

161

"Turk, get some clean sheets and a change of underthings," I whispered, "I'll stay here."

Turk looked happy to oblige, rushing down the passageway with Johnny. I dipped the cloth in water, wrung it out, and wiped Rory's brow again. Even now she looked beautiful to me. *Don't let anything happen to her…*

"WM. I need WM," Rory cried. "He's the only one…"

"I'm right here," I said. I didn't understand what Rory was talking about. The only one for what? To give her grief, perhaps. I didn't have time to ponder other possibilities.

Minutes later, Turk reappeared. By that time, Rory was resting quietly, her forehead cooler too. "I want to put new linens on the bed," I said to Turk. "These are wet and dirty from hanging on the ground."

We undid the ends of the existing ones. Turk took one end, I took the other, and we lowered her, sheets and all, to the floor. After changing the bed, I knelt beside her and whispered in her ear. "I'm going to move you and remove your damp underwear. It's only me." She didn't wake. Even changing her underthings caused no disturbance. I covered her with the green-girl blanket and turned to Turk. "Thank you. Bring the portable heater from the meeting hall back before you turn in. It's cold down here. I'm going to stay with Rory tonight. She might lose her balance if she gets up on her own." *And I can't leave her unless she's safe.*

****

I insisted Rory swallow the ibuprofen when she woke a few hours later. She refused at first. I had her repeat the submissive prayer.

"I accept your domination, submit to you and will obey your orders," Rory recited in a husky whisper.

"What do I want you to do, Rory?" I asked.

"Take this medicine."

"Roger that. To keep your temperature normal."

She took the pills feebly from my hand, swallowed both with a gulp of bottled water, and lay back down. I smoothed her hair back gently.

"Don't leave me," she whispered, her eyes wavering, tears welling. "I don't want to die."

I held her hand. "I'm not going anywhere. I'll be here by your side if you decide to leave this earth. But believe me, you're getting better."

She clutched my hand back. "Will you please me too, WM?"

"What's your desire, sweet one?" I teased.

Her face flushed. "Will you hold me?"

"How can I refuse?" I squished in, almost on top of her. Damn, these twin beds were small.

Rory nestled inside my arm. "Would you mind touching me, WM?"

What did she mean by that? "Can you be more specific?"

"Touch me like a man touches a woman," Rory replied, walking her fingers up my arm, eyes glinting red from the light in the hall.

Electricity shot through me. Whoa. "I'm not sure. You might be delirious and—"

Rory put her finger on my lips, whispering, "Hush," stopping me from saying anything further. She closed her eyes and whispered, "Please me."

Clasping my hand, she slid it between her legs and placed it on her lace-covered crotch. My mind presented various adverse outcomes. I wanted to push every one of them away, along with Rory's panties, but I couldn't. I brought my hand back to my side and watched Rory's chest go up and down, her eyes slowly shutting as she drifted off to sleep. I stayed the rest of the night and the following day, too, until her symptoms were gone.

I went to shower around dinnertime and returned to her room later that night. I found her by the window, standing on her stool, staring at the night sky until she heard me. I handed her the amoxicillin. She washed the pills down quietly, no more fighting. She lay down on the bed, grasping my hand. The only light came from the moon shining in. "Rest with me," she said.

I didn't wait for her to ask me again. I nuzzled her neck, playfully nibbling her earlobe, and whispered, "Do you still want me to touch you?"

"Yes," she said, the moonlight resting on her eyes, creating stars.

I moved her panties aside and rubbed her small wet flower with my thumb, teasing it. My fingers spread her, stroking her as moisture formed. I shoved my index finger into her dampness and moved deeper, bringing it out halfway and then back in, fucking her with it. "Am I touching you like you want, little one?"

Rory moved against my finger, opening herself wider. She became wetter and thrashed against my hand. I pushed a second finger in, and she squeezed tightly around it. "Oh, yes," she replied, moaning.

I moved them harder and faster, quickening the pace. Rory's moans grew louder still. I considered forcing in a third until she turned the tables. She unbuttoned my jeans, and my erection, demanding freedom, jumped from my pants into her willing hand.

She wrapped her fingers around my cock, and it filled her fist, pre-cum forming. Her hand slid up and down a couple of times until my cock escaped. Laughing, she said, "Come back here," and recaptured it.

Rocking against her, I caused her camisole to hike up and expose her breasts. I brought her closer. The smell of sex and her soft skin was intoxicating, filling my senses. Within minutes, my cock was ready to explode. Where had she learned to give a hand job like this? I made a to-do list in my head to keep myself from coming—wash the bike, purchase stock and organize my CD collection. She knew what she was doing. Her *coup de grâce* was squeezing my balls, and not a light touch either. The pain was excruciating, hurting me badly, and so damn good.

I took my medicine and a howl escaped my throat. I came, spurts of cum landing on parts of her lace cami and her bare skin, but she didn't grouse about it. I hoped no one had heard. "Thank you, little one," I replied gruffly.

Once again, I took hold of her slippery clit and rubbed slowly, softly, building up more friction and speed. Her little inhales and gasps came closer together. If the other girls were awake, maybe they'd think she was still with fever. Better yet, maybe they were still out working.

Rory's eyes burned red, closing and opening in unison with each stroke, lit by the emergency sign in the hallway. Her body tensed beneath me. She threw her head back and then forward, arching her back, thrashing against my hand. I pinched her clit tightly. She tried to get away, to escape her sweet pain, and I didn't let her. Finally, with a quiver, she released her honey into my hand, clutching my hair, whimpering my name—"WM, WM, WM,"—in my ear until my name de-evolved into "mmmmm." Her eyes were half-opened, diamond bright as her lips parted. She mouthed, "Thank you."

I brought my fingers containing her essence to my mouth, tasting her, and then to her lips. "Taste your sweetness, sweetness." The tip of her tongue appeared, and she licked my fingers and her lips clean. I stroked her head with my other hand, losing it in a mass of wild curls.

A few minutes later, she left me, falling into a peaceful slumber, an angelic smile on her lips.

Chapter 12

Life is Suffering

I never found rest in her bed. Usually, I preferred to be the one dispensing pain, but I had enjoyed what she'd done to me. I needed to be honest with myself. I'd never become this close to any other girl who had worked for the Knights. Rory said she shouldn't be here. The better part of me believed it. The other part of me knew I couldn't give her up. What was I doing? I needed to get a hold of myself. I couldn't use her like this. Or was she using me?

Rory woke at dawn. Her temperature was still normal. Unfortunately, I couldn't say the same for myself. There was nothing in a bottle to appease my fever. Cowboy had better not learn of my attachment. He'd have my head and balls, and there'd be no way of holding Cowboy back from Rory if he found out what we'd done.

****

The aroma of freshly cooked bacon and eggs smelled enticing. I handed off the pills to Turk as he stood in the kitchen with some other members. "Probably won't need the ibuprofen unless she runs a fever again, but give her the antibiotic twice a day," I instructed. "The next dose with breakfast. Keep it light. And give her plenty of fluids today. Inform Mike too, if he takes over. I'm catching some Zs. Any change in her condition, call."

"No problem. I'll take care of it," Turk said as I stepped towards the door to leave the kitchen.

"The prospects reported Rory's ill," Cowboy said, entering and opening the cabinet and grabbing a mug.

"Yeah, a sky-high temperature. Normal now, most likely a bacterial infection. Going to be a few weeks before she's totally well." I said, not meeting his eyes. I tried not to play with my ring.

"The girl's got more lives than a cat. What's this, two come-back-to-life experiences since she's been here? A record for our club. She must have good karma. Or is it bad karma if you keep living the same damn life?"

"I don't know a lot about Buddhism, Cowboy."

"I think it's not a bad deal if you're born again, but according to them, it's bad because life is suffering. But I think if you're born into a great situation then it's good." Cowboy closed his eyes.

"I'll take the perfect situation and no suffering," I said.

"She's with us, so she's damn well gonna suffer." Cowboy shrugged, taking a sip of coffee. "'Cause that's what we're about. Pain is our thing. Most of our girls are masochists and into it, so it's symbi…something. Works out well, yeah?"

"Symbiotic. But it's our job to keep them safe. Give them what they want, get what we want, and not let things get out of hand. Conversations like this open my eyes, but I need sleep, what with nursing the girl and all. I would love to discuss this in-depth with you later." I was determined to get out of the kitchen without tipping him off and wondered what else I could say.

"Of course, later is fine. But we've never harmed any of them badly, and no complaints from any either. Maybe a scene in the dungeon with two girls would put some pep in your step, WM. Or you could go to sleep first. Do you want me to check on the girl for you?" Cowboy asked, patting my shoulder.

"You definitely don't want to catch what Rory's got." *I didn't want Cowboy anywhere near her, and this was the perfect excuse.* "She's highly contagious. It might be a good idea to post a sign on the kitchen door about her illness too*."*

"Speaking of suffering and the girl," Cowboy said, pouring more coffee in his cup. "I read something yesterday. Made the front page of the *Sun*. The cops think Rory killed Landry. Isn't that killer? Found the harassing texts he sent her and interviewed the best friend, who said there were arguments between the two. Blue put two and two together and came up with wrong." Cowboy laughed and took another sip from his cup.

"Really?" I asked, concealing my shock. "They reported earlier they wanted to talk to her. Now they think she did it?"

"Rory can't think of going back to Vegas, or she'll end up behind bars," Cowboy said. "She can't run, either. No money. Double jeopardy deal. Works well for us. She'll commit now." He nodded his head up and down. "Don't worry about the poster. I'll have Louie make it."

She's wanted for murder now. *Fantastic.* And if that wasn't bad enough, the next thing gave me pause. Louie stared at me with a less-than-friendly expression. Then he turned to Cowboy and said, "Didn't you have a question for WM about the missing stuff in your office?"

"Yeah, right." Cowboy turned back to me. "After you waited in there alone the other day, a couple of things disappeared."

The whole kitchen settled. No one poured coffee, no dishes rattled, no one moved about. All eyes were resting on me as I stared at Cowboy.

I looked him in the eye. "I don't steal. And I would never take anything off a brother." An unsettling heaviness traveled throughout my chest and my mind raced back to that day. I couldn't recall if anyone else had been outside his office before or after my visit.

"Of course not," Cowboy said, his face in a scowl. "Did you see anyone else hanging around?"

"No."

"Humph," Louie said as I exited the kitchen, everyone's eyes following.

****

A movement made Rory jump.

"Relax, only me," Turk said. "I'm here because WM wanted me to keep a careful eye on you. Are you feeling better? Hungry?" Her throat was scratchy, and she couldn't get the words out, so she nodded. "I'll go upstairs and whip something up." He pulled the folding chair behind him, leaving it in the hall and fastening the door.

Rory pushed up from the mattress, finally standing, and sponged off with the fresh water in the bucket. She picked up the clothes she'd worn the previous day, damp and wrinkled. She brushed her teeth using the water in her bottle, and combed out the tangles in her matted hair. Then she sat cross-legged on her bed in easy pose and practiced Ujjayi breathing, her energy level increasing.

Turk returned and slid a plate with two pieces of gluten-free toast and a green protein shake in front of her. He always seemed to know just how to meet her needs. The memories from the previous two days jumped into her head. Her face heated in horror as she replayed forcing herself on WM. The idea of dying alone, having enjoyed no one of the opposite sex, bothered her. And in her delirium sha had tried to do something about it.

WM, the perfect gentleman, had done nothing that night, *but* last night was different. She swallowed a piece of bread, and it lodged in her esophagus as she remembered. Choking, then coughing, she forced the toast out. It was unbelievable what WM's touch did…explosions. She shouldn't think of it now, shifting her attention back to Turk, his smile shining down on her. "Thanks for taking care of me. I wasn't at my best," she said.

Turk belly-laughed. "You ain't kidding."

"Well, maybe we can put it behind us and forget about it." Anything to shift the subject.

"You were like out of a horror movie, a real-life zombie. Super strength. It's burned in my memory forever."

Scorched in Rory's, too, but not for the reason he was talking about. *The first orgasm I didn't give myself.* She felt her face flush. "Stop it. You're embarrassing me. What were you doing to me?"

"We weren't trying to hurt you." Turk's expression turned serious. "You were out of your mind with fever. We needed to give you ibuprofen and get the dropper into your mouth."

"I appreciate everything, Turk."

"You should thank WM. He stayed with you the

entire time. Even sang to you."

"Really? WM sings?" Rory asked. *He cared.*

"Yeah. Ever heard the quote about music soothing the savage beast?"

Rory blushed and stammered, "Was I that bad?"

"You were as strong as three men. Supernatural."

"What did WM sing?"

"'An Irish Lullaby.'" Rory's eyes welled up, and tears ran down her cheeks. Her throat closed as she tried to hold them back. "Why are you crying?" Turk asked.

"My mother never believed me when I told her I didn't feel well. She accused me of faking. It touches me that WM cared." She hadn't thought for a long time about the way her mother had treated her. The truth? Her mother hadn't acted like other mothers, and not just when Rory was sick. Her mother had never even packed a school lunch for her.

Rory's mood got lower as the afternoon slipped away. Turk sensed her sadness and asked if she wanted to take a shower. "I have nothing clean to put on," she said.

"Usually WM gives me the clothes, but I don't want to wake him. I'll go find something," Turk said.

Rory waited. She was always waiting for something or someone. The room was an icebox, Rory pulled the green-girl blanket closer, fighting the cold, falling in and out of slumber. A spider devoured a tiny bug in its web above her bed. She looked closer and hallucinated Cowboy's head on it.

Then she began remembering fragments of George's maneuvers. She did her best to push them away, made it a priority to forget. She'd never discussed what he'd done to her with anyone, except once. Her mother had stopped her, and her stepfather, George, used threats to keep her quiet. He'd said no one would believe her, and even if they did, it was her they'd blame. She had fought him off as she had gotten older, and things got even worse. George broke her things and told her mother lies. She had stood her ground, at the end becoming Goddess of Fire, Hephaestus. *They gave me a life of hell and I returned the favor.*

The hair on Rory's arms tingled. She turned toward the open portion of her door. A figure masked by a billow of smoke hovered in front of the gate. Had she died and gone to hell? She blinked and rubbed her eyes. The vapor dissipated, and a tattooed muscular body and the bluest of eyes emerged.

Cowboy—the newest devil in her life.

"How ya doin', little girl?" he asked in a raspy voice, vapor coming from his mouth. "Ya feelin' better?"

"Fine, Sir." Cowboy stood outside her room, not inside. Should she stand or not? What was the protocol?

Cowboy said, "I'm glad you're well, little filly. Worried about you. Why don't you come over here?"

Rory didn't want to make him mad enough to come into the room, and he had requested something. She moved to the door while taking the cover along and wrapping it around her body. "Graceful, the way you did that," Cowboy guffawed, "but I prefer seeing you without the sheet. Drop it." He barely got the words out before reaching between the bars, seizing her hands and tugging her forward. Cowboy released her and propelled her away, causing the cover to fall. "Hmm, that's better, girlfriend. Why do you play coy with me? It's not like I haven't seen your ass and tits in your tight yoga gear."

Rory turned red, plucked the cover off the floor,

draping it over herself, and wondered if there was any truth in his words, as she yelled out, "Why are you so rude and crude? Every time you open your mouth to me, you say something mean and insulting."

"Is this how you see things? I'm just honest," Cowboy scoffed. "I would come in there and show you some more of my truths, but with your infectious condition, I can't."

Rory wanted nothing to do with Cowboy, and would've liked to see him disappear, but she remained silent. He didn't seem bothered, and if he was, he tackled it head-on.

"I'm sure you harbor resentment because of what happened after you ran, but you need to take responsibility for what went down. Hopefully, you learned from it, and I won't have to resort to that kind of punishment again. You can't ever talk back in front of my men. It would've been the end of my presidency if I didn't do something. It's how things work here, and in corporate America, too."

Rory stared at him. *I'm sure the CEO doesn't rape his employees to put them in their place, asshole.*

"Of course, ours will never be a storybook romance, like the ones you like to read about. You'll need to be down with that. You gotta earn your keep by bringing home the bacon and becoming a top earner. Do that and learn how to please me," he smiled, "and your situation could change. You could be my woman exclusively. We'll see."

Shocked by his declaration, words poured out of her. "I'll never do that, ever! I'm a Buddhist." And she backed further away from Cowboy, a rushing sound in her ears as lightheadedness attacked her.

"Bless your heart. Of course you are. But WM has ways of gettin' a girl's head straight. I bet he's already gotten you to do some things you'd never imagined yourself doing." Cowboy chuckled. "Big news. Looks like staying here is your only option." He passed Rory the newspaper. "He hasn't shown you the article, I bet."

"What's this?" she asked, scanning the article. *What's WM gotten me to do?*

"Now simmer down. There's no going back. Accept it. You're here for the duration. Best if you thought twice about getting feisty with me. You never know which way that's going to go. I let you slide this time 'cause no one's here, and you amuse me." Cowboy threw his cigarette on the floor, stomping it out with the heel of his boot, and walked away.

She fought back nausea as she clutched the newspaper and read it again. *Will I belong to Cowboy and have to sell myself? Why did WM hide this?*

****

I threw the pillow off my face, reached for the phone, and checked the time. A whole day, gone. I hobbled out of bed, one hand on my waist, my back out again. I needed to make it to the shower and loosen it up. *Come on, soldier, pick up the pace.*

The water splashed from the jets on my spine, an easy reminder of why all this fancy stuff was worth every penny spent. How could I function without it? Especially now. Squeezed into a twin bed with an old, skimpy mattress two days in a row, and sitting on a metal chair for hours on end, didn't do my body any favors. I smiled, remembering the good part. My erection was taking over. A simple hand job, mind-blowing. What would it be like to go all the way with her? *Stop. I can't go any further. Cowboy will nail me to the cross in the dungeon if he finds out. It can't go anywhere. Even if I like her.*

A Guitar Shorty CD played in my room, and it sounded good. I had less time to relax and listen to my favorites since the girl landed. My life was becoming chaotic. I was losing control of everything I enjoyed, like listening to the blues, riding my bike, and working on my stock portfolio. But last night, in her bed, more than made up for it. I'd endure less control to have that again.

I stopped myself. She's in my head, full circle. Crap.

****

"WM, I gave some things to Turk for the new girl," Anna said, stopping me in the cellar corridor. "She'll have enough outfits to last quite a while."

"What kind of wardrobe? How many things?" I asked, attempting not to display my anger.

My mouth tightened as Anna reported the details. "Turk acted like he was doing this under your direction," she stammered, the color in her face draining and the whites of her eyes growing larger.

Arms crossed, I stared into Anna's eyes. "I'll discuss it with Turk. But in the future, so you never make this mistake again, I don't want a new girl having extra clothing. It suggests ownership. She owns nothing. I own her, understand?"

"Yes. I won't let it happen again, I promise," Anna said, hurrying away.

I found Turk mopping the tile in the shower area. He made the error, and he'd need to fix it. I wasn't going to be the bad guy this time. "Turk, we need to talk," I said.

"About what?" Turk's eyes questioned as he leaned on the mop.

"All those clothes you gave Rory. She can't have

them," I said, holding my coffee in one hand and a banana in the other.

"She needed something to wear, boss."

"Yeah, she does, but they need to come a little each day. Her having these things all at once isn't right. We need control of her and everything she does. If I give her stuff she didn't earn, she'll never do what we want."

Turk's face lit up, and he nodded. "I understand. Part of gaining authority over Rory is making her wait."

"Exactly. Take them back. You can do it one of two ways. I can take Rory out of her room for some bogus reason. You go in and remove the apparel, and she won't know what happened. Or you can be upfront about it. Tell her you made a mistake and you need them back. Your choice."

Turk walked up the hallway slowly, his hands shoved in his jeans, his head down. A few minutes passed before Turk returned, his lips curled downward, carrying a large pile of clothes.

"Did she cry?" I asked.

"No crying. But she wasn't happy," Turk said. "She'd already folded and put them away neatly. She wouldn't look at me."

"Remember, decisions have consequences, and you don't want to hurt any girl more than you need to. You want to give them the strength to survive here, not make it worse. Let me see them." I divided the clothes into two piles. "I don't want her wearing some of this. She looks best in fitted clothing. Rory's petite with an athletic build. I like lace on her sometimes, and her favorite color is purple."

"Where do you want me to put the ones you selected?"

"On the top shelf," I answered, "by the hairdryers, and take the other stuff back to Anna. It might be a good time to change the soap the girls are using. I don't care for the smell, too medicinal. Send away for some samples…something with citrus or a woodsy scent."

"I'll work on it," Turk said, picking up the mop with a scowl.

Moving past him, I walked down and into Rory's room, pretending to know nothing about the clothes. I tossed a banana toward her. Even with her head down and on her knees, she still caught it. When she looked at me, her eyes were red and wet. I ignored them, plastering a smile on my face. "Your hair's great, like Farrah Fawcett's. Did you curl it?" Maybe my compliment and the conversation would bring her out of her funk.

"Yeah," she said.

"Yes, what?" I corrected her, but she said nothing. "Rory, what's the problem? Something's bothering you, since you seem to have forgotten most of the rules. Again. And remember to keep your answers short."

Rory's face transformed into one of confusion, as she tried to figure out how to tell me about the clothes in a shortened version. In my experience, girls and some fellas had a hard time keeping things on point. They wanted to give a long song and dance.

"Turk gave me some outfits to wear. A few minutes ago, he came and took them all back. He said I couldn't have possessions because I am, in fact, a possession. Sir, you had a thing for Farrah Fawcett?"

What the hell was wrong with Turk? He shouldn't have been that direct. "Not really. I used to watch old reruns of the show she was in, *Charlie's Angels*, at a friend's house, and I bought a vintage poster of her too."

I lied. I did have a thing for Farrah—a serious one. I jacked off to her image every chance I got, fantasizing about her. "Do you think it's true what Turk said?"

Rory closed her eyes, wrinkling her brows before responding, "Right now, I can't make any decisions. I'm dealing with a force more powerful than myself. Everyone's possessed by something or someone greater than themselves."

No doubt about it, she considered things deeply. One of the things I admired about her. "Did those garments mean that much to you? I thought Buddhists weren't into material possessions."

Her eyes glinted like stainless steel. "Every day I lose more of myself. The clothes made me feel safe, normal. You're stripping away who I am and changing me into something and someone else, but you know this, don't you? Do you really think complimenting my hair is going to make me feel better about what you're doing?"

"Rory, why don't you spend some time alone. I'll come back later when you're feeling better." She's defying me, and no interaction was better than allowing negative ones.

She got off her knees and came at me, further challenging me. Her arms were crossed, and her face was turning red. "You mean, you'd rather I don't voice my opinion, keep my feelings bottled up and play the Stepford Wife for you, Sir. Or would you prefer I pretend I'm Farrah?" She flipped her hair. "You never told me the cops think I killed Lloyd, and that I can't ever go back to Vegas." She reached for the folded-up newspaper on her bed and hurled it, hitting me in the head.

What the hell was a Stepford Wife? And yes, I

would prefer she played Farrah. "That's going to garner punishment," I said, turning my back. An error. Rory bum-rushed me and knocked me off balance, causing me to slip. Déjà vu. The keyring slid from my hand, coasting and halting in the hallway.

Rory followed the keys' route, running through the door, bringing her arm up, and stopping me in my tracks, a gun pointed at me. "Don't move," she said, calm as could be. She reached up and shut the gate, squatting and scooping up the keys, then smiling sweetly. "Maybe if you stopped pretending you are a god and took on actual godly traits, like empathy and caring for others, I wouldn't be doing this. You can't change the fundamental things about a person unless they want to change, and I might as well break it to you—I don't."

She bolted down the passageway, selecting the door with the stairs leading further inside the clubhouse. I didn't have the keys or my phone...they were in my jacket, hanging on the back of the chair in the kitchen. But that wasn't the real problem. *Shit, where the hell did she get a weapon?*

****

Rory pressed her ear to the door. Nothing but quiet. The keys on the ring were plentiful and cold, in contrast to WM's hot body. "Hee-hee hee," poured out of her mouth until she caught herself. WM must have fancied himself a dungeon master.

The passkeys weighed as heavily in her hand as her conscience. His opinion mattered. *What did he think about me making the first move the other night?*

She tried several before finding the one that allowed the knob to turn, then cracked the door enough to slip through, walking on tiptoes. Turk was sitting at the kitchen table, a newspaper open in front of him and a glazed donut in one hand. "What are you doing up here?" he asked, eyes squinty.

"WM sent me to prepare some dinner for myself," Rory said, heart racing, stomach churning, the handgun held in one hand behind her.

Turk's eyes narrowed. "Where's WM?"

"Downstairs, of course, waiting for me." She aimed to keep up her pattern of bullshit as long as she could.

"I don't think so," Turk said, putting the donut down, closing the newspaper, and rising. "He'd never let you up here by yourself. Not yet, anyway or without telling me."

"Go down and ask him," she replied, hoping to get Turk to leave her alone.

"That's a good idea, but you're coming with me. Let's go."

"No." She brought the gun up and aimed it at Turk.

He swatted her hand aside and the gun clattered to the tile. He then pushed Rory into his chair. "Sit," he said, pressing his mouth tight, picking up the firearm, and placing it on top of the refrigerator. "Now let's go." He pulled her to her feet, squeezing her shoulder, directing her down the steps to the basement.

Turk started dragging her when they reached the passageway and she refused to walk. She leaned back further, pushing her heels into the ground, making it as difficult as possible. *I don't want to face WM.* He unlocked the entryway to her room, allowing WM out and pushing her in. Rory looked at the floor, avoiding WM's steely stare.

"You went too far," WM said. "We had an agreement." His voice deepened. "You didn't keep it.

181

There'll be consequences." He slammed the gate closed, and the two men's footsteps faded away. WM's threat swam in her head.

Consequences.

Chapter 13

Dungeon Master

I bought Turk a drink at our bar, which was the least I could do for him after he prevented Rory from making a colossal mistake, bringing her back and freeing me from her room. The saloon was crowded, so none of our brothers could overhear our conversation.

Cowboy showed and sat down beside us. "We'll talk later," Turk said with a smile, winking at me over Cowboy's shoulder and walking away.

"Did ya see the sign I posted in the cellar about Rory's illness?" Cowboy asked, motioning the bartender for a beer. I nodded and he continued. "How much longer will Rory be contagious? I want to drop by and check on her again." He smirked.

I bet you would. "I don't imagine more than a few weeks." I decided right then to milk this as long as I could. I only hoped Johnny would keep his mouth shut.

Cowboy brought the beer down from his lips. "Wow, that long? What a downer. How's the trainin' going? You seem to be piddlin' along."

"She's in a snit at present." I explained about the mix-up with the clothes. I didn't appreciate being grilled by him, but there was little I could do about it.

Cowboy grimaced. "The prospect messed up. We shouldn't have them down there. They're undependable."

I shot back, "We've discussed this before, Cowboy. Full members are even worse. Less likely to listen to me. Turk made an error in judgment; he's learning and rectified his mistake."

"He's set you back, and she's a tough nut to crack."

"He's not the first and he won't be the last to impede her training," I said, meeting Cowboy's eyes.

"I deserved that, but we don't always agree on how things should go. I also have a love-hate thing going on with this one. I might be a little obsessed. She's different."

"I think we established that the first hour she was here. Remember, Rory's a business investment for us. You said you wanted her for our high-end Dom clients. You have to be clear—am I grooming her for *you* or *the club*? I'll hand her over right now if she's for you, and you can do your thing. I'm not working this hard to turn her into a plaything for you." A bluff. Could I actually hand her over?

Cowboy lit his cigarette, took a drag and stared at me, baby blues unblinking. "WM, I'm surprised by your attitude. From the first day, I've been honest about my interest in this girl. I got a tiny taste the other night before being interrupted, and I'm willin' to wait. Our client base is into the same kinds of things as you and me, and I don't see where there's any conflict. I have a question for you, too." His eyes turned into deep wells, and his head tilted to one side. "Exactly when were you going to tell me about her pulling a piece on you, and what are you going to do about it?"

I looked down at the table and snapped back, "I was going to inform you about the situation after you told me about showing her the newspaper, naming her the prime suspect in the Landry case."

Cowboy laughed, the kind that wasn't one, getting closer to me. I smelled the smoke on his breath. "You're pushing things, brother. I'm in charge. And I don't owe you anything. You're callin' it a situation, are you? A sneak attack is more like it, and she needs correction."

"You need to stop interfering."

"What you call interference, I call keeping an eye on things."

"A speed bump, is all. I hope you don't catch anything from her," I said.

"I didn't get close. I watched the whole thing on video and it was no bump. Aiming a gun and locking you in her room again. More like a sinkhole. Either you punish her, or I will."

"I said, *I'll handle it*."

"You better. This is going south because you're too easy on the girl. The other problem children you've had, came to my office every week, crying and complaining. You know it's true. You've got a little over a month to turn things around. She's gone if she doesn't perform as she should. I got first-class guests coming. I won't be embarrassed. Ask her how she got the gun too. Who gave her access? Where is it now?"

"In my room. It's a Luger."

"Could be mine." He shrugged. "Drop it by." He stabbed his cigarette on the bar, then flicked the butt on the floor "Do the job on her or…" He pushed the chair out, picked up his beer, and joined Louie at his table, leaving me to imagine what the 'or' would be.

****

Rory couldn't take her eyes off WM's hand, and the

ring on his middle finger. As he twirled it, the gold flashed. "Come. Follow," he said after unlocking her room, but not meeting her eyes, his face placid.

They stopped at an unassuming door, the secret one, between the two doorways that led to the stairs. She'd never been there before. *Take this off my bucket list.* WM used a key shaped like a skull to unlock the door. He grasped Rory's arm and walked her inside. A metallic clanking sound made her jump when WM closed the door behind them.

The space was dimly lit, and there was a rustling behind her as WM lifted something on the wall. There was a loud bang when rows of lights hanging from chains on the ceiling snapped on, light flooding the room, sounding like a starter's gun going off and revealing the contents of a nightmare. The walls were lined with cabinets that held whips, paddles, and other things she didn't want to see. She spied an enormous cross with leather straps attached, various tables with chains, and several cages that could hold human beings.

Rory clung to WM and screamed, unable to stop herself. "Please, please, take me back," she said, pawing at him. She ran back to the door, pulling on it, trying to get out. It wouldn't budge. *He isn't just a whoremaster; he's a dungeon master.*

"Calm down, it's not as bad as it looks," WM said. "You need to be punished. Deep down, I think you even desire it. I warned you." He pulled himself away from her and leaned against a wooden contraption that looked like some demented horse.

He did warn me, but he didn't understand me. Or my reasons. "I'm sorry for escaping again, WM, Sir," she said, fearing she'd faint. Her eyes traveled around the space, searching for a way to leave. A set of stairs led up to a door across from her. She ran towards and up to them, pulling on the door frantically.

"It's locked. There is no way out. Now come down and calm yourself," WM called. Rory walked down the steps hesitantly. Once in front of him, he proceeded. "I think you realize it was more. You pointed a loaded weapon at me. Unlike Cowboy, I don't act out of anger. I prefer to wait until I'm calm."

"I promise, I won't do it again, Sir. Let me explain—"

"Much too late for promises and explanations."

"Please believe me. I'll behave."

"I have one question. Do you consent to the punishment as you once agreed to when you accepted my dominance?"

"Yes, Sir, but—"

"Good. You aren't leaving this place until I'm done with you." He looked straight ahead, acting like he didn't recognize her or want to.

I can say no. I can change my mind, but I won't. If I want to embrace the light, I need to embrace darkness too.

****

"Leave your shirt on," I said to her. "Take everything else off." Rory's eyes pleaded with me, but I couldn't stop even if I wanted to, not after Cowboy's threat. If I didn't punish her, he would, and it would be so much worse.

"Do it," I said, refusing to look at her. She removed her shorts and panties, folding and presenting them as a gift. That's what submission was…a gift.

I placed them in the cubbyhole designed to hold the

clothing of subs. Her body's roundness and paleness contrasted with the angular lines and black padding as she mounted the bench.

Cowboy was right. I don't treat her like the others. I remembered Lydia. The other girls were always on time, but not Lydia. I warned her several times, and she continued to disrespect the other girls, making them work late because of her. I had taken care of it, assigning Lydia the worst johns and the most extended appointments until she finally went to Cowboy in tears, and he called me off. Lydia never did anything else that I didn't like again. I have my father's trait of getting even. After I left the military against his wishes, I haven't heard from him since, over six years now. I have a little over four weeks to turn Rory out, or she'd burn, and my own life would be in jeopardy too.

"Normally there's ritual and protocol involved with this," I explained, "but I'm not inclined to provide instruction right now. Safety's my top priority. Let me know if things get too out of hand with you. We use safe words. We're going to keep it simple. Red is for stop. You say 'red' if it gets too much. Truth is, I don't expect any problem. This is just a spanking. For your spanking tonight, I'm using my hand and a paddle. You're being punished for disobedience and unacceptable behavior toward me. Do you understand the safe word and accept punishment of a spanking?"

Her eyes blinking, chin trembling, she blurted out, "Yes, Sir."

"What is the safe word?"

"Red, Sir."

I realized I needed to cut my spiel short. The sooner I got Rory through this, the better. Her face was pale, and her eyes searched for some way out. I didn't want to chase her if she bolted. Maybe it would be fun, but perhaps I'd scare her worse. And I didn't want that.

"Climb on," I said, motioning toward the bench. Her body shook as she straddled the padded middle section tentatively, knees on either side of the support and her arms at the top of the sides. "You can back down and rest your head on the bench. I can place a bolster under your head to make it more comfortable if you'd like."

She scooted down, laying her head on the padding, then turned away from me. Her beautiful butt was displayed high in the air, an easy and motivating target. I usually enjoyed making subs sigh, squeal, and eventually, scream, but this didn't feel right. I didn't want to use a spanking as a punishment, but how could I get out of it?

"You can't use physical force against me ever again," I instructed. "That includes aiming a gun at me. I won't tolerate it. Have I ever physically abused you?"

"I told you I was sorry."

"Where did you get the weapon?"

"I found it."

"Where?" I asked skeptically.

"In my room. Someone left it on my lunch tray, but—"

"Enough. Don't talk anymore. No comments, pleading, nothing. The only thing I want to hear in this room is 'yes, Sir' and what I direct you to say." I didn't believe her. Who or why would anyone leave her a weapon?

I slapped Rory's ass lightly, much like beating a drum, part of my warm-up routine. Her skin was like a baby's, delicate—I needed to be careful. She squirmed as her skin turned pink and then cherry. The light spanking would enable her to get used to the sensation and prepare her for more.

"I suggest you don't move," I warned. "I don't want to hit the wrong place unless you wish to be restrained."

"No, please don't. I'll be still," Rory promised.

Her movements ceased even when my blows became heavier and her ass turned crimson. I changed it, altering the pacing and pattern, giving her soft hits and then harder ones. These things leave a sub's mind a mess, becoming fixated on guessing what would come next. The scene built up suspense and tension. An expectation of more pain overrode the actual level received. This being her first time, I held back. Down the road, I wanted her to find enjoyment in spanking, and I didn't want to hurt her.

She moaned out, "Ahh."

I walked around and examined her face. Tears were forming, and one eased down the side of her cheek. Her eyes were squeezed shut.

"Does it really hurt, or do you think it will? Don't make noise, it's distracting." I should've been enjoying this, but I wasn't. I wanted this over as quickly as possible. My heart was beating out of my chest.

I removed a giant wooden paddle from the rack, ebony and round with a long handle. Extra-wide paddles were more comfortable for subs to tolerate. The hit spread out across the cheek rather than targeting a smaller surface. Rory wouldn't know this. To her, it looked like one nasty motherfucker. We called it Big Bertha.

I walked to her side. "Look, I saved this for last. Give it your full attention." Rory's eyes grew enormous as she stared at it. "I'm going to smack you three times. One wallop for talking back, one for threatening me with a gun, and the last one for your escape attempt. You're going to count them out, and after each one, you're going to say, 'I'm sorry for,' and give the name for each transgression. Do this correctly or you'll have to do it over. Understand?"

"Yes," she replied, taking a big breath.

"Yes, what?"

"Yes, Sir."

I returned to the bottom of the bench and positioned my body sideways. I kept my arm slightly bent, targeted Rory's right butt cheek, then buried it behind my body as I swung, providing more power. I struck my target in the center of her already red cheeks but held back just enough.

"Ah!" she screamed out. "One. I'm sorry for talking back, Sir."

No broken skin, but she would develop a lovely mark. I aimed the paddle on the left side of her butt. *Swoosh, smack*. Big Bertha made contact. The skin turned white, compressed under it, and then beet-red when I lifted it. Another beautiful bruise would form. That pale skin of hers provided a perfect canvas.

"Oh," she sobbed, gulping for air. "Two. I'm sorry about the weapon."

"Stop crying, you're supposed to be quiet. Hard to understand you. It was more than that. You threatened me with a gun. I never figured you a liar. You forgot the 'Sir,' too. Do that one over."

"Please, George, don't make…" Her body shook while she held her breath and hands, gripping the arm supports. Stress was taking over. *George?*

"Don't hold on so tight. And inhale. It's more painful when you don't breathe. Use your breathing techniques from yoga." I had a bad feeling in the pit of my stomach. *I can't continue*, I thought to myself. I put the paddle away in the cabinet. I knew when she brought George's name into this that a spanking wasn't suitable for her. "I think we'll stop now. Apologize."

"I'm sorry for everything, Sir."

Thank God it was over. For both our sakes. I helped her up and walked her to the aftercare area, filled with comfy chairs, beds, and a couch. "Lie down," I said. "I agree with what you said earlier. 'You can't alter the fundamental things about a person unless they want to change.' I believe I've provided motivation. Rest and reflect. Another thing you should realize, I didn't know about the article until Cowboy told me about it, and then I went to bed. I was waiting for the right time to tell you. Truth."

I walked to the small refrigerator we kept in the dungeon and removed two ice packs, a water bottle, and a straw from the drawer. I placed the compresses on her ass, now the color of the maraschino cherries she loved so much, one of the few things that made me smile. I unscrewed the cap off the water, hurled the lid toward the trashcan on the opposite wall, and sank it. Usually I'd be happy about it, but today I was miserable. I dropped the straw in the water. "Drink," I said, holding it to her lips.

She refused and wouldn't look at me.

I took a few sips instead. I was afraid she was getting too close to me. Now she wouldn't. Rory looked small, alone, lying on the enormous bed. Her skin was splotchy red, fragile. I did that. She'd submitted. Would she keep trying to defy me? She needed to submit to survive here. Her submissive side was there. I saw it. Would I have to do this every time to see it?

I lay down beside her and met her eyes, but only briefly. She looked away. I tried to hold her hand. She pulled away. *I'm like my father. I destroy everything I touch.*

****

The glass turned from frosty gray to blazing yellow, the sun pouring through my ceiling, attacking me with its brightness. I enjoyed spanking women, and all of them had liked it too. Until last night. Maybe that was why I found no pleasure and stopped. I didn't want to harm her. I suppose I wasn't as big a sadist as I thought.

The slip in the dungeon when Rory called me George's name had become a splinter; at first it had been easy to ignore, then it burrowed deeper, calling attention to itself, eventually festering, becoming the only thing I could think about. I thought back to when Rory had been sick, when she had mentioned photographs and her stepfather, George, while hallucinating. Perhaps Worm could investigate. The name for his handle was no accident. Most of the time, he slept all day and stayed up all night, working. His domain was technology.

It was only eight-thirty a.m., early by club standards, but late by Worm's, and he was still up. The room was full of his love objects—computers, jacked from all over Vegas, running at a fast hum while contributing to the Knights' hefty electrical bill every month. One reason the membership was considering going solar.

"I need a favor," I said to him. "When Rory was ill, she referenced her stepfather and something about pictures. I think they could be inappropriate ones taken as a child."

Worm got a somber expression. "I hate dudes who hurt children. What do you want me to do if I find something?"

"Come get me if I'm available. If not, copy whatever you find and give it to me later. I have enough stuff interrupting my sleep."

"Sure, WM, I'm on it," Worm said, hunched over his keyboard.

****

Bam, bam. Not even two hours and Worm was at my door. "I found her," he said, hustling through the doorway, laptop under his arm, setting up camp on the desk. "I downloaded quite a few pics off the dark web—these guys share. To make it easier, I dropped them into a slideshow program."

She appeared ten or eleven years old. We got to one image, and I covered my eyes, my stomach suddenly upset. She was eating a vanilla ice cream cone with a cherry on top. "Worm, stop. I don't need to see anymore," I said. Guilt overwhelmed me. I thought I would never feel as bad as the day the vehicle I had been driving ended up blown to pieces, and my friends died. My heart raced. Did I traumatize her too?

Worm asked, "What do you want me to do?"

"Nothing. I'll keep the flash drive. I want to check something else." I Googled 'Stepford Wives' and pulled up the Wikipedia entry. "Rory's afraid of transforming into a brain-washed, zombie-like submissive. God, she has my number."

"I've seen that movie," Worm said, looking over my shoulder. "A weird one. A remake came out, not as good. I'm surprised you never heard of it."

"The first one was before my time. My father never let me watch movies or TV. Thought they were frivolous, time wasters. I was probably in Afghanistan when the new one came out, who knows?"

"Your dad must be a ball of fun," Worm said. "Make sure you delete all this crap. Better yet, destroy the flash drive. This kind of trash is illegal, and you don't want to get mixed up in anything like that." He looked at the thumb drive in my hand and closed the door, his computer clutched to his chest.

Rory kept reminding me every day, with her smart-aleck comebacks and challenging ways, that she was one up on me. Most likely, she was brighter than I was. We didn't have another girl like her; or maybe we did, but because I was so full of myself, I didn't realize it. I stewed all day and all night because of my actions, my stomach tossing and turning. A mess. Should I confront her about her past and ask for forgiveness, or leave her alone?

I stopped by Rory's room, surprised to see she wasn't asleep. She should've been. I had a set bedtime hour for all of them when they weren't working. I would think she'd follow the rules by this point. I spoke through the gate. "Rory, put the journal away. It's two a.m. Why are you still awake…and what did you do to your hair?"

"I clipped it off, is all. I'm an insomniac. This is normal for me. I'm amazed Turk didn't tell you. A couple more minutes, please, WM, Sir." Her hand raced across the page.

"I would think you'd have learned something the other night. To do what you're told and not argue. You didn't clip it; shaved is more like it. Why?"

"I learned physical abuse is preferable to mental. I

deserved it. I hope spanking me makes things right between us. Hair is a symbol of seduction and attraction. I want to rid myself of that."

She'd lost it. What did she think she's here for? "You consented. I spanked you. I didn't beat you. These don't sound like yes and no answers, and no 'Sir' either."

"Once you picked up the paddle and stopped using your hand, Sir, it became a bashing, and once on the bench, there was no escape from the burn of the wood. I'm not cut out for this. Wisdom means knowing which pain is worth enduring and which is not."

"You gave consent and could have said the safe word. Next time you ask before changing your appearance. I need to remind you, part of your function here is looking attractive. A shaven head is an extreme look, not to everyone's liking. We discussed your discomfort. It's not your call." *You're not the only one not cut out for this.*

"Yes, Sir," she said, looking away.

I sighed. "I didn't come down here to argue or rehash the night before last, although I admit I made an error. I should have found out if your background prevented a spanking. I apologize for my actions. I'm here to discuss something else."

She put the pen inside the notebook and slid it under her bed, staring at me. Why did she have to be so lovely, even with no hair? Her eyes looked even more prominent, like the green marbles I had hid from my father and used to entertain myself with. I unlocked the entryway and sat down on her stool. "Last night during the spanking you screamed 'George,' and when you were sick, you said other things about your stepfather groping and photographing you."

"I don't remember."

"You don't remember saying those things, or you don't remember him doing those things?"

"I don't want to talk about it. You can't control everything. No matter how smart and strong you are. You can't fix me. Too late for that."

"What are you talking about?" I asked and scooted the footrest to face her. "You don't need fixing. It's that scumbag who did those things. Something's wrong with *him*."

Rory stood, pacing back and forth, gesturing with her hands. "Of course something's wrong with me." Her voice was now high-pitched. "I'm not normal. If I were, I wouldn't be here."

I felt like gagging and jumped up. "You don't believe that, do you?"

"Yes. Yes I do." She sighed and lowered her eyes.

I cradled her. She fought back, pushing me away with her hands, soft cries escaping. I didn't let go. I rubbed her back and said, "I'm sorry, you're right; I can't control everything. But I want to make things right between us."

Her body relaxed into me, no longer fighting off my embrace. Once she was cushioned in my arms, I continued. "Cowboy wanted you for one reason. He thought you the most beautiful girl he'd ever laid his eyes on. Told me that several times. He may be a complete moron, but on that he's perceptive. I see it too. He wasn't just talking about the outside of you; your inside radiates out to your exterior. There's only good in you."

I took her hands and sat down on the bed, guiding her with me. "You cut your hair off, but it didn't change a thing." Touching her cheek, I continued, "You'll always be a beauty. Any bad thoughts in your head, an evil person placed them there. Any time you want to share what happened, I'll listen, but I'm never going to force you."

I got on my knees before her. "Forgive me. I apologize if what I did caused additional grief. In my world, a spanking is stimulating. If you ever want to learn more, I'll tell you. Last night I wielded it as correction, but I didn't mean it to be a beating, and again I'm sorry I did it. Next time, if there is discipline—and hopefully there won't be another time—but if there is, we'll come up with something else. Together. Remember our deal. I *will* take you home if you aren't happy, and I mean it, but home might need to be a different place."

Rory looked down on me and met my eyes. Her eyes danced with light, searching and beaming like she'd found something important. Then she came to me, got on her knees too, lay her head against my chest. She wrapped her arms around my neck, and whispered, "Thank you," before returning to her bed.

I squeezed in beside her, stroking her head and embracing her. She didn't pull away. I kissed her eyes and nose. She kissed me back. I breathed my words into her mouth: "I'm so very sorry."

"I know," she said.

No one had given me a gift like that since my mother. I read faith and admiration in her eyes. I prayed I wouldn't disappoint her again. Like I'd failed others. I had both happy and gloomy feelings when I left her room. Happy she'd forgiven me, but sad she didn't feel better about herself. Was Rory right about the paddle?

I closed the door behind me. Shit, I needed a smoke.

Chapter 14

Cloak of Invisibility

"It's done," I said, stopping at Cowboy's table in the bar. "She's punished."

"How did it go?" Cowboy asked.

"Fine." I pulled the Luger out of the inside pocket of my colors and placed it down. The gray matte metal finish contrasted with the top of the bar's shiny, black marble counter. "She said she found it on her lunch tray."

Cowboy examined it. "Mine. A remake of the classic. Do you believe her?"

"I didn't at first, but she doesn't wear a cloak of invisibility, and she's locked in her room. How could she take it?"

"True, she couldn't, but someone could have helped."

"Can I bum a smoke?"

Cowboy handed me the last one out of his pack. "Started up again, huh?"

"Off and on." I walked out the door to the porch.

****

Cowboy tapped a new pack of cigarettes on his palm several times, and then opened them, taking out a cigarette. "WM's punishment was a joke. I watched it." He gave Louie a quick look.

"You got a camera in the dungeon?" Louie's

eyebrows shot up. "I never knew that."

"You ain't the only one that doesn't know. I can see everything from my office. Entertaining. Not just the dungeon. The only problem, I don't have a recorder. Got to be in my office to watch, but I can see anything that happens anywhere in that cellar." He took a sip of his beer.

"What did he do, anal penetration?"

"What the fuck, Louie? Good God, no. Not yet. Hammer, get me a beer. Thanks." He bounced his fingers on the bar and swiveled his stool back to Louie. "Basically a lot of nothin'. Some swats with his hand and he brought Big Bertha out, gave her two hits. Over and done."

"At this rate, she's gonna be barbecued at the barbecue," Louie said, downing his shot.

"You're worse than me." Cowboy shook his head. "How the girl got the gun, I'll never know. I wonder if she stole her license back too. WM needs help. Maybe he's getting old, or he stuck his stick where he shouldn't have, and her pussy's magical like a unicorn."

"Who will you bring in to help?" Louie asked as the sound of billiard balls hitting each other rattled in the background.

"I could go two ways. Outsource it or stay in-house. A couple of months ago I was visiting our chapter in Oregon. The prez there, Dog, went on and on about their newest prospect. 'The kid can bed any woman,' he said. 'It doesn't matter what the age or inclination. He can get them out of their skivvies in no time flat.' Dog's words. The kid's one of those metrosexual types from GQ with the man bun, long and lanky frame, waxed chest. Uses body wash. The type of guy young girls like Rory seem to go for."

"Sounds pretty," Louie said.

"Shut up. The only problem is time. We have little of it. It'll go faster if we stay in-house and use one of her handlers. The new one, maybe, the Irish guy, Mike. Or the other one, Turk. She's known him longer. I also won't owe no favors."

"What ya gonna tell WM?"

"The truth. I want Mike or Turk to help. Simple as that. One will get their ticket stamped, and if they don't, you know what they say?"

"What's that?"

Cowboy smiled. "If you want something done right, do it yourself." Chuckling to himself, he raised his beer. "Call downstairs, Louie. Have them bring Rory up to my office in ten minutes. I want a chat with my girlfriend. I should be done with my beer by then."

At the appointed time when Rory walked in, Cowboy pointed at a gray metal chair in his office. "Sit yourself down over there. Good God, what the fuck did you do to your head? He removed a cigarette from the pack, shoving it in his mouth, his eyes never leaving her. Louie flicked the lighter, a flame appearing as Cowboy leaned into it.

Rory's hands itched and her stomach flip-flopped. She wanted to run. The only thing keeping her from bolting was the idea of two hundred and fifty pounds of Louie tackling her, and the punishment Cowboy might bring upon her. He was his same cocky self, one ankle propped on a chair, cowboy boot hanging off, different ones today, these black. She'd never seen him wearing anything but cowboy boots. Maybe that's why he's called Cowboy.

"Louie, wait outside, I want to talk shop with Rory." Cowboy took a drag off his cigarette, then stared at his fingernails as if he was thinking. *Did this guy think? Did one of his girls manicure them, or did he go to a salon?* His fingernails were in better condition than hers. Seemed a little feminine for someone like him. *Should I tell him that? I think not, Rory.*

"I told you to sit and I asked you a question. Where's your hair?"

"I shaved it off." Rory couldn't help fidgeting.

"Obviously. Britney Spears meltdown or what?"

"No."

"Don't do it again." He paused. "Tell me about your mother."

"I don't have a mother."

"Everyone has a mother. She dead? Is that what you mean?"

She shrugged. "Yep." Her face was hot and she crossed and uncrossed her legs nervously.

"You gotta learn how to hide your feelings, 'cause I can tell you're lying. Try again. I want the truth this time." He put out the remainder of his smoke.

"I...um...I don't...because she's dead to me." Rory's hands sweated.

"Stop babbling. Had a mother-daughter spat, did ya?"

"Uh-huh, but I'm not discussing that with you." Her mouth was dry.

"Tell me about your dad, then."

"He's dead."

"Stop lying."

"It's the truth. He really is dead."

"Stepfather, then."

Truth Moon

"You didn't ask about him."

"Now I am. Your parents didn't burn up in the fire, and they didn't move back to the trailer park, 'cause I checked. They're still looking for the suspected arsonist. Could be you. Impressive if it is. You demolished a boss, and you're a firebug too." Cowboy's eyes were studying her.

She jumped up and pointed at him. "You killed my boss."

"That's not what the Man thinks." Cowboy smirked and walked around to where she stood. "Sit." He pushed her down in the chair and pulled out another cigarette, sitting and facing her.

Talking in a slow, sing-song way, while staring into her eyes: "You look innocent, but I'm thinkin' you're not. More my kind. I like killin' too." He ran his hand up her thigh, taking hold of her kneecap and squeezing. "I like the sound skin makes. The way blood forms when you first cut into it. The surprise in their eyes when they realize you don't have feelings like them. Exciting stuff." His gaze didn't leave her eyes. "How about you? You like the way skin crackles when the fire reaches it? Seeing the skin change color and smelling the burnin' flesh, baby? Hearing them cough and cry for help? How 'bout it?"

"Ah, no—yes." Her boldness wilted as she looked into the bluest eyes of any person she'd ever met and the evil that came with him. *Contacts?*

"Some Buddhist monks light themselves up, protesting. Sure, you've heard about it, being a Buddhist yourself and all. No attachment to their physical selves. Not like us, with our credit cards, fancy phones, need for bodily pleasure." He ran his other hand up the inside of

203

her thigh.

"How do you know anything about that?" Rory asked.

"You think I'm stupid. I'm not," Cowboy snarled. "All you Millennials are the same. Think you know everything. Would you have pulled the trigger on WM? I think if he'd forced the issue, he'd be dead. 'Cause again, you're like me. Don't like being fucked with. Too bad, 'cause that's what I aim to do." He smiled. "So answer the question."

"It's hard because you keep talking. I'm not—"

"I wouldn't talk back if I was you. You know I don't like it. Answer the question."

"I'm not sure," she said, avoiding his eyes, landing on Cowboy's thick, long fingers and her kneecap changing hue, becoming rosier.

"I believe you. You're still figuring out who you are. A crazy thing, a scary thing when you first see your shadow self. If you'll embrace it, you'll become whole. Difficult to do…it doesn't align with society's laws of right and wrong, what you've been taught and all your yoga shit." He paused, bending forward, bringing his mouth close to hers, whispering, "I can help you."

"I don't need—"

"Your mom's address, give it to me," Cowboy growled, his eyes beating her up. His fingers continued to crush her leg, the pressure increasing, the pain building, but it didn't weaken her resolve, strengthening it instead.

Rory said, "I have no idea. And even if I did, I'd never tell you. Ever."

"I like you like this. Turns me on when you fight back. How did you gain entry to my office, and what did you do with your license?" He pressed harder, her knee now on fire.

"I don't know what you're talking about," Rory said, trying not to squirm.

Cowboy got closer, breathing into her ear, "Leave." Releasing her knee, he pushed her away.

Gladly. Scooting back the chair and walking out of the room, she repeated her new mantra to herself. *Don't run. Don't run. Don't run.*

****

"What ya think?" Louie asked, walking back into the room after she'd left.

"I'm still thinkin' Kitties is a good fit for Rory. Remind her who's holdin' the reins and what's expected of her. She'll turn to Turk for comfort afterward. Might help him. Opinion on that, Louie?"

"I like it. And I'll see her without her top on again." Louie held his hand up for a high-five. "But how are you going to get her up there?"

"No problem. Give her something to make her more agreeable."

"Last time she almost didn't make it."

"Johnny ain't touching her. I'll do it myself." Cowboy pulled out a Ziploc sandwich bag of weed. "This here's the ticket. Ever seen a broad after she's eaten a couple of pot brownies?" He laughed. "Two servings should do it. Perhaps even one. She *is* on the small size. If they have too many, they walk into walls or don't move at all. Of course, they gotta be gluten-free for the princess. I'm not sure about her new hairstyle. Might have to slap a wig hat on her."

"I like it," Louie said. "Looks commando. Reminds me of Jack from that game, Mass Effect 2. She kicks ass.

Like to see her with a short leather skirt or a plaid one. I'm partial to plaid. And a vest, combat boots and automatic weapon."

"A real one?" Cowboy's mouth opened wide. "I don't know about that. She's already pointed a gun at WM."

"Nah, a fake one. She might shoot me too, for holding her down," Louie said. "But I like the look."

"You might be on to somethin'. Sexy," Cowboy said, placing his hand up for a high-five and connecting with Louie's. "But forget the real armory, too risky."

****

Rory paced back and forth. Cowboy insisting on her parents' address didn't make sense, or him accusing her of gaining access to his office. What did Cowboy want with her mom? She'd most likely would tell Cowboy to keep Rory. She couldn't leave her room, unless she acquired superpowers like some goddess.

Rory punched the pillow twice, laid down, looked at the ceiling, and thought about what WM might not be telling her. *How can I care about someone who doesn't speak the truth?*

****

I savored Rory's quick response. She responded immediately, coming to her knees and dropping her head, hands to her thighs. She got confused when I instructed "at rest," though. "Rory, that means you can stand with your hands at your side or clasped behind you."

Rory rose from the floor in one movement with no stumbling. She was the most graceful submissive I'd ever trained. She appeared healthier, had gained a couple of pounds, and her skin was radiant. I wasn't keeping my mind on business again, one of the reasons Cowboy made me stop seeing her. It nearly killed me to do what he asked. "Tell me about Cowboy. Someone said he's been sniffing around down here late at night and early in the morning."

Rory turned a dark shade of red, words tumbling out in turrets. "He doesn't come in my room because he says I'm infectious, but he wakes me up and makes me present myself. He describes what he's going to do when I'm healthy again. I'm to perform sexual acts on men to earn my keep. The last time he visited, he told me there would be a coming-out party at some barbecue. Forget that. Other times, he doesn't wake me but stares at me, and I pretend I'm asleep because I don't want to listen to his crude comments."

Short answers they weren't. What the hell was wrong with Cowboy, planting thoughts into her head? Rory had enough stuff scrambling her brain. "Is this a problem for you, Rory?" I figured I might as well float it out there and witness what tsunami came back. I studied her eyes. The best way to gauge how a submissive was feeling was their eyes. Hers darted back and forth, telling me in no uncertain terms that she wasn't ready for male clients or Cowboy. "We've discussed this a little. Cowboy can't make you do anything you don't want to do. I'll see what I can do about his visits, but you should have told me earlier." Cowboy needed to keep his mouth shut, and he better watch his step if he didn't' want a RICO charge. The Racketeer Influenced and Corrupt Organizations Act was a federal law initially used to go after organized crime like gambling, bribery, kidnapping, money laundering, drug trafficking, human trafficking and other illegal activities. Federal

Prosecutors had already indicted members of other motorcycle clubs like the Hells Angels, Pagans, and the Mongols for RICO act violations.

"WM, are you avoiding me because you're afraid of being honest or don't want to be with me?" Her voice broke up. "How can I tell you anything if you're not here? You haven't visited me in weeks."

"Are you accusing me of something, Rory?"

"No, I'm explaining what's going on, and I want you to be straight with me. I don't think you understand how things are down here, left in a room by yourself, with no one to talk to but the one man you're most frightened of."

Starved for human contact, she poured herself into my open arms, laying her head on my chest. Encased in my arms, I brought her closer. Her lips—pink, quivering and needy—required my attention. I placed mine to hers, kissing softly at first, then pressed harder, parting them, slipping my tongue inside her moist mouth, probing deeper. Then a skid of lips and teeth clicked, an incisor scraped my lip and our noses smashed. Hadn't she French kissed before? Or was it nerves? Or was she out of practice?

Thankfully, she relaxed, her tongue darting in and out and around until I got dizzy trying to keep up with her. I squeezed her tightly to my chest for control, and got distracted by her scent. No aroma of burning wood like before. The smell of peppermint instead. I suppressed a grin. I had told Turk a citrus or woodsy soap. Seemed he had his own ideas.

A different kiss now, more like after a heart attack when medics used a defibrillator to bring you back to life. This kiss sent electric currents through me. This wasn't what I had planned. Was I responding to some need in her or myself? Yeah, my need. I missed her. Nothing ever went the way it's supposed to when I was with her.

We stayed wrapped in each other's arms until I pulled away. "Never doubt that you matter to me. Rest easy. I've got a meeting, but I promise I'll be back after lunch. I'll take you up to the bar to work with Hammer too. He's been asking about you." I hugged her again.

"You're not angry at me anymore?"

"I could never stay mad at you. I wish things would get easier and I could help you more." I turned to leave, and then realized I couldn't. Unable to straighten up. "Ouch, goddamn. My back."

"Again?"

"Yeah. I'm fine"

"I can see, Sir. Could be your body's not the issue. Often other problems manifest themselves in physical hurt."

"More yoga mumbo jumbo?" I scowled.

"More yoga *wisdom*," Rory said.

****

"I called you into my office to discuss Rory. Did you stay clear of her, like I told you to?" Cowboy asked.

"Yeah, like you wanted." My eyes moved across Cowboy's desk. How did he function? It was covered in newspapers and discarded food wrappers stuck with old cheese, empty stacked pizza boxes, ashtrays filled with cigarette butts and old cigars, beer bottles mingling with several unfinished containers of sweet tea, topped off by a bottle of whiskey, one-quarter full, dead center. All of this kept the desk unused for meaningful tasks.

"Good. I want Turk involved. A pinch-hitter is best. I pulled the other two prospects. He'll be the only one down with her. Teach Turk what to do. I want your little chick up and running in time for the party, and this guy's the way."

A girl in white, wearing hot pants, at least a Thirty-eight triple-D, representing the month of July in the calendar, stared back at me. The calendar was over two years old. Cowboy lived in the past, too lazy to purchase a new one.

"What are you talking about, my little chick?" I was distracted and mesmerized by July's body.

"Come on, WM. The way you act with this one is like a mother hen. Work with my new man. Do your job."

"He's not your man. I selected him."

"Then you should be happy. I like Turk too, but I want him to do more than deliver her entrees. Let him bake a cake. If he gets lucky, he can expand her horizons and pump her rump too." He chuckled.

"With her background, we need to go slow. I mentioned it earlier. I think she was sexually abused. Plus you usually want to be first on the girl's hit parade. When did that change?"

"Abuse just makes them more agreeable to becoming sex workers. As far as me taking first, I think it's best someone else bats early, what with my history with the girl. After Turk cracks her open, I'll take my turn." Cowboy put his butt out between his two fingers and stared at his hand, as if trying to understand something difficult. Cowboy felt nothing, and his heart was calloused too.

I argued, "For some women, it can work the opposite way and make them unsuitable. Worm went online to check, and what he found is worrisome."

"You're making too much of it. She's not a child."

"I'll show you." I passed Cowboy my phone.

Cowboy sat stone-faced, shifting in his seat, clearing his throat as he scrolled. Finally, he shouted, "WM, *enough*! I can't handle another second and I'm not looking at another photo. Who's the pervert motherfucker that did this to her, and where is he?"

"It's her stepfather, most likely?"

"We need to track the guy down. Call a local chapter and let them loose on the guy. Anyone that hurts a child needs to be dealt with. Simple as that."

"What do you want to do with Rory?"

Cowboy closed his eyes and drummed his fingers, pausing for a few seconds. "I don't know, what do you think?"

"There may be problems with her ever working for us. Maybe we should let her go…"

"No fuckin' way. She knows too much about our operation."

"Wanted by the cops too," Louie volunteered. "She could use us as a bargaining chip."

I had no chance to respond to their concerns. Cowboy said, "She stays. Get Turk on it," and pounded on his desk. "No excuses. Tick tock. You can go now."

****

"Do you believe him?" Louie laughed, watching WM close the door. "WM expecting you to let Rory go?"

"I'll let her go after she lights my fire, or I light one with her in it," Cowboy sneered. "Now I really do need her mother's address." He slammed his fist down.

****

"Rory, I brought you some popcorn as you requested," Turk said.

"Ooh, goody. But you should have waited until mealtime to deliver it. Won't WM be mad you're down here?" Everyone in the Knights was fearful of Cowboy, WM and Louie, in that order, but now Turk didn't seem afraid of anyone. Unusual for a prospect, even she knew that much, and she knew little about the inner workings of motorcycle clubs.

"You worry too much," Turk said, throwing her the bag of popcorn. He had started as someone who delivered meals and clothing, nothing more. Now he was a friend, turning into a friend with benefits if she didn't put a stop to things. He woke her gently in the mornings and turned his back when she disrobed in the bathing area. And he visited several times a day.

Turk spread lazily across her bed, his long legs hanging off the end, jiggling one leg up and down as they discussed the reason he didn't have a nickname. "They haven't come up with anything yet. Hopefully not a stupid one, when they do."

Rory balanced on the bed's edge. "Leave it to these nitwits and they will. Come up with your own is my advice. Maybe for these guys, Turk is a different enough name."

"A handle can't be your actual name or something you've used before. I can't say I want to be called Popcorn and presto, that's my name. It doesn't work like that."

"No, you *have* to do it this way. Find a name you like, and then set it up where they think it's their idea to call you the name you picked. Problem solved. I kind of like Popcorn. Popcorn it is." She nailed him in the head with a kernel.

Turk sat up quickly. "Please, Rory, don't joke about

that." He picked the piece out of his natural hairstyle. "If I end up being called Popcorn, I'm quitting."

"Don't worry, I won't call you that. Does the name Turk mean something?"

"My mother's Turkish. It means 'from Turkey.' It's a nickname my childhood friends called me and to be truthful my mother isn't too keen on it."

"Why do you even need a handle?"

"Just a way to keep your proper name away from law enforcement. Makes it more difficult identifying you." A line appeared between Turk's brows.

"What kinds of things do you plan on doing?"

Turk smirked. "None of your business, nosy britches."

Turk brought her snacks and books to read. *Am I using Turk? Probably.* She liked him, but knew it should be more than 'like' for all the kissing and touching they were doing. Yet when she closed her eyes, Turk, her teddy bear, morphed into WM. *I shouldn't be turning Turk into someone else.*

With WM gone, her loneliness had gotten the better of her. No excuses. The feelings she got with Turk were akin to stomach pains, guilt most likely.

Chapter 15

Kitties, Pussies Galore

"She likes you, Turk," I said.

"I like her too. But honestly, WM, she's out of my league. Cute, perfect skin. And those eyes, they look right through me. I don't think she'd give me the time of day if she wasn't on our lockdown program. On top of that, when we're together, she spends the entire time talking about you."

"Don't under-estimate yourself. She's a girl that judges a guy by what's on the inside. She's all about a man with brains that can make her laugh too."

"Is that a way of telling me I'm not much to look at? Should I shoot myself in the head or sign up for plastic surgery?"

"I'm just saying she needs more than a fuck boy. One of the reasons I picked you and not the new guy."

"I enjoy spending time with her. I can't say that about most girls. Rory is the smartest girl I've ever been with, hands down."

"Yeah, but don't become attached. Remember Turk, you're not dating her."

"I don't get you. You want me close, but then you warn me when I do it. Decide."

"I'm reminding you she belongs to the Knights. It's difficult keeping it straight. Your relationship isn't real.

You're playing the pretty boy role to draw her into our world." *I should take my own advice.*

"I understand." Turk's eyes grew angry.

"Friday's the night. There's a visiting OMC. Everyone will be upstairs working. I'll give you the high sign to take Rory back to her room. You'll have privacy. If it feels right, get it done."

Turk patted his package. "Great, because my system's ready to blow. Thankfully you gave me access to Ivy."

"I had to remind Ivy to keep her mouth shut, but she was all about it because she thinks Rory likes you. Remember, don't rush her. 'No' means precisely that, got it? Use a condom. Get her consent for everything. You lay a hand on her in a way she doesn't like, I'll cut it off. I mean it. Understand?"

"You know me. My parents didn't bring me up like that. Besides, wouldn't you like a little Turk running around here, WM?"

"No. I wouldn't. My friend Porkie-Pie is on stand-by, ready to spill drinks and otherwise bother Rory on Friday night, to make sure I have an excuse to send her back to the room early. Insurance."

I was worried. Cowboy and his plans. Turk was a good guy, and Rory was someone unique. Truth, I was more concerned about myself. Could I handle Rory being with someone else? I couldn't believe I was asking myself this question.

****

"Tonight's our night," Cowboy said to Louie. "Make those brownies and get Turk to deliver them with dinner. We're taking Rory to Kitties. I'm makin' sure Friday goes the way it's supposed to. We've got two days to drive her into Turk's arms." He passed Louie a bag of weed.

"How long will it take for her to feel anything?" Louie asked, putting the grass in his pocket. "I smoke it. Never done edibles."

"Usually about half an hour. We'll give it forty-five minutes. We'll smoke a blunt in the van if she needs some extra courage. Call Cookie, have an outfit sent over. I want her dressed for success, one of those satin numbers with the sequins. Tell him white for her maiden voyage."

"No black skirt, vest and machine gun?"

"We'll buy that costume ourselves and have Rory give us a private lap dance another time, when she's more experienced. Now leave. I got other business."

After the door closed behind Louie, Cowboy picked up his phone.

Cowboy—*U in town? Still on 2night. Princess showg skin. Kitties, Pussies Galore, I-15—*

—Hits stage @ 9—

—B in back—

MM—*B there w/friends—*

—I stop by afterward—

Cowboy—*No. My man w/me. Knows nothg abt :(—*

MM—*All know eventually—*

Cowboy—*Wait until club—*

****

Gluten-free brownies, OMG. Yum! Rory was whacked. She had written the same sentence in her journal for half an hour, over and over, and still didn't understand a word. *What's wrong with me?*

"Hey, little filly, got a surprise for you," Cowboy said. "I'm taking you out."

216

Minutes later, stripes of scenery zipped by the window, and a hula girl on the dashboard jiggled, straw skirt shaking. *I'm not scared, and I don't have questions. In La La Land. How lovely.*

"Put this on. You gotta look proper, like all the other girls." Cowboy leered, handing her a hanger covered with a plastic dry-cleaning bag. He lit the thin smelly cigar. *Not a cigar. Weed.*

She tried to shake her head. "I can't put…Too revealing," she said as she unwrapped the garment, coughing and then rubbing her eyes.

"Put it on, or I'll dress you. Your choice."

She turned away and slipped the halter top on under her shirt. She held the satin ends in her fingertips by her throat. Cowboy's hands stole them away, tying them in a bow at the back of her neck and pulling her outer garment away. "Mmm, spectacular. You need help with the bottoms?" He nuzzled her throat. She swiveled away and pulled on the white hot pants and black fishnet stockings, his eyes following every move. *Oh my gosh. Shoes, stilettos. For real?*

"Mmm, let me help you with those." Whisking them out of her hands, Cowboy bent down, picked up her foot, and placed the shoe on. "Check it out, Louie. I'm Prince Charming. Give me the other blunt."

The vehicle filled with smoke. Cowboy pulled her on his lap, holding tight, exhaling smoke into her mouth and not letting go. She coughed as the two men laughed. The lot was packed. The van bucked and groaned as it went across gravel and potholes. A neon sign blinked in red and pink colors through the windshield:

Kitties
The Ultimate Dance Club.

217

Pussies Galore

"Weigh next to nothin'," Cowboy said, licking his lips, hunching over and removing a bottle of tequila from under the seat. He took a gulp and shoved the bottle into her hand. "Drink up."

She rested it on her knees. "I don't drink." *I wish I weighed a thousand pounds right now and would crush his lap.*

"You do now." His eyes were intense. She took a small sip. It burned her mouth but warmed her. "Take some more," he said, his eyes boring into her.

After many more sips, he let her be. She felt wonderful. The entire van was dipped in gold, all the rough edges gone, nothing scary. Cowboy and Louie changed into clowns with giant noses. She started giggling, but they didn't seem to mind.

Louie's cell buzzed, and he looked down at the message. "I think they're ready."

"Too bad. I'd like to stay and get to know her better, now that she's in a relaxed state," Cowboy said. "She's good like this, Louie, don't you think?"

"Yep, definitely. Less dangerous, no hitting."

Cool air chilled her skin when they got out. Sequins were fluttering and shaking in the night breeze, but the heels proved difficult. Cowboy held her hand and caught her. "Be careful, honey. You almost tripped."

After that, her mind floated. She remembered nothing until she was suddenly up on a stage with other girls. Cigarette smoke in the air stung her eyes. In the dim room, she barely deciphered men's faces, and after that, just haze. Loud music thumping, colored strobe lights bouncing off, in, and around them all. She felt beautiful, bathed in pink and purple. *I'm a fairy.* The other girls removed their clothing, laughing. Rose draped Rory with strings of beads as she moved, shouting words of encouragement, pointing with long crimson nails at her top. Everything was in slow motion. The ties around her neck were loosening, and suddenly someone grabbed it. She saw Ivy giggling and flinging her top into the crowd, Rory's breasts now exposed. *Not a fairy anymore.*

The noise was deafening, clapping and yelling from the audience. Men pushed forward, hands in the air, eyes everywhere. And then she smelled him—lemons, nutmeg and musk. The only scent he ever wore. Her mind protested the stench, heart pounding, drumming in her ears, hands shaking.

And then nothing.

She woke up in the van. Her hair and her skin stank of smoke and alcohol. The ride home, she leaned on Cowboy's shoulder, in and out of consciousness. She was a sea of jumbled thoughts. Cowboy's words rang out. "Push the accelerator, Louie."

"I can't. It's already touching the floor," Louie's voice boomed. The van sped up and swerved into the opposite lane, and then back in its own. *I hope I don't throw up.*

"We can't outrace them, but we outweigh them. Run them off the road." Cowboy's teeth shined. A loud, long ringing noise rang out, followed by scraping metal as their vehicle hit the bumper of a white car, pushing it toward the shoulder. She dimly heard Cowboy's laughter. "Good job, Louie. We stopped those motherfuckers."

"Who were they?" Louie asked.

"Could be the Cobras, or interested patrons from

Kitties that want more. Windows were tinted. I couldn't see who they were." Cowboy laughed. "I got the plate."

****

She woke up in her room hours later with a headache, hunched over, vomiting on the floor. "The best thing you can do is get it all out, sleep, and drink water," Turk said, bending over her.

A bad couple of days followed. By Friday night she felt somewhat better.

Rory dropped a tray upstairs in the bar, spilling her drinks. WM was acting jumpy tonight, kept telling her to do a particular task and then changing his mind, insisting Turk take her back to the cellar.

"You're so beautiful tonight," Turk said once they were alone. "I would've loved to walk the guy outside that touched you, but WM said it was none of my business. Are you feeling any better?"

"It's an improvement over the first day of my hangover, but it's still bad. I never drank before."

Turk rubbed her back softly and put his hand under her shirt. Her stomach heaved. She shouldn't be doing this. *I don't like him in that way.* "You've got to stay out of anything involving me," she said, lifting his fingers away. "You're a prospect. I want nothing to impede you from becoming a full member if that's your goal." She tried to put his mind to other things. "You better go. What if WM finds you down here with me?"

"WM's busy upstairs." He kissed her. "You smell nice, Rory." He undid the button and zipper on her shorts next, placing his hand on her underwear. He'd attempted a lot of stuff like this the last couple of days. She stiffened and Turk waited her out, his smile like the Mona Lisa, sly and mysterious. She'd read somewhere the Mona Lisa was a self-portrait of the artist in drag, the painting a giant hoax on the viewer. *I shouldn't be kissing Turk if I'm daydreaming about the Mona Lisa.*

Turk stroked her through her panties, and she stopped him again, pushing his hand away. "I'll help you take your shorts off," Turk said, and before she could stop him, he jumped to the bottom of the bed, and like Houdini performing a magic act whipped her bottoms off in one move.

What the hell?

Rory laughed at the absurdity of Turk's move. "Hold it, Turk. We've got to talk. Give me my clothes." Turk had become a constant companion in a short amount of time. Abandoned by WM, Turk had filled the void. So much for her Buddhist principles. In here, her very foundation was eroding. Turk may want more than a friendship, but she didn't. He was cute, honorable, sweet, and funny, but just a friend. *And a jailer. Don't forget.*

"I need to be closer to you. Please," Turk begged.

"I'm sorry. I can't," Rory voiced loudly. "I want my pants."

"Come on, baby, don't be like this."

"Turk, if you don't give me my bottoms, I'm going to tell all your Knight brothers that your handle is Popcorn. Now give them to me," Rory threatened.

"Fine. But if anyone asks, we fucked."

"What?"

"WM's job is on the line. Most girls are earning in a few weeks." Turk's face was red, pointing his finger at me. "And Cowboy wants it done."

"I can't believe this," she said, eyes widening.

"This isn't a college dorm room." Turk scratched his

head. "What did you think you signed on for?"

"Yes, but—"

"Cowboy will send someone else down here if I report I didn't do it. Do you want that?" Turk's eyes locked on hers.

"No…" Rory said. *Maybe, if WM comes…*

"We'll talk about it again tomorrow. I probably shouldn't have told you any of this, but I'm trying to protect us."

****

"It's done," Turk said, sliding onto the stool next to me. My heart sank, and I got angry but pushed it down. "I don't think I should have left. She seemed upset," Turk said worriedly.

"Don't concern yourself. I'll check on her," I said. My mood was in the basement too, but not for the same reasons, I was sure. There was no way I was going to let Turk stay with her afterward and cuddle.

I kicked a black bag over to him with all the tools he'd need for the next month. He looked down at it but didn't pick it up. I removed the rope and held it out to him. He clutched the cord. "What if she doesn't want to?"

"Don't push her. Just leave her alone. You can ask her the next time. You're building trust and confidence in you," I said, watching Turk wind the cord around his hand. "If she goes along, don't do anything else she'd find objectionable. Every time you have sex, keep adding the restraint in, but increase the complexity. Tie her hands tighter, then bind her hands behind her back. You're getting Rory acclimated to bondage. After you do her hands, add her feet. Eventually, she'll be used to bondage, at least with you." I gave Turk a book on knots and ropework, demonstrating essential ties so he wouldn't be fumbling around. "Read the safety protocols section carefully, it's important. Never put anything on her neck, for instance."

Turk nodded his head up and down, continuing to wind the rope more tightly around his fingers. *Hopefully, he won't tie Rory like that.* "Eventually, when we move her through restraint, we can add pain stimulation," I said.

"I'd rather not harm Rory," Turk said.

"Do you think I want to hurt her?"

"Possibly not." Turk's eyes were glued to the tabletop.

"No, I don't. You agreed to do whatever I told you when you asked to work down there. No questions asked. Now you're telling me how to do my job."

Turk's eyes were still down. "No need to rage. I'm worried about her, is all."

"You can't do this job if you're going to get involved with the help, and if you're going to play a bigger role with the girls, you need to harden yourself. As their Dom, you need to understand that the line between pleasure and pain is a thin one." I stared at Turk's right hand. The red rope twisted tightly around three of his fingers. I whispered, "Let go," and watched as Turk released it and the rope unraveled, flopping on the counter. Turk's eyes and mouth opened wide as he examined his fingers, now white from cutting off the circulation in his hand.

Yeah, don't get involved with the help or you'll end up fucked like me.

Leaving Turk behind, I snuck down the dark passageway of quiet. Rory's shoulders were wrapped in a sheet, and she was sitting cross-legged, hunched over her journal, writing, her eyes wet. I backed away before she spotted me. I couldn't deal with her emotions or my own.

I went to my room and tried to sleep. I rose from the bed, punched the wall, then paced, unease taking over. I held no illusions about myself. It wasn't Rory's sorrow upsetting me; It was more the idea of Turk with Rory. I should never have gone along with Cowboy's plan, but what choice did I have? I had to cooperate if I wanted to remain whoremaster. I didn't want Turk staying with Rory because I didn't want them getting attached. That's how gone I was over this girl. I was jealous.

Perhaps I could exorcise her from my soul by spending time with her. Nothing like seeing a woman more to make a man realize everything that's wrong with her. I lost interest in most girls or them with me in a couple of weeks of full-on dating. Sometimes less than that before they're gone. Rory, crying, only proved emotional neglect. My spending time with her might improve her mood, or it might go the opposite way. Shit. I hoped that didn't happen.

I wet my skin, applied shaving gel, ran the blade toward the hair growth on my face. I rinsed after each swipe and splashed with water. I ran my hand over my jaw, smooth and silky. I didn't want to irritate any of Rory's sensitive spots. A smile crossed my face. I went to bed satisfied, with a new plan already swimming in my head.

****

I presented the two-piece swimsuit, jeans, shirt, and sneakers to Rory after breakfast. She was quiet at first, turning her back and then dressing under the toga-tied sheet. I accidentally-on-purpose spied her ass. Glorious. The only disappointment was the bruises still there from Big Bertha, faded and slightly green on each cheek.

Rory followed me up the steps, taking them two at a time to keep up with me until we reached the door and the blinding sun. Once there, she tilted her head toward it, soaking in its rays like a sunflower. She skipped around the yard like a child with the widest of grins. I put on my sunglasses and handed her a pair. "Put these on," I suggested, placing a borrowed helmet on her head. Her face lit up with another smile. I balanced the bike and motioned for her. "Just so you know, this is not a date," I said as she climbed aboard.

"Well, what is it?" The grin disappeared.

"An outing."

"Fine, an outing it is." A small smile reappeared.

The house sat low on flat land, a Mid-Century Modernist dwelling by itself with no other homes for miles. I disarmed the alarm. Rory's eyes darted back and forth like a cat burglar breaking and entering. "The guy's a friend of the club. We have permission," I explained, guiding her out through the sliding doors of the great room surrounding an expansive pool.

Rory's eyes sparkled like green pearls, seeing the pool for the first time. "I love swimming! You're away from the world when you submerge yourself. All the noise in your head goes away. Much like meditation, because water keeps you from connecting with the world above. You're alone with your thoughts."

"I thought you'd be all about working on your tan."

"Redheads don't tan." She grinned. "Burn, maybe." Then she ran at me, catching me off-guard. *Whack.*

"Argh," I cried, losing my balance, falling into the

pool. My feet settled on the bottom as I pushed up to the surface, sputtering. "I can't believe you did that."

"Why?" she asked with hands on hips. "Too cool to get wet?" The sun was blazing behind her.

****

Rory had never heard WM laugh like that. Most of the time, he never cracked a smile. She was filled with joy, knowing she'd done something few could—made him laugh with abandonment.

All the chatter in her head disappeared. She stripped her clothes off, leaving her in only the bikini, before diving in after WM. Rory stroked the water, coming to the turquoise surface, as the sunlight spread rows of scissored patterns, then flipped on her back, her body suspended in aqua color, body and mind now at rest. Everything wrong with the Knights washed away. Rory thought back to last night. She was grateful to Turk for helping her after Kitties, but she didn't have feelings for him. Not like she did for WM. And with WM showing up in her room this morning with the bathing suit, it felt like an answer to her prayers.

WM swam to her and pulled her through the water. His body was lean and tan. Their limbs became entwined and his arms came around her waist. "What am I going to do with you?" he asked, his lips smiling mischievously.

"Something fun, I hope."

They both left the water to catch some sun beside the pool. Their skin glistened as if sprayed with gold glitter. "WM, could you please put some suntan lotion on my back?" she asked, stretching out beside him. She imagined herself a cheetah.

Squeezing the bronze, oily mess into the palm of his

hand, he said, "This shit is disgusting," and dropped the golden globs on her back, moving his palm across her shoulders, the oil gliding and melting into her skin.

"I need the protection to keep from burning."

WM spread the lotion lower on her back. His hands were powerful as he massaged the oil into her flesh. "Mm" and "oh" escaped her lips, and a tingling sensation spread between her legs. Unable to stay still, she sat up.

He stared into her eyes and like pressing a button on a bomb, her need for him was ignited. Their chests came together first, then their mouths. They were in unison initially, then out of sync. Her body, slick with oil, slid against his. Like animals in the heat of battle, they pushed and pulled and worked against each other. WM reached around her, untied her top, and threw it toward the water. The bikini cups, billowed by air, drifted into the pool and lazily floated.

"I surrender," she shouted, laughing, the sun shining down on them.

Chapter 16

Swim Date

Their hands explored each other's mountains, bumps and crevices, fingers sliding over smooth skin. Rory knelt and eyed WM's cock. Her imagination was set free. *Is it winking at me?*

She remembered a few short weeks ago when WM made her kneel, and she had been scared thinking she might have to do what Ivy had done. Now? Now she was hungry for him. Her lips opened, taking him in while she cupped his balls. She made a series of tiny licks around the head of his cock, like a kitten lapping up milk. Then she shifted to longer laps down his shaft, her tongue swirling around the head. His tautness was in her mouth, shaft swollen, suddenly choking her. She looked up at him, his smiling eyes upon her. *I'm happy too.*

WM teased, "Too big a mouthful, little one?" Her response was to force her throat open wider, taking him in deeper. "Good girl. I'm going to come f you keep going. I don't want that yet." It pleased her, knowing the power she wielded.

"Your turn. On your back, knees up," he said, ripping the bottom of Rory's suit off, diving and wedging himself between her legs. His fingers ran over her clit. "Pretty and pink, like a dewy morning." *What a strange thing for WM to say.*

WM pushed two digits in and brought them out again, nuzzling her thighs, his face smooth against her skin. His tongue teased her, licking and sucking, and every few times his teeth would nibble lightly, making her quiver and body hum. Noises escaped from her mouth, sometimes cries. She tried to close her legs and wiggle away, the feelings were so intense.

"Next time I'll bring something to help you lie still," he joked, moving on, exploring another opening, darting his tongue in and out, making her want more. Every time she seemed close to coming, he stopped and moved somewhere else, eventually up to her nipples.

Her body burned with desperate desire, wanting him and seconds later wishing to escape. Torture. He put his fingers in, testing. "Do you want me, little one? Are you sure about this?"

"Not without a condom," she said.

"I don't need one. Hurt in combat. Worn a condom with every other woman. Nothing to fear from me. I'm also sure you, little one, have had very few partners, and I bet they'd worn one. Correct me if I'm wrong." He trailed his finger along the lines of her pussy.

"Are you telling the truth?"

"Yes, and you know by now I don't lie. I'm not into rape scenarios. Your call, stop or go?"

"Go."

"Maybe I've changed my mind. I have a different hunger now."

She was confused. Was WM hungry? *No, he's teasing me.* "I'm hungry too. I could go for mac and cheese."

"I believe I gave you something to eat earlier, little one, and it was dairy- and gluten-free," he chuckled.

WM came back to her, eased part of himself inside of her. His hugeness stretched and filled her to her limits. She was correct when she guessed, WM was well-endowed. He pulled out a bit and went in more deeply this time. After a few gentle thrusts, it got more comfortable. He put his arms around her, cradling her. "I'm not hurting you, am I?" he asked, drawing his eyebrows together and listening intently, for her answer.

"No."

Their eyes locked together. WM thrust in and out again, slowly, and out. After a few times her tightness eased, and she snugly fit around him. He came out of her all the way and, with one decisive stroke, plunged in as far as he could go, as if digging for something. *My soul?*

He pulled out and repeated this move. Rory arched her hips, meeting his thrust. She took everything he gave. WM's eyes never left her. Finally, WM pulled out, just giving her the head of his cock, teasing her, and then ramping up the tempo again, going full throttle.

She squeezed herself around his cock as he twisted one of her nipples. "Does this feel good?" he asked.

"Not so hard," she said on a gasp.

As WM touched her again, her pussy clenched. "Yes, bear down, squeeze my cock." He parted her lips, his tongue dancing with hers, and then he stopped, acting like he had remembered something important. "Anything I can do to make this better for you?" He nipped her bottom lip, waiting for her answer, her hands pinned to the cement. "Tell me." His eyes studied her.

Rory felt her face redden and not from the sun. "I haven't done much, but I'm interested in trying a different position."

"Which one?"

"From behind," she said softly.

His eyes lit up. "Roger that." He left her and snagged a towel off the lounger and placed it on the cement. "Get on your knees," he said, pointing to the towel. WM entered her with enthusiasm, almost knocking her down. The towel kept her from scraping herself. "Normally, I would hold some of your hair in my fist, but we'll wait till you have some. I have to admit, your new do is growing on me."

Rory moaned in response. "Does my little one want me to ride her hard? Do you want it deep?" She didn't answer, couldn't answer.

WM kept talking. He seemed to talk more during sex than any other time. He spoke of all the different ways she would serve him and what he would do to please her. All the while he kept a steady pace, moving inside of her. "Rory, take hold of your clit, help me give you an orgasm," he said, continuing with his dirty chatter.

She did what he suggested. She rubbed herself and then pinched her clit between her two fingers, making her body shudder as she screamed out, bucking into him.

With another hard thrust, WM erupted violently. "Take it," he said, his voice rough.

She held him tight, her pussy wringing every drop from his pulsing cock, his wetness flooding into her. They folded together as they collapsed, lying on their sides, not wanting to come apart. She wanted to keep him inside of her forever, until her mind drifted to Turk. And to the dance club. She glanced at WM and then away. Guilt flooded her. *I should confess to him.*

****

With the others, I didn't desire intimacy. Couldn't

wait to disengage. Today, it wasn't me who broke the mood. I thought a young girl like her would need reassurance and cuddles. She sought none, which was a surprise. Maybe she thought I wasn't down with it. Truth, I wanted to hold her in my arms, but Rory cleaned up instead in the outdoor shower, dove into the water, and swam in the nude alone.

I went inside to fetch refreshments and couldn't help comparing Rory to the other women who worked for the Knights. I'd had all of them before. Rory's muscle control went well beyond theirs. It must have been the yoga. Truth, she kept up with me. She'd be a moneymaker if I could harness any of this for our BDSM clients, and when Cowboy had her, he'd go insane. What was I talking about? I didn't want customers fucking her or Cowboy either. *If anyone touches her, I'll kill them.*

I stopped myself from thinking further. I checked text messages and prepared cocktails, stepping back outside. I noticed the quiet, and everything inside of me froze. Rory lay still on the pool floor. I did a double-take, disbelieving. "No, it can't be," I muttered, attempting to figure out what had happened.

I dropped the tray. The plastic glasses bounced and rolled on the cement, the pomegranate margaritas spilling and staining the concrete. I dove into the water, just as Rory's eyes popped open. I latched on to her, pulling Rory toward me, but her body was too slippery to hold. She climbed from the water, hardly making eye contact.

The nightmare from that first night, the drowning in the pool, was nothing. It had all been in my head. She was very much alive.

I wanted to have her again and have the closeness

between us back, but she dressed, her eyes never landing on me. I tried talking to her. She blushed and said nothing. I didn't let it go. "Was this a mistake for you?" I asked. "Didn't you enjoy what we did? Did I hurt you somehow?"

"No, I liked it, a lot." Her eyes crashed to the ground, embarrassed to meet mine, as she put one hand in the other and pulled her fingers. No matter what she said, I read regret. Not mine. I was in the crosshairs.

I placed her against the fence. "Look at me." Her eyes questioned, but no words came out. I pinned her arms behind her. "We aren't going anywhere until you tell me what's wrong." I brought my lips to hers. She turned her head so I only grazed them.

"No," I said, kissing her again. This time I made direct contact. She struggled under me until I got my tongue in her mouth and drew her out, drawing her back to me. Her skin was damp, from the water or the heat I wasn't sure. I put my hands under her shirt, no bra or bikini top, just her bare breasts. Her nipples were erect as I brushed against them. I brought my head down, swirling my tongue around them.

No more moving away, she finally moved toward me. "Mm," she said.

"Take your jeans off, Rory." I let her hands free so she could. "Blouse too." She stood naked before me. "Do you still want me to take you from behind?"

"Yes," she said, face reddening.

"This time, you're not getting what you want. *I* am. And it's something I need. I believe you need too. Now, down on your back."

The sun was lower in the sky, disappearing behind the roofline and the landscape. The grass became her bed. I unzipped my pants and climbed on top. "Open your legs wider," I instructed, pushing my finger into her still sweet honey box. "Seems your body still wants me."

No fooling around this time. I got down to it, sliding in, working my way, searching for the bottom of her. "I'm not fucking you so you can push me away," I said. Rory turned her eyes to the sky, but I touched her face and said, "Keep your eyes on me. You're going to have to look at me this time. I want to watch you come and make sure you're enjoying this."

I moved up her body, pushing my love rod deep inside of her. I brought my hand up to her clit and flicking it, pushed her juices toward it. She thrashed against me. There was no mistaking her enjoyment as her pussy clutched and squeezed my cock, moans emitting from her throat, her eyes sometimes closing.

"Eyes open. Don't close them," I ordered as her body first fought against her sweet pain, then surrendered to it. Her eyes were wild and unashamed as she challenged mine, then they softened beneath me.

"I'm sorry," she said. Her words freed me, my body spilling into hers. I stroked her head, lying on top of her, sealing everything in. I cleaned her with my shirt. I didn't let her return to the pool or shower this time—no washing away the evidence. She belonged to me.

****

Rory's stomach churned the entire way back to the clubhouse. She was so close to WM, smelling leather and smoke, but she couldn't be further away. Guilt swept through her like an infection. The noise from the engine was the only thing soothing her.

Two men in her life at one time wasn't in keeping with her Buddhist precepts. She hadn't told WM about

Kitties either. She should have. He'd given her an opportunity. Within twenty-four hours, she'd kissed two men's lips—and done more with WM—but she couldn't remember what happened after the strip club the other night. Thankfully, Rory was sure she hadn't slept with Turk, but she couldn't continue to lead him on. She only wanted *one* man in her life, and she knew the man she wanted. Had wanted since the first time. *I just had sex with WM, and not on a date: on an outing. Lordy, how far down will he take me?*

The wind blew his hair, and she stared at the Knights patch on the back of his jacket. Instead of the sea of blood, she imagined herself in the pool again, swimming free. Intimacy with WM was the best she'd ever experienced, and Rory couldn't imagine doing anything like that with anyone else. He pulled something primitive out of her. She'd never forget what had happened between them. No longer a child or a victim, not someone having something done to her, like in the past. WM made her a participant, asked what she wanted, and gave it to her. WM took what he wanted, too, and somehow he knew she needed to see him. *I don't hate myself. Not this time.*

A blasting siren and blue and red lights flashed behind them. "Shit," WM swore, slowing the bike and bringing it to the side of the road.

"Driver's license and registration, please," the police officer said.

"Why did you stop me?" WM asked.

"You were speeding, sir. Does the young lady have identification?"

"Not on her. We went swimming at our friend's house. Didn't need it. She wasn't doing the driving."

"She looks young." The cop's eyes scanned her up and down.

"She's over twenty-one and my old lady. I'll drive home and get her ID and bring it to the station, if it's an issue." WM flashed a look of disgust the cop's way.

"You married to him?" He stared at her. His hair was blond. His name tag read Darryl Duggan. His hand hovered over his gun strapped to his belt. A fly landed on his ear, and he brushed it away. The cars whizzed by, *whoosh, whoosh, whoosh.*

She could be free from the Knights if she said no. *But I'll end up in jail when the cops find out who I am. WM could go to jail too.*

She could say yes. *And be trapped with the Knights if I do.*

Both men waited, their eyes on her.

"Yes," she said slowly. "He's my husband."

****

When she was back in her room, Turk didn't ask where she'd been all day. Instead, he pulled out several pieces of red rope and asked, "Can I tie you up?"

"Don't be ridiculous. No." Rory's mind raced. *Who put Turk up to this? WM?* Every time she started trusting WM, he'd do something to destroy it. At any point she could have gone with the police officer and never come back here, but she didn't. Not only that, she talked the policeman out of giving WM a ticket too.

"You can fasten my hands first if you want." Turk's arms stretched in front of himself, grinning.

"It'll be more fun tying your hands to the bed," Rory smiled, waving the cord like a hypnotist in front of his face.

"Sure," Turk said, leading her toward her bed. He

laid down trustingly. She bound each hand to either side of the bedframe, using the bow knots she'd learned in Girl Scouts. All the while Turk's legs dangled precariously off the bottom of the bed.

"Rory, the knots you used are pretty, but they're kinda tight," Turk whined. "Will you loosen them?"

"I can't." She bolted out of the door, rushing down the passageway, metal crashing and clamoring from her room like cymbals clanging.

Turk's pleas rang out. "Help me! She's getting away!"

Halfway to the door with the steps, the dungeon door sprang open. WM stepped out into the corridor, appearing before her, a sly smile pasted on his face. "I wondered when you were going to try something again," he said, blocking the passageway. Rory halted and watched him warily.

WM spread his arms wide and planted his feet, motioning her to try to pass him, and then suddenly changed his mind, running forward and tackling Rory, bringing her body to the floor. A sinister smile formed on his lips as he lay on top of her, but she didn't let it stop her. She fought him, kneeing him in the groin. "Ouch," he called out, letting go of one of her arms.

She aimed a punch at his nose but only grazed his face. "Ack! Stop it!" he yelled, grasping both hands and pinning them to the floor, his body weighing her down so she couldn't move. When she stopped shifting her body, he said, "You're getting smarter, knowing when to quit." Rory lifted her head and brushed her lips against his, and he answered her, placing his on hers, slipping his tongue in, then stopped. "I thought after today I could trust you," he said, his eyes softening.

"You betrayed me," she replied.

"I did, but I did what had to be done." WM removed his hands from her wrists and held them palms-open. "Don't you understand the position I'm in?"

"Yes. The same one I'm in, but a bit different. We still have a choice," Rory said.

WM gripped her hand, pulled her to her feet, and walked her back into the room. Once there, his dark brown eyes glared. "Don't move until I say otherwise." He sauntered over to assist poor Turk, transformed into the Wicked Witch of the East, mattress and bed now covering his body, him pinned underneath them and his boots the only thing sticking out. WM untied Turk and righted the bed. WM's eyes bounced to hers. "You're going to be punished for this. Turk, go to the bar and wait. I'll meet you there shortly."

Turk looked at her, confused. "Rory…" He rubbed his wrists. "Why?"

"I'm sorry, Turk." Her eyes locked on WM instead.

"Turk, go," WM ordered. Turk sulked out the door and down the hall.

Finally, WM addressed Rory. "Your eyes are too much. Stop staring. Keep them on the floor."

"WM, I don't know what you were trying to do exactly, but to involve Turk and make him do your dirty work is deceitful. I'm thinking you're not a good man." Defeated, Rory placed her hands between her legs.

"I'm aware." He slammed the gate and turned to look at her. "And you're right." He briskly walked away.

Rory had a flashback to the discussion with WM the morning after Cowboy's rape attempt. "You'd be wise not to trust any man," WM had said. *I should have listened.* She fished under her bed, spreading her fingers, feeling for her bracelet. She needed comfort.

But it wasn't there. She lifted the mattress: not there either. Did it fly to the floor during her tussle with Turk? She searched the entire room—gone. *Did WM steal it back?*

****

I took the enemy down when they ordered it in Afghanistan and never thought twice about anything I did, but the things I did to Rory made me feel shitty. Guilt. I poked my head in Cowboy's office. "I need to speak with you about Turk."

"Where the hell did you go all day yesterday?" Cowboy asked, busily stacking his health supplements on his shelf.

"Went to Carl's house, swimming."

"Ain't that sweet," Cowboy said. "So what about Turk? Take a seat, WM."

"Turk planted his flag Friday like we planned," I reported. "Last night another story. Turk tried bondage. Things went wrong. Rope went on the other pelvis."

"What?" Cowboy's facial expression changed, his mouth turning into an O shape.

"Rory tied Turk to her bed." I lowered my eyes. I didn't want to watch his reaction.

Cowboy burst out laughing. "Rory's a bondage expert too? What style, Midori or Shibari?"

"I'm not sure."

"We can't allow her to turn the tables on the guys if we expect to make a submissive out of her."

"Agreed."

"We have little time left and I have something else that needs doing," Cowboy said.

Trouble. "What's that?" I asked.

"Go recruit a new girl."

"What are you talking about? You just got this one."

"This one's slow, and we're not certain she's going to make it, although I got her over one hurdle," Cowboy said, his eyes lighting up.

"What?"

"The touchin' thing. I got Rory up on the stage at Kitties. Possibly I can handle the bondage trainin' too."

"What about Kitties?"

"Surprised she didn't mention it. Danced a few nights ago. They loved her. I took a video. Removed her shirt too." Cowboy passed his cell to me. "Sexy, huh? They want her to come back. A crowd stopper, even without hair. What ya think?"

"Ah, interesting..." I had plenty to say, but not to him. I returned his phone instead of smashing it like I wanted to.

"Yeah, she was awesome, but when you recruit another girl, no redheads. They're too much trouble. Take Johnny and Turk too, show him the ropes. Hopefully Turk will be better with this kind of rope, lassoing a new one." Cowboy guffawed.

"About the restraint. I'd rather handle it when I return," I said.

"Sure," Cowboy nodded.

****

"Gave WM something to think on. Girlfriend didn't tell him about Kitties." Cowboy chuckled.

"Maybe she doesn't remember," Louie said, teetering on two legs of his chair. "She was messed up, barely able to walk when we left there."

"I've heard what WM's had to say about how delicate she is 'cause of her background. Bullshit.

Resourceful more like it, and her actions with Turk proves it. Restraint is my forte, and I can guarantee one thing, I won't be the one tied up."

"WM's not gonna be happy," Louie said.

"I don't care. I'm not pleased with WM, and he's the reason this went bad. WM's in the pink with her, having sexual relations, and who knows how long it's been going on?"

"How do you know? Could be just training sessions," Louie said.

"Nope. Carl called me this morning. Gave me the blow-by-blow. Got an electric eye on the pool. He's a voyeur. Said it was quite a show. WM needs to pay for his betrayal, tapping her before me. I'm going to straighten it all out, WM included. I'll deliver Rory to our world when WM's gone. A little rope play, a little bit of pain stim, and the job's complete."

"Can I join the party?"

"Not this time. Call Turk up here. I want a word with him before he leaves with WM. Schedule a prospect to clean my office too. It's a bloody mess."

"Yeah? Whose blood?"

"An Irish asshole who didn't know better. Check this out," Cowboy said, holding up a double cord bracelet with angel wings hanging from it in front of Louie's face.

Chapter 17

Arguments and Two-Timers

WM was wearing his tight black jeans, the ones with all the buttons, and the belt with the dazzling silver buckle, that Rory liked. *The one he said he'd tie me up with when he talked the dirty talk.* "We need to talk," he said.

"Yes, Sir. Let me put the journal away. Is it about Turk, Sir?" She expected a lecture and a discussion on her punishment.

"No. Provide a yes or no answer to my question. Did you take your clothes off and dance at Kitties?"

"I don't know what happened, I—" The words wouldn't come, and she stammered. *I should have told him.*

"I thought you were different, and you aren't. You pass yourself off as some innocent, with your Buddhist precepts. All an act. Just like everyone else, say one thing and do another. You're like my two-timing ex," WM said, pointing at me.

"I can't believe you," she said and stalked towards him. "One shitty girlfriend, and you're taking it out on all womankind—"

"Don't change the subject. We're talking about you, not me," he said.

"You don't get off that easy, buddy."

"Buddy? Who do you think you're talking to?" He asked, as he loomed over her and forced her to back up. "Forgetting something?"

"Oh, how could I forget, Sir?" she spat out, "I'm speaking to a stone-cold narcissist. I understand everything now. No faith in me. In fact, you don't trust or even like women. That's why you're whoremaster with the Knights…a way to control us and make us pay." She flapped her hand as a dismissal, but he just stood there glaring and provided no room for her to flee.

"Enough," he finally said. "Yes and no answers, remember? Monitor your volume and stop that accusatory stance. Remember you're in the wrong here, not me. At least I don't have to concern myself with your welfare anymore. No more shield of chastity over you either. From here on in, whatever happens, happens."

"Are you threatening me?" she asked, her body becoming still.

"You're not different. Just like all the rest," he continued and slammed the gate closed. He never gave her a chance to explain. Rory sat down and bowed her head, but how could she answer when she didn't understand what had happened herself.

****

No one delivered breakfast. Louie came to her room instead, and his dour expression made her run. She didn't get far, only halfway down the corridor before Louie picked her up and threw her over his shoulder, like Santa Claus carrying his bag of presents. *And I'm the present.*

Rory didn't struggle as he took her through the clubhouse. The shirt she wore already revealed too much of her backside. She hung upside down, looking for help. Her eyes landed on Hammer behind the bar. Their eyes connected, and he dropped his gaze to the counter, unwilling to watch. *I'm alone. Is this what WM meant? Whatever happens, happens.*

"Special delivery," Louie called out when he reached Cowboy's room.

"Put her on the bed," Cowboy said. "I can handle it from here." Louie left without a backward glance, the door closing behind him. Cowboy turned to Rory. "See Rory, I sent my man on his way. I hope you appreciate the gesture." She tried moving off the bed. "Not so fast. Like before, you want to leave before I'm done."

He pushed her back down, her body bouncing on the mattress. "Seems you're not taking my advice. Been actin' out again." He clutched her right foot and, before she could do anything, slipped a pre-tied rope around her ankle attached to the bed. He got another one on the other foot too. Cowboy climbed on top, straddling her torso, pinning her arms to the bed, leaning over her. "Settle down, Rory. This is going to happen." He flashed her a cruel smile. "Got a lot of practice breaking wild ponies like you. Did it with my pa. You're like them—rear, buck and stomp, give those crazy eyes. They put me in the dirt and bloodied my nose too." He chuckled.

Stop talking, please.

Cowboy snared her left hand with a cord, letting go of her right hand to do it. She lashed out, punching at him. Cowboy snickered and snatched hold of her hands, holding them down against the mattress again. "You've punched me in the nose twice. Payback time. Since you insist on starting with the pain part first, I'll accommodate."

Smack. Cowboy slapped the left side of her face. Her ears rang. Her cheek stung. She squeezed her eyes closed, refusing to cry, but ceased to struggle, instead laying still. He slid the rope over her hand. "Now you're learnin'. You behave, I won't hurt you, at least not badly." He placed a rope on the other hand too, then tied another line around her waist, through her thighs and down through the frame of the bed. Now she couldn't move at all.

Cowboy smiled from above. Her breaths grew shallow. "Hmm, don't worry your head about nothin'. I'm only tying you up this time. No dirty dancin' for us. You got a fan of yours mighty obsessed, not that I can blame him. I got a call yesterday from another one who wants in on your dance card. Truth be told, it's getting a little crowded. I'm interested too." His eyes raked over her prone body. "You're calming down, good. Getting bound will do that. Puts you in a good mental state. Safer too. Less likely to end up hurt. And you'll notice somethin' else, you'll *feel* things more." He unbuttoned her blouse and flicked her nipple. Rory glared up at him. *I hate this man.*

He scrutinized her, as if selecting the best vegetables at the farmer's market, then touched and squeezed different parts of her. She tried to move away but couldn't. "I have clamps to toughen them up," he said, twisting her nipple. "Probably too soon for that."

She closed her eyes, wishing she could close her ears. He ran his fingers down her neck and whispered in her ear, "Look at me." She ignored him. "Suit yourself. Listen, instead. I can't prove that you're the daughter suspect in the article, at least, not yet. Worm's still working on it. You can start my fire though." He thrust his groin against her. "I hope they're not offering a reward. Tempting. But I enjoy having you around. At least so far."

Cowboy's hair dragged across her face, dry as straw. *Please let me leave my body, rise up like I did before.* She strained against the ropes, feeling his breath on her face, long exhales escaping from his lips.

Suddenly, he stopped, loosened all the ties, and put his arms under her body to turn her. "Let's take a gander at the back of you."

"No, don't, I promise I'll be good. Please—" Rory cried out.

Bam! Cowboy's door burst open, splintering away from the frame. WM's voice rang out. "I didn't agree to this." His face was red, clothes and hair in disarray. "Let go of her!" he yelled, shaking his clenched fist.

Cowboy's footsteps moved away. Rory turned her head to the side, watching as Cowboy sat down on his weight bench, shaking his head, mumbling and reaching for his smokes. WM came to her, slid the ropes off, and assisted her off Cowboy's bed.

"You kiddin' me, kickin' my door in?" Cowboy asked, lighting his smoke and staring down WM. Rory looked for something to slip on, eyes landing on a pile of clean T-shirts. She took one off the nightstand and pulled it over her head and down her body, covering herself. "You need to calm down, WM. Have a cigarette."

"No thanks."

Cowboy's eyes landed on Rory. "Shit, My Sons shirt. That's one of my favorites." He moved his attention back to WM. "If I take this to the brothers, they'll concur you're not fit for the job anymore. A shame. Something's gotten into you. Or maybe it's the other way around."

"What do you mean by that?" WM moved closer to

face Cowboy.

"You stuck your pecker somewhere you shouldn't have, before your time."

"We'll talk about it later." He turned to Rory, jabbing his finger towards the exit.

"Give me the T-shirt back," Cowboy called out. "And what about my door, WM? What are you gonna to do about it?"

"I'll write you a check."

"My office tonight at seven and you better be there." Cowboy shook his finger and stared at WM.

"When haven't I shown for a meeting?" WM asked.

"You're doing a lot of things you've never done before." Cowboy cocked his head and raised an eyebrow, a tight smile forming, shaking his head back and forth as WM escorted her out.

****

After settling Rory down in her room, and talking with Turk and Johnny, I finally trudged up the stairs. Cowboy was seldom on time, but tonight he was sitting in his office early. I could see the top of his desk for once, and the floor was swept too. Was Cowboy sweeping everything else away as well? Trouble.

"Your recent behavior has been surprising," Cowboy said once I sat down. "Not knockin' before coming into a man's bedroom. I chose it on purpose over the dungeon, because it's not so intimidating for Rory, and you come bustin' in like the Hulk. You don't bring a new girl back either. You realize bondage is a regular part of what we do, right?"

"You said you'd wait. And I never agreed to anal sex with her."

"What are you talking about? I didn't touch her. Did

she say somethin' different? Besides, I don't need to run things by you. Our clients aren't gonna like a girl who will do some things and not others, no matter how cute she is. They get that at those amateur clubs in Vegas. They're paying for our professionalism, and it's your job to make sure the girls deliver."

"Yeah, those public places are crawling with bored housewives," Louie interrupted. "They all read that popular book, you know the one—"

"Enough, Louie." Cowboy spun back to me. "Louie's right about one thing, though. These women who frequent those public clubs think they want to be submissive, but the truth is they don't. They want things their way, the kink without the stink. Rory's the same. She needs to accept restraint to do the job."

"She can't work here if she doesn't," Louie added, taking a sip from his water bottle.

"Louie's right. We have standards. The Knights of Steel are known for having the best submissives around."

"What are you saying?"

"What I've said since the beginning." He stared at me, then pounded the table. "She either does it or she blows across the desert."

"We discussed Rory becoming an escort or working in films if the dungeon didn't work for her."

Cowboy tapped his fingers on his desk. "Not your call. The brothers will decide. In my opinion, doubtful she can do any of it. And I'm gonna tell them that."

"They'll be mighty disappointed, I'm sure," Louie said, twirling his thumbs. "Most of them had their hearts set on nailing her."

"She goes if she can't put out." Cowboy's voice was raised. "We don't carry hangers-on."

"Think, Cowboy," I argued. "They'd never vote to off her."

"We aren't under any obligation," Cowboy shot back. "She came here, and now she doesn't want to perform? Not our problem. The members take my lead. My suggestion is to make her keep her commitments. You can go now, WM."

****

Cowboy waited for the door to close. "Hold on, let me send this," he said, glancing at Louie and then down at his cell.

Cowboy—Had it w/handler—
—Problems w/Princess—
—Had her in my bed bound, as you demanded—
MM—*Nice—*
—Like the sound of that—
Cowboy—*Princess got freaky—*
—Handler 2—
—Gave him warning—
—Girl submits to restraint & rest or goes—
MM—*LOL going regardless—*
—I'm taking—
Cowboy—*Don't recall that—*
—We don't give assets away—
MM—*Now u do* ;)—
Cowboy—*Did you try for visit, run us off road after dance show?—*
MM—*No.—*

"Something's definitely off with WM, yes?" Cowboy asked Louie.

"No doubt about it," he said.

Knock, knock. "Enter." Cowboy looked up from his phone. "What you need, Ivy?"

****

I called out, "Psssssst, Rory, wake up." She stared into space, eyes glued to the ceiling. She looked nothing like the girl at the pool from four days before. The one who swam with a smile on her face. The one I tried to find fault with that day and couldn't. I would have freeze-framed her face if I could have, like Poseidon did with his wife Amphitrite. Today I couldn't hear her when she answered. Rory's voice was whispery and weak. "I'll come in," I said.

When I got close enough, I could finally hear her. "Remember you said Cowboy wouldn't do anything without my consent?" she asked.

"Yes," I replied, my eyes following hers. I needed to vacuum that ceiling; dust in the corners.

"He didn't ask, he just tied me up and then…he turned me over and I thought he was going to spank me like my stepfather did. If you hadn't come back—" She rose from the bed and paced, her voice gaining strength. "Why is he like that? He seems hellbent on destroying me."

"He's always had his issues, but I don't understand what's wrong with him. I think he'll leave you alone now."

"Memories I'd forgotten flooded into my head when he restrained me, but I can't talk about it." Her eyes got damp as she paced. "Will you train me now?"

"We'll see." No way could I reveal Cowboy's plans.

Her eyes darted around nervously. I touched her shoulder and her body trembled. She wept and then stopped herself. "I'm sorry for crying. What's wrong with me?"

I whispered, "Don't apologize," patting her back.

"Please snack on something. You haven't eaten your dinner."

"Yes, you wouldn't want a hysterical girl on your hands," she spat out. "Especially one who removed her clothing in front of a room full of men." She pulled away, tumbling onto the bed, yanking the blanket over herself as she faced the wall.

"Turk told me what really happened when we were in the van together today," I said.

"I stripped." She turned her face.

"Cowboy drugged you," I corrected. "Made you drink. And one of the girls undid your top."

"Ivy did it. She's mad at me because you don't visit her anymore."

"She said that? Did she threaten you?" That bitch.

"Not exactly, but I'm thinking she'll be better now. She got even by making me pay. I don't remember leaving Kitties or coming back here." Tears were spilling down her cheeks again, her face red. "More could have happened. I don't remember."

"I shouldn't have said what I said. There's usually more to a story and if there isn't, who am I to judge? I'll talk to Ivy."

"No, don't. Leave her alone. It's over. I don't want things to start up again. There was something else weird that night—I think my stepfather was at Kitties."

"How could that be?" I asked.

"I smelled him. His aftershave, before I passed out." Rory buried her face in the pillow.

"Lots of men wear the same cologne. Get some rest." A drawing of a bird in silhouette on the cover of her journal, wings spread far-reaching, lay on the floor. I scooped it up and tucked it underneath my jacket.

She lifted her head. "People can wear the same scent, but it smells different on everyone. It was him. He was there. I'm sure of it."

"Did you see him?"

"No, too hazy because of the smoke." She lifted her head and stared at the floor. "I just know."

"I realize you don't understand what's going on. It's called sub-drop, all hormonal. Caused by what happened with Cowboy. Pain and stress can change endorphin, adrenaline and cortisol levels, and then create an emotional crash. You'll feel better if you rest and eat something." I took a step to the gate. "I'll talk to Cookie. We can check the crowd. We'll see him if there are tapes from that night you were there. I'll stop by later. Everything's going to be fine." I didn't know if Cookie had cameras or if everything would be fine, but it was all I could come up with to reassure her.

****

I sat in the van and waited for the women to line up for the evening run, my mind exploding with memories. Men's heads open on the ground, shattering bone, glistening and splattered brain matter everywhere. I thought I'd never want to see those things again, but it would be a delight to have Cowboy's remains dripping on my boots. I stopped myself from taking it a step further. I was losing it.

Rory was, too. The sobbing in her room and telling me she thought her stepfather was at Kitties. Even the near-rape with Cowboy hadn't affected her this badly. I pulled out Rory's notebook hidden inside my jacket and opened it, thumbing through the pages, looking for signs of distress. I shouldn't have been snooping in her journal but under the circumstances, I needed to check on her emotional state. The most recent entry was from four days ago. A drawing of a crow above the writing. Strange looking. I examined it closer. It had the eyes of a human being. I realized they looked familiar. Like mine. I started reading:

I love WM, or it's lust. It makes little sense. How can I have feelings for someone if he doesn't share them? I guess that's how it works sometimes. WM fucking me meant nothing to him. I'm just another one in a long list of conquests. He's older and more experienced, and I'm...well, let's say I'm a messed-up girl from a trailer park. But today at the swimming pool, being with him, was something special.

I realized what sex is with someone you care about. It proved I could enjoy sex and showed me the difference between genuine passion and going through the motions. With Turk, it's just a friendship, but with WM it's fireworks. I need to cut things off now, but not hurt him. Dishonest to mislead Turk.

Rory loved me. My chest felt heavy. I flipped through the pages and went further back before picking an entry at random and reading it.

WM spanked me tonight. He took me to the dungeon. A terrifying place that held all kinds of tools and equipment for torture. He spanked me on my exposed rear. Words that came to mind—mortifying, shameful.

My stepfather invented untruths to give me spankings, using his belt mostly. My mother never stopped him. I fought back when I got older. The last time, when I was eleven years old, I knocked his glasses off and broke them.

I didn't fight WM because I deserved the punishment. I should never have aimed a gun at him. I could never forgive myself if something had happened. I don't think he believed me about finding it in my room. I didn't tell him how Mike gave me my lunch bag, and there was a gun in it.

In the beginning, when WM first used his hands on me, I enjoyed it. It sounds crazy, but WM touching me this way was a turn-on. I felt warm all over. I want a spanking from WM again, but he took it too far, like everything he does.

The paddle was too far. He humiliated me when he made me count out the blows and apologize after each one. I hated him for that—not for the strikes, but the humiliation. I don't think punishing me made him feel any better. After it ended, he stole my words and used them against me like a saber, a stronger pain than the spanking.

She liked me spanking her with my hand. It had made me happy. She didn't like humiliation. Good to know about. It was hard to believe the gun just happened to appear when Mike gave her the lunch bag.

One of the earliest entries was on a separate piece of paper, torn in several parts, scotch-taped back together, tucked inside the journal.

I can't believe the men here. The way they treated me last night, like a bug for dissection or some oddity on display in a traveling freak show. WM stood guard next to me. But WM's like the rest of them. Why did I feel like he was different?

I couldn't read anymore. I didn't want to spy on her, only to make sure Rory wouldn't harm herself.

Ivy, Lily, Rose, and Daisy climbed into the vehicle, and I closed the journal. "Hey, WM, remember, whatever happens in Vegas stays in Vegas," Rose said, winking. "Ha. So maybe my girl, Lily and I stay at the Bellagio and order some spa treatments at the end of the evening."

"Either of you hit fifty K and I'll pay for a day pass at any spa your heart desires," I said, opening the door to step out, then addressing the two prospects who had come along for protection. "Guys, you handle things. Here's the hotel and client list, all repeats. I have something I need to take care of."

"Is it about Rory?" Rose asked before I even got the door half-closed.

"Why?" I asked.

She sighed. "A sweet girl. Helped me with my hip pain. Always has something inspiring to say. She's so sad lately. Something's got her all down, but she's not a complainer and didn't say who or what."

"I wasn't aware any of you knew her that well."

"Now that she bathes with us, we've spent time with her. A bit too sweet, if you ask me. I can't for the life of me figure out why she's here. Not like us. We chose to be here, have an end game. Rory doesn't seem to have a reason. I hope you don't mind me saying so, but honesty is the best policy."

"I value your opinion, Rose, and thanks for letting me know your concerns. And yes, I do plan on checking on Rory." My eyes drifted to Ivy, her head bent down, eyes on her lap, refusing to look at me. "You take the night off too, Ivy. Come with me." I motioned her out of the vehicle. "Call me if you run into any problems," I said to my guys, glancing up at the red sunset. Beautiful tonight.

The van pulled away, down our gravel driveway. Both of us watched it. Ivy swallowed loudly enough for me to hear. "I noticed you had nothing to say about Rory," I said to her.

"No one else but Rose did either," Ivy replied, face white.

"Yeah, but they don't have a problem with her. They've never had words with her or tried anything."

Ivy's eyes wavered. "I…I had feelings for you, and you treated me like—"

"You shouldn't have any feelings for me. Did I at any point ask you for anything? Or lead you to believe you were anything more than—"

"No, but—"

"You have a beef with *me,* not Rory. I'm only going to say this once. There is nothing, nor will there ever be anything, but business between us. Is that clear enough?"

"Yes, Sir."

"You are going to make nice with Rory. She's going to be your new best friend. If you do anything, and I mean anything, to cause her further grief, you'll suffer. Understand?" My eyes were glued to her.

"Cowboy told me to do it. I did what he said to do." Ivy licked her lips as her eyes bounced everywhere but on me.

"What did he tell you to do?"

"To-to make things difficult for her. And to take her top off."

"Well, now you're going to make amends and tell Rory why you took it, so she understands you don't have a problem with her. Then you're going to do everything in your power to become her best friend."

"I was just—"

"I don't want to hear it, Ivy. Take the night off and think about your apology." I walked away, leaving her standing in the parking lot.

****

Clang. Her door opened. Rory squinted at the shadow as a man who was not WM walked in. "Hey Rory, you remember me?" he asked.

"Worm, right?" He'd ordered Tito screwdrivers and his laptop had porno pics.

"You got it. Mind if I take a seat?" He didn't wait for her answer. Walked right over and sat next to her on the bed, crowding her space. Rory tried to get up, and he blocked her legs with his own and turned to face her. "Don't go anywhere. We need to talk." He placed a hand on her arm, holding it. She said nothing. She looked at the floor, but Worm's closeness left Rory uneasy.

"You're not like before, with stuff to say and angry eyes. The training must be working. Not surprised. WM is one of the best," he muttered to himself before speaking louder to her, "Here's the deal. Cowboy wants the scoop on you. I've held back for now. I found everything, even the phone number of the detective handling your case. Arson is a serious offense. Even a first conviction can lead to some serious jail time. You play ball, I won't give Cowboy or WM any of it. You're in bed now. It makes things opportune. Take your clothes off and we'll get to it." Worm moved his hand on her naked thigh.

Rory felt behind and underneath her pillow for the familiar cold shape, wrapping her hand around its handle.

"Don't make me say it a—" he began, but she didn't let him finish his demand a second time. She drove the knife through the back of his hand.

"You bitch!" he screamed. The knife was wedged in

deep, the point sticking through his palm, blood oozing from the exit and pooling at the shaft. He bolted from the bed, blundering and blubbering toward the door.

"Is it still opportune?" Rory asked out loud as Worm cried incoherently, and WM watched at the gate, eyes open wide and mouth open.

Chapter 18

Four F School

I placed the tray on her table. "I made you a snack and a drink." Rubbing her eyes, Rory scrambled up. "I'm returning this to you as well." I passed her the journal. "I was afraid you might hurt yourself. Didn't occur to me you'd harm someone else."

Rory brought the notebook close to her heart, glancing up at her window. "Did you read everything?" Rory asked with an expression of worry that turned to anger.

"Only a couple of paragraphs," I said, shifting my attention to her window and then the floor." *No way am I fessing up to how much I read.*

Rory frowned. "You had no right."

"I had to. I was worried about your emotional state."

"What parts did you read?"

"Your journal is private, and I care about you. Let's not discuss it further."

"In your way you do, but I don't believe happily-ever-after's are possible in a place like this. This isn't a romance novel. I have to face reality."

I rubbed her back, sitting beside her on the twin bed. "You'll have the happily ever after you deserve."

"There are only so many pages left in this notebook to make that happen. Which parts did you read?"

"There are larger powers at work. Drink some tea and eat the sandwich. I can always purchase you another journal. Why did you stab Worm, Rory? Were you frightened?"

"Answer my question first."

"The entry where you came to church, and the one where I spanked you."

"What did Worm say?"

"Not much, but he had a knife sticking out of his hand, and what with the crying and Johnny having to drug him, he was hard to understand."

"Worm tried to fuck me."

"Are you talking figuratively or physically?"

"Both." Rory's mouth pursed, and her eyes narrowed.

"Where did the blade come from?"

"The bar."

"I have to be honest. I don't know if I can get you out of this." I turned my eyes toward the window. "You stabbed a brother."

"I don't need your protection. I protected myself. I can't do this anymore. I quit. Has it been two months yet? I want to go home."

"Understood." I faced her again. "Come here." Our eyes met. I brought her closer, wrapped my arms around her, and she laid her head against my chest. "I have something to tell you."

"What's that?" Her green eyes stared up at me.

"I love you." Too late to take it back now, but I didn't want to.

"Got a funny way of showing it," she said. "The proof of the pudding is in the eating. One of the few things my mother ever said that I agreed with. Someone else told me not to put trust in what a man has to say. I think he meant I should judge him by his actions." Then Rory gave a heavy sigh and raised her eyebrows.

****

I knocked on the door of the dungeon, and Louie opened it. One of my girls was on the spanking bench, and another one was chained to a table. Cowboy was by the display racks, selecting a flogger. "We need to discuss Rory," I said to Cowboy.

"I'm tired of talkin' about this chick, and your timin' sucks. All tied up at the moment, or should I say they are." He winked at me and pointed over his shoulder.

"I won't keep you, but here's your T-shirt back. I think I should buy Rory from the club."

Cowboy's eyebrows shot up in surprise. "Shit, what did she do to my Sons of Anarchy T? She drew flowers all over it with colored magic markers. Did you see this? There's a flower growin' where the guy's dick is supposed to be."

"Nah, I didn't notice."

"How am I gonna wear this? Better yet, where?"

"While smiling," I said.

"South Beach," Louie cackled.

"You jerkoffs! I'm going to enjoy myself with these other two ladies. I need a diversion. I love watchin' a girl dominate one of her own, don't you?"

"Definitely," Louie said.

"Too bad Rory isn't into this. Now she's gone and stabbed a member. Gone further than I thought possible. How can a man produce an erection if he thinks a woman's going to bring a blade out?"

"Yeah, a switch is one thing, but a *bitch* with a switchblade's a whole other animal," Louie said, tilting his chair back and balancing it on two legs, watching.

Cowboy picked up his bullwhip, untied Freesia, and handed her the whip. It seemed he had gotten himself another redhead; Freesia was no longer blonde. In a conspiratorial tone, Cowboy said to her, "I want you to start on her ass, go between her thighs, then move up her back and keep movin' around between those three places. Vary the strokes. Shoot for twenty, hon." Freesia smiled and strode over to the other girl, Gladys, a brunette with a beauty mark above her left eye.

Cowboy whispered to me, "I'm going to make sure whatever Free dishes out comes back double to her. Then we're going to screw the both of them. Red's gonna pay the 'stiffer' price." He winked at Louie, taking the 'King Kong' dildo off the shelf. "My bitch mother had red hair too. Why don't you join us, WM? It's been a while."

I looked at the toy. "Not today. I have some things that need my attention. I'll see you in church."

"Don't break the door on the way out," Cowboy said, chuckling. "Take the T-shirt with you." He threw it at me. "Give it back to Rory. She can wear it at her comin' out party. Or her funeral." His laughter followed me out of the room.

****

"After stabbing Worm, she needs an adjustment," Cowboy said. "Do you believe WM thinks he can buy her? What the fuck is that about? He's changed. He used to be from the Four F School when it came to women."

"What's that?" Louie asked.

"Are you a dummy? Find 'em, feel 'em,' fuck 'em and forget 'em. I need a new whoremaster."

"The members will support some kind of punishment this time for sure. Plus, I forgot to mention something that happened earlier today."

"What?" Cowboy asked.

"Two detectives from Vegas showed up asking about Rory. Said they traced her phone to a tower near here some time ago. Asked if we'd seen her. I kept them out on the porch. They were flashing her picture around. We don't need the heat."

"You're right, Louie. What do you expect me to do?"

"Dump her."

"I can't, even if she is a pain in the ass."

"Why?" Louie asked.

Cowboy sighed. "A guy's been threatening my brother's life. Said if I didn't hurt Rory, he'd kill Whiskey. This guy wants her. And Louie you can't tell anyone."

"Who is he?"

"I have no idea, but if I ever find him, he's dead meat. Another thing—I found out about the car that tried to ram us. Our friend inside the police said it was a rental. One Patrick Kelly leased it. Don't know him. Sounds Irish. If he is, it's the second one in the span of a few weeks we've come across. WM coming back early before I was done with Rory, that's no accident either."

"Who squealed?" Louie asked.

"Not Johnny. No spine. That prospect, Turk, most likely. He knew what was happening. I told him to monitor WM and report back. He didn't. He's got to pay for opening his mouth and not following instructions. You need to put a scare into him so he doesn't go against me again. He's visiting his parents this weekend. Perfect timing, off club property."

****

"Hey there, little killer. You're full of surprises," Cowboy said, unlocking Rory's door. She hurried off her bed and stood, backing up against the wall, eyes going down. "Nice. Remembering the rules, you're learnin' something here. Unfortunately, not everything you're picking up is going to work for us. Can't think of a single one of our clients that enjoys being stabbed, although it works for me." He laughed, "I love knife play."

"You want to be stabbed? Hand me a knife and I'll see what I can do."

"No, but I enjoy watchin' others get hurt. Can't believe you stabbed Worm. Whenever I lose interest, you do somethin' to lure me back. Did you like hurtin' him? Did you enjoy watchin' his blood escape? Takes guts to do it, or the crazies." He ran his hand up her arm. "Which one is it?"

"You're a creep." Rory lifted her eyes and snatched her arm away.

"Yes, and you're a failed killer. Couldn't pull off burnin' Daddy up in bed, either." Cowboy chuckled. "But you've managed to light my fire. I'll tell you what, I'll assist you with Daddy Dearest if you want, but you gotta help me." He massaged his groin.

"I don't need help. It was my first time. I'm learning. Next time I try to kill someone, I'll be successful." She poked her finger into Cowboy's chest. *I wish I could destroy him.*

"Mmm, you're getting me hot and bothered. Ever hear the expression, 'If you play with fire, you'll get burned?' Be careful, little one, unless you want to present your backside to me again."

"I can cool you off." Rory picked up her water bottle and splashed him with it.

"You sure are feisty tonight." He shook his hands, the water flying from them. "And you sure like to live dangerously." He grabbed her and turned her body, pushing her stomach flat against the wall and pressing himself against her back, making her breath hitch.

"You too, Sir." She struggled to turn herself and push him away.

"You got more weapons in here?" He breathed heavily in her ear. "Knife play with you might be fun." He ran his fingernail down her neck.

Ring, ring.

Cowboy removed his cell from his jacket with one hand, examining it. "Enough playtime for today," he said, removing his body from hers. "We'll get together again soon. I got some news to share with you." He tried to kiss her but only grazed her neck as she escaped. *Asshole.*

Cowboy walked the corridor, speaking on his cell. "You interrupted me. Why you callin'? I said no calls, just texts."

Pause.

"Yeah, leaving her room now. What do you want?

Pause.

"She's a hard case. Stubborn. By the time you take her, she'll be sorted out. Tell me how you met her."

Pause.

"You still there?"

Click.

"Motherfucker," he mouthed to himself. "You're not getting her. She's growing on me. Not givin' her up without a fight."

****

I listened from the bathing area. Cowboy's phone

265

call provided little, but it verified everything I'd suspected. Some of the things Cowboy had done were not like him, like going back on his word and not getting consent from a girl when playing.

He was out of his mind sometimes, but he followed the rules regarding scenes with the subs. At least, he always had before. Why and who was Cowboy communicating with? What did this person want with Rory? What did he have on Cowboy? I squinted after his fading figure, the creak of the dungeon door followed by a click.

****

"Rory, are you all right?" a female voice asked.

But Rory couldn't be less 'all right.' She walked toward her gate to see who was speaking. *Ivy*. Did she come to gloat or do something else? "Please, leave me alone," Rory cried.

"I have something of yours." Ivy shoved her open hand, palm up, through the bars, something glittery resting there.

Eyes widening, Rory jumped from the bed. "My bracelet." She scooped it out of Ivy's hand. "Where did you find it?"

"Cowboy had it. I gave it to him, and I stole it back. I'm sorry for taking it, and I'm sorry about the other thing too. I shouldn't have agreed to help him." Ivy turned to leave.

"Don't go. Cowboy's a hard guy to say no to."

"He is, but I was mad about WM and you. I just—"

"Don't explain. I don't blame you for anything. Thank you for bringing my bracelet back to me."

"You're welcome." Ivy put her hand through the gate, taking and squeezing Rory's hand before walking away.

****

"Rory, are you awake? I brought you some reading material," Anna said.

"Wow! Thank you." Books—a lifeline. "I can't wait to reread these," she said, as she took *Alice in Wonderland* out of Anna's hand. There were other familiar spines in the woman's hands too. Wizards and wardrobes, the stories of her childhood. "Love it!"

"I think it's time for you to leave, don't you? I don't think you belong in our world."

"Why would you say that?"

"Do you think you're part of this?"

"I don't...I think..." Rory stammered.

"Who are you staying for, WM? He'll follow if he loves you. And if not, you have a purpose. To live your life."

"I tried to leave. It didn't work."

"Try again. You can have a life. You stay here too long, and you won't be able to leave. 'You may feel comfortable here, but it's time to move on.'"

"Are you talking about you or me?"

"Do you need another gun?"

"That was you?" Rory's eyes widened.

"Yes."

"Thank you for helping me, but I think a gun is a bad idea. I don't know how to use one."

"You just aim and fire," Anna said.

"There's more to shooting someone than just the pulling of the trigger. Do you want to come with me?"

"I can't leave. I'm needed."

"What should I do with the books?"

"Savor them and carry them inside of you." Anna

267

moved back down the corridor.

****

I logged into my brokerage account and made sure the stock deal had gone through, and that the proceeds were in my drip account. Then my cellphone vibrated, the caller ID reading Turk. "Turk," I began, "good to…" Then I stopped and listened. "What? No. I can't believe it. I'm so sorry. He was…I understand. Yes. Was the road damp? How about the other driver? I'll call back tomorrow. Thanks for notifying me."

Hit-and-run. Turk was in critical condition. A white cargo van, a few miles from Turk's parents' house. I punched the wall and leaned my body against it, forehead pressing, rocking back and forth. My knuckles were bleeding.

I walked to my deck, scanning the parking lot. The Loser Cruiser was missing. I went downstairs and scouted the bar, the porch, the hall, and the dungeon. One member not accounted for—Louie.

Later that night, I was leaning against the wall while Church started. Cowboy brought the gavel down—*whack*—bringing the meeting to order. He announced Turk's accident and proposed, "In honor of all the sacrifices he made for the Knights, I suggest we make Turk a full member. He earned his patch." All the men stomped the floor and clapped in agreement. "Unanimous," he continued. "Turk is now a full member of the Knights of Steel."

My head was on fire; I found a seat next to Hammer. Was this how we treated a wounded brother? A few claps and stomps on the ground, and a patch on a cut he might never wear again? Cowboy was the one behind Turk's accident, but I couldn't prove it, and I couldn't say anything. If I did, I wouldn't make it through the night.

Chief asked about Rory's road-readiness. Only a couple of my Knight brothers were aware of the stabbing. The lights in the room were positioned at intervals, and one spotlight appeared over Cowboy's head like he was a suspect in an interrogation. In a way, he was.

"Things have not gone according to plan," Cowboy said. "She attacked a brother, Worm, two days ago. Because of that, I need all of you to approve punishment."

Hammer interrupted. Only the oldest members had enough guts to ask some questions. "Wait a minute, don't we need some dialogue on this?"

Cowboy's face got red. "Consider this a discussion. She's got issues. We've gotta do something. She's gotten aggressive. What if she hurts one of our visitors from another club? Or a client?"

"Perhaps we can sell her," Phil said.

"Possible, and something we're considering." Cowboy nodded his head up and down. The room erupted in conversation. "What's wrong with you guys?" A scowl appeared on Cowboy's face. "We aren't choirboys. She agreed to come here, and now she's gone crazy. Requires correction before she hurts a client, and if she can't do what we want, she's got to go."

My brothers discussed the issue among themselves. Louie waved his hand and exclaimed, "We've got another problem with her that comes into play. I reserve the right as sergeant-at-arms to pull the plug if she attracts unwanted attention from law enforcement."

"What ya talking about?" Hammer said, getting out of his chair. Louie shared the news about the cops' recent visit, and Hammer continued, "Why would they be looking for her?"

"She killed her boss," Louie said.

"We sure know how to pick 'em, don't we?" Phil said, laughing.

"Bring it to a vote," Louie yelled.

"How many brothers are ready to show hands?" Cowboy bellowed. Hands went up around the room, enough to vote on it. "How many members believe she requires some correction?" He started counting hands. I tallied along, praying. Cowboy won the vote by two.

"We've got it. She's toast," he said, leaning over Louie. "We'll carry out the correction as soon as possible. WM and I will come up with a plan. I want permission to act if she doesn't shape up by our chapter run, and possibly arrange a buyer. Who's ready to vote on this action?" All the brothers raised their hands. "Raise your hand if in favor of selling Rory to a private client if she doesn't work out."

Hammer whispered to me, "Why don't you say something?"

"Why? Would they listen? They think she whacked her boss, and now she's stabbed Worm."

"Say something anyway," Hammer said. "Put something on record."

I raised my hand and stood. "We've never sold a girl before. Do we want to go down that road? Get mixed up with trafficking? Our women come here on their own, *and leave on their own.* Why can't Rory?"

"The girls that left contributed and did their five to ten. Rory hasn't." Cowboy's face was beet-red. "She's been nothin' but trouble. We've discussed this before. She's wanted by the law and might tell the cops about us to reduce her time."

My brothers' heads went up and down in agreement with Cowboy's assessment. He called for the vote, and I looked around the room. He triumphed again by two. The rest of the meeting was standard stuff, except Phil's treasurer report outlining our best month ever—our X-rated films and our new chat lines were raking in lots of extra dollars.

At the end of church, Cowboy motioned me over. "Stay. We need to iron out a few things." After the other members filed out, he gave me a steely stare. "Now you appreciate what's what. The sooner she's punished, the better."

"You want me to do it?" I asked.

"Of course, who else? Do your job, WM. Straighten her out or it will end up costing her. Might cost you something, too—your position. You've forgotten that you need us and owe us. Where's your loyalty? You're nothing without us."

"Don't talk to me about allegiance. I'm a Ranger. I gave my life to this country, and the last six years to our club. I made the Knights profitable after your brother went to jail, gave you a business model and the girls to do it with. I don't owe you anything." I shook my finger at him. "*You* owe *me*."

"Do your job," Cowboy said, jumping from his chair. "Punish her or quit being whoremaster."

I removed the check from my pocket and dropped it in front of Cowboy without glancing back.

"Come back tomorrow," he shouted after me, "and we'll discuss the punishment and schedule for getting this done!"

"What's the check for?" Louie asked.

"My door," Cowboy said.

"Is it any good?"

"Don't be a numbskull, Louie. Would a brother give another brother a bad check?"

Ring.

Cowboy answered his cell, glancing over at Louie. "You again. What?"

Pause

"Yeah, if you still want her, she's yours. Leave my brother alone."

Pause.

"When? Come before the run or after, but if you want her to have the whole treatment and pull a train, she stays until the end of the week. How many friends are you bringing?"

Pause.

"All right, before the run, in our dungeon with you and your three buds. Then leave her for us and come back and collect her on Sunday. I got something else you want...that bracelet you asked about. I found it, but you ain't gettin' it for free. Call the dogs off, my brother."

Click.

"I don't like this," Cowboy glared at Louie. "This guy likes to twist the knife. I'm not giving him Rory unless I have to. She's mine. Once she's punished, she'll come around. I wouldn't even speak to this jerk if Whiskey wasn't being threatened. Something's wrong with this whole deal. The jewelry—it's important. Now I have something to bargain with."

"I thought you said Rory was WM's woman," Louie said.

"Shut up, Louie. I never said that. Never lost against anyone." Picking up his bottle of whiskey, Cowboy poured a drink and opened the drawer. "Where the fuck did I put that bracelet?"

Chapter 19

Once a Wierdo

I realized all of this had something to do with Whiskey, as I listened outside the hall, but how? Cowboy's brother was locked up in federal. Whoever was involved was coming to see Rory before the barbecue. It didn't matter now what I did or how well she did. Cowboy's plan was to get rid of her if he couldn't find a way to keep her for himself. Cowboy would take me out, too, if I tried to stop him.

The man terrorizing Cowboy must be powerful. Who was he? And what did her bracelet have to do with any of it?

****

Rory felt better, like WM said she would. Raindrops struck her face as she climbed the stairs to his place. On reaching the landing, she couldn't believe how large his plants had grown. "Your flowers are like something out of a Rousseau painting. All you need is the tiger," she said.

"You're the tiger," WM mumbled.

Rory remembered when she'd first moved to Vegas. She'd felt like an animal set free, able to do anything. *Now I'm more a wild beast than ever, ferocious. I scare myself. I hurt someone yesterday.*

It was quiet inside WM's room, except for the

soothing sound of the raindrops hitting a glass ceiling. "You don't need ambient music when you have this." Rory looked up.

"Sit, please," he said, pointing to the chair by his desk. "I need to talk to you."

"Is this why you brought me up here?"

"Yes. It's about Turk."

"What about him?"

She watched WM's lips tremble before he answered.

"I can't sugarcoat this. He's seriously hurt. Massive injuries due to a hit-and-run near his parents' home. He can't even have visitors. I'm thinking Cowboy's involved somehow."

Rory jumped up and covered her mouth with her hands, tears forming. "Cowboy likes hurting people and turning the screws," she said, and couldn't stop from pacing, as she held back tears. "Cowboy told me so himself. He's doing it to me, but I thought there's a rule against going after your own peeps. Poor Turk." She couldn't hold her tears any longer and they flowed down her cheeks.

"What's he got on you?" WM held her shoulder.

The sound of rain got louder. She paused, deciding whether to speak. "I'm not who I say I am. I…I used a fake license and someone's social security number on a job application."

"How would Cowboy know that?"

"He heard my boss accusing me. Knocked him out in my apartment. Cowboy said he was going to tell the police I did it."

"I knew it. This whole thing's been sketchy since day one. Why didn't you tell me?"

"You never wanted my explanations. Always yes and no answers, remember?" She motioned with her hands. The flow of tears stopped as she pulled herself together. "Turk didn't deserve it."

****

"Truth." I threw himself in the chair, frustrated. "Cowboy betrayed me, the club, and you, with his lies. He's worse than I imagined."

"Lies are what the world lives on," Rory said. "Cowboy's not totally bad. He's read things about Buddhist thought."

"You can't be serious." I laughed. I needed to get her out of here before she completely lost her way.

"Do you think Cowboy knew Turk lied about sleeping with me?" Rory asked.

"What?"

"I refused to sleep with Turk. Turk explained that we needed to pretend, and that if we didn't, Cowboy would send someone else. Turk said your job was in jeopardy too."

"I'm certain Cowboy doesn't, because *I* didn't know either. I'm glad you didn't go through with it." I took her hand. "I have two questions. Who are you, and what are you running from?"

"I don't know anymore," she answered, her eyes steady on me. "I did when I arrived. I'm different now. I could ask you the same thing." Her eyes were still wet with tears.

"You're right. I've got something for you," I said, changing the subject. I crossed over to my nightstand, opening the drawer, removing the gift, and presenting it. My timing was off for giving her the present, but I didn't know how much time she had left.

"What is this?" She took the jar from my hand.

"Cherries in liquor from Italy. Like maraschino cherries but better."

"You remembered," she whispered. "The ceramic jar is beautiful. I can't eat them now. I'm depressed about Turk."

She should try to enjoy them. It may be the last time she'll have them. I watch as Rory paced back and forth, holding the gift with one hand next to her chest. "Turk getting hurt might be-be my fault—"

"No, it's not." I took her other hand and stopped her from moving.

"How do you know? Maybe Turk didn't do something he was supposed to do involving me. Or Cowboy thought he didn't, and they wanted to make him pay."

"Only been here a couple of months and already figured out how this club operates," I said.

"Maybe we can prove Cowboy had something to do with it, and tell your friends."

"No," I said strongly. "I didn't tell you about Turk so you could do something about it. Truth, Cowboy wouldn't hesitate to kill you to keep you quiet. Watch yourself. Now is not the time to do something. Understand? For once, listen to me. Keep your head down."

"I will," she said quietly. I reached out and wiped a tear from her cheek. "Go along to get along," she said. "Cowboy's advice to me."

"Exactly. I'm going to make a quick call to Turk's father. I told him I'd call back and see how he's doing."

I removed my cell phone from my pocket. "Hi, WM here. How is he?" Pause. "Wonderful. Encouraging news. That's a relief. Let me know if I can do anything, and when he can have visitors. Thank you." I hung up and turned to Rory. "Turk's going to make it, but he's going to face some physical challenges."

"It's not right, what happened to him."

"No, but you realize the world isn't fair, and things don't always go the way we want."

"Sometimes they do," she said, unscrewing the jar. "I'll try just one, to celebrate Turk's second chance." She popped a cherry in her mouth, tiny drops of pink juice staining her lips, eyes shutting then opening as she chewed. I stood there, watching her. "Thank you, WM, Sir, these are delicious, even better than maraschinos." She ate another one. "I'm still hurt about what happened to Turk. I hope nothing I did caused it." She swallowed. "Mmmm. I might eat this whole thing."

She ate about halfway through the jar before I thought about taking them away, even though watching her consume them was the most beautiful thing I'd ever seen. She smiled with enjoyment, savoring each one. It was better than watching a sunset over Lake Huron, a star-filled night in Flagstaff, or fireworks on the Fourth of July by the Washington Monument in Washington, DC.

"Stop. Enough," I eventually said, reaching to take the jar away from her.

"Oh, can't I have one more, Sir, please?"

I had thought those green eyes could bring a man to his knees when I had brought her back to life in the pond. I was right. "Save the rest of them for later." I would let her eat all the cherries, if they didn't give her a tummy ache. I waited for her to pass them back.

"All right, *Dad.*" She hesitated, her face darkening.

"What are you going to do?" She asked as she handed over the jar. "There must be something…" Rory's forehead furrowed as her voice trailed off.

"Sleep on it," I said.

****

She didn't take off all her clothing before entering WM's bed. *Once a weirdo, always a weirdo.* They stared at each other, lying on their sides. After WM had told her about Turk, guilt had seeped in and she couldn't get rid of it. *Am I responsible for what happened?*

WM seemed to know her thoughts. "Don't concern yourself with this. I'll do the worrying." He reached to the bedside table and turned the lamp off. The room was black except for green and red marks dancing on the glass, like a spinning carousel, from the colorful bulbs tracing the windows.

"Can you take this off?" He touched the sleeve of her shirt.

"Can you help?" she whispered back.

He fumbled with the tiny buttons on her camisole, finally freeing her. "How does this feel?" He ran his fingers across her shoulders.

"I think it feels, hmm…"

"What if I do this?" He burrowed under the covers, opening her thighs.

"I like it," she giggled.

"You know what I'm about, what I'm into, yes?"

"The Dom thing?"

"Yes." He snickered. "That, and you forgot the Sir."

"Yes, Sir."

"Do you agree to do what I ask without question or hesitation, and submit to me tonight?" As her eyes grew accustomed to the darkness, his eyes seemed to invade her entire being.

"Yes, Sir," she breathed out.

"Present your hands. I want to handcuff you."

"I'm not sure…"

"Didn't you agree?" Flashes of red patches from the window bounced on WM's face.

"Yes."

"Do you trust me?"

"Yes."

"Then put your arms in front of you." She held her hands out. "Don't worry, I have the key," WM chuckled, snapping the cuffs on her wrists. "Are you ready for me to fuck you hard, Rory?"

"Yes," she said, her cheeks warming. Was it the cuffs, WM asking for her submission, or him telling her he would fuck her hard, that was making her clit throb?

Climbing on top and straddling her, he said, "Lie back, relax, and remember, don't move unless I tell you to." Aroused already, she twisted away as he sucked one nipple and his fingers squeezed the other, making them swell and harden. "Did I mention I enjoyed the taste of your pussy the other day at the pool? I can't stop thinking about you and that day."

The shadows in the room hid Rory so that WM couldn't see her blush. Sometimes she thought about that day too. *Not sometimes—it's more like several times a day, and a few times I touched myself re-imagining it.*

He pinched her nipples firmly and twisted them. Her back arched, making her hold her breath. "Breathe, Rory," he said. *How did he know?* He flicked his tongue side to side across them before moving down her body, licking her with long strokes, coming to her belly and delivering smaller licks at her belly button, down her legs and between them. She couldn't stop moving. The anticipation was driving her crazy.

"Lie still," he ordered. "Open your thighs for me, pretty one." WM crawled down, walking his fingers around her fleshy parts, separating them. He ran his tongue around her outer lips into the inner ones, shifting back and forth. She squirmed against him, dampness spreading.

"Be still," he warned again. "Bend your knees and keep your legs open. Remember, your pleasure will come through pleasing me." WM moved back up to her breasts and squeezed them again, harder than before, taking each nipple between his teeth, hardening them. The ache was exquisite, her sex clenched.

He moved to her pussy again and dipped a finger in, and then two. She trembled as he put his tongue on her clit, flicking and sucking her with his lips, causing her hips to shoot upward off the bed. "Still," he said, bringing his arm across her abdomen and holding her body down. He kept going, driving a third finger in until an orgasm swept her along like an ocean wave, leaving her thrashing and screaming out, engulfing her, as she was lost in ecstasy. *How does he make me come so quickly?*

"Good girl," WM said, removing the handcuffs. "Thank you for trusting me enough to try this." He held the cuffs up. "Next time we'll use something else, and restrain your feet too. Our relationship will grow if you're willing to experiment. If you don't like something, we'll never do it again." He ran his shaft up and down her overly slick clit. "Does that sound fair?"

"Hmm, yes," she said. *I'd agree to anything to keep WM doing this.*

WM kept rubbing her clit with his cock again and again, but he didn't enter her, increasing her need. "Do you want this?"

"Yes," she whimpered, attempting to move her body to capture him.

"You'll have me when I'm ready," he laughed, "and I'll decide when you're ready, too."

Embarrassed, she looked away.

"Your eyes on me," he said. He palmed her ass, getting her attention, bringing her to him. He pumped into her hard, pulling out again, making her gasp. He plunged in and out again, his rhythm building. A violent attack, her senses were shattered, his cock growing harder and more prominent every second.

She bucked back, gripping him like at the pool. She began seeing colors in her head and felt her pussy clench around his cock as it pounded home, vibrating and expanding. WM whispered into her ear, "Go, baby, go." There was no more talk about not moving, just his exploding and flooding inside of her.

Afterwards, laying side by side, she rested her head in the crook of his arm and looked up into his sleepy gold-brown eyes, touched by the dots of colors from the lights. He took her hand. "Hopefully you liked it. I didn't hurt you, did I? I realize what I do is not the warm and gentle kind of love, not for everyone."

"No, I'm fine," she said. *No doubt about that.*

"Was it all right? Did you enjoy it?"

"Uh-huh, yes, Sir." *It could be there's something wrong with me. What he did was perfect.*

"We can discuss all this in more detail, what you did and didn't like, tomorrow. Submission doesn't mean you don't have a voice. My responsibility is to choreograph everything, but I'd be a fool not to consider your needs and desires." He kissed her lightly. "This is just a starting point for discussion." He brought her closer.

Then things went wrong. "I'm going to give you some tips on dealing with clients. Some women think it's about opening your legs. You need to listen to their personal problems, give advice, but only if they ask. Make them think nice things about themselves. You already understand this from teaching yoga." Rory said nothing. Distressed, she feigned sleep. "Did I lose you?" *Yes, he had.*

After he fell asleep, Rory gazed out the window. No Truth Moon tonight, only dazzling lights.

****

"Wondered if you were going to show, WM," Cowboy said. "I got up early for you. It's unlike you to be late, WM. Come up with a plan for girlfriend yet?"

I scanned Cowboy's office wall. The calendar page was still stuck on July, and July's eyes looked more tired than last time. I was sure sharing a space with Cowboy aged a person. Even if she was just a picture. Her eyes reflected how mine felt. I turned back to him and imagined a bullet bursting through the middle of his head. "Yeah, I got it figured out."

"Great. I want Rory back on schedule. We're behind. I have a test for her before our chapter run. A private client."

"Who?"

"A friend, that's all you got to know. The other thing, Cookie wants Rory back. Put Kitties in her datebook. No more bar. She dances every night until the barbecue. Make a prospect take her if you're busy on hotel runs or managing the dungeon appointments."

What bullshit line would I run on Rory to get her up on the Kitties dance stage? Or would I drug her as Cowboy had? "What prospects? Mikes disappeared and Turk won't be back."

"Shit, Mike. Don't even mention that guy. I'll give you some new ones. Now, what's the punishment and when?"

"This evening. In the dungeon. But first I'm taking her out." What happened to Mike?

"Wow, that fast? My man." Cowboy glanced over at Louie and back at me. "Tell me about it."

"I'm going to take her to that hotdog stand thirty minutes from here. Last meal kind of thing. On the way back, near the clubhouse. I'll stop and have a picnic. Mickey Finn her drink with some Rohypnol. Drive the rest of the way back—"

"What if she falls off the bike all drugged up?" Louie asked.

"I'm taking the van," I said.

Cowboy's eyes lit up, glistening like Christmas lights. "She trusts you, too. Are you sure you don't want her fighting back? I like it when they resist."

I wish I could take away your last breath. "More chance of hurting her. It could put her out of commission. Do you want that, with friends coming? This way is clean."

"You're right. Always sensible." Cowboy smiled. "You do it your way, without the razzle-dazzle. Perhaps I'll come in and join." He opened a drawer and took a pocketknife out, scraping underneath his nails.

"You don't trust a brother?" I asked, becoming angry.

"Of course I do. I like doin' it in nature. After you

drug her drink, she'll be relaxed. I can flip her. She'll earn her brown wings." Cowboy cackled.

I hated this motherfucker.

****

Any doubts about Rory' willingness to submit to me disappeared last night. I got her through a bit of restraint and even tested her pain tolerance. It wasn't bad, probably from the yoga. She was used to discomfort from getting into those yoga poses. She was coming around. She came fast with the handcuffs and the stim.

I screwed up at the end. I hadn't lied about who I was, but the way I treated her had been stupid. Instead of enjoying my closeness with her after our scene, I pushed her away with my words, all because I was jammed up with Cowboy and the Knights. No woman had felt this good and meant this much to me before, and I pretended otherwise. I treated it like it was nothing more than a training session and she meant nothing to me.

When I returned to my room, Rory was running a bath and waiting for it to fill. She needed clothes, too, and before leaving to locate them, I remembered her purse, the one I wanted to dump. I should have done it weeks ago. I headed downstairs with the bag under my arm, stopped in the kitchen for matches, and then went outside, the door slamming behind me. I threw it in the fire pit, sprinkled it with lighter fluid, and lit it up. A lump developed in my throat as I saw it shrivel and burn. I turned my back on the fire and went back inside. Would it be better for her to die than to end up traded away as a slave? I'd check on it later to make sure there was nothing left.

All this was much worse than anything I'd been part of before. Rory shouldn't even be here. All the others had come of their own accord. I may have facilitated a girl to sell herself in the past, but I'd never coerced one into doing so, nor came close to human trafficking.

Rory was in the Jacuzzi when I came back. I knelt beside her and picked up the cloth. "I'll clean you," I said. She argued but I ignored her protests, and eventually she went along, settling in and trusting me. She shouldn't. I could push her head under and hold her there, and she wouldn't have to suffer. *What's wrong with me?*

She was quiet this morning. Why wouldn't she be, after the way I had treated her last night? I started at her head, working the shampoo into her scalp, little hairs making an appearance. I made sure none of the shampoo got in her eyes, rinsing it out carefully, moving to her neck. "I'm sorry about what I said last night," I finally said. "You won't be entertaining clients. Not if I can stop it." I moved the cloth to her back and then to the front of her.

Rory's eyes measured me. "I figured you were frightened of your feelings and wanted to make me not like you."

"Did it work?"

"No, but it still hurt."

"Can you forgive me?" The water hit the slate on the fountain, making a soothing noise.

"I'll give you the answer you gave me once. I can never stay mad at you." She reached up and kissed me. I cleaned her abdomen before moving the cloth between her thighs and down to her toes. Then I thought of Cowboy putting his hands on her hips. I let the water out of the tub, left with the thought that I'd prepared Rory for Cowboy's onslaught.

"Thank you, that was relaxing," she said. "No one's ever washed me before, at least that I can remember." Latching on to my hand, she stepped out, the soon-to-be sacrificial lamb to Cowboy's perversions.

I located the washed, white, cotton good-girl panties she'd worn when she first arrived. "Gosh, panties I like," she said as I handed them to her.

"Was there anything last night you didn't enjoy about our scene?" I asked.

"You mean the sex?"

"Yes."

Her face turned pink. "I liked it."

"Good. From now on, before I do anything new with you, we'll discuss it first. There will be things you've never done or seen, but you have to believe I would never do anything to harm you, right?"

"Yes."

"Do you understand the difference between pain, pleasure, and injury?"

"I'm learning," she said. "Last night when you were really pinching me, it ached, but a certain part of my body seemed to like it." Her face got redder. "Even though I didn't want to. For some reason, it made everything more intense."

"You mean your orgasm?"

"Yes. It left my whole body shaking, and I saw different colors in my head."

"Pain releases endorphins, a kind of chemical reaction. The idea is to give you a high but not to injure you." Rory looked away. "Does talking about this make you uncomfortable?"

"To be honest, talking about sexual things of any sort makes me uncomfortable."

"To do what I do takes some discussion. I'm responsible for keeping you safe during our time together. That takes awareness. And if we're going to be together, you're going to have to accept and get used to talking about these kinds of things…"

"Expect a lot of yes and no, answers, Sir." She giggled, giving me a wink.

"You got me on that one." I chuckled.

Chapter 20

Loyalty

"Three things cannot be long hidden: the sun, the moon and the truth." ~ Buddha

Rory Dressed and got ready to work in the bar as I went out on the deck and extracted the last cigarette in the pack. I'd tried quitting before, but it always came back to this. How fitting, being down to my last one again.

I smoked it, watching the white cylinder decrease in size, and listened to my brothers' bikes come to life in the yard. I considered whether I could put Rory's welfare above that of my club brothers when I hadn't known her that long. I could help her, but if I did, I'd have to return to my old world, one of failure. I'd have to leave the Knights and my job, where I'd escaped my past and become somebody new.

What would I do if I went? What if my ideas about her were all in my head? She might not be suitable for me. I could end up being too much for her. What if I was making more of her than what was there? There'd be other girls. I could change my mind about her the first time she did something I didn't like. And maybe I'd get over what happened to Turk. How did I know for sure anyway that Cowboy had anything to do with it? Even if he did, perhaps that's the end of it now. Turk was still alive, anyhow.

I stopped thinking this way as soon as the cigarette burned my fingers. What an ass I am.

I grabbed our jackets from the chair, packed a helmet in my backpack, and carried the knapsack and duffle bag to the door. The late afternoon sun streamed through the transparent ceiling and left shadows shaped like daggers on the wall. I thought I'd feel worse, closing the door to my room. But after I got this done, nothing would weigh me down.

****

"Where you off to?" Louie asked, eyes landing on my bags, body blocking my path.

"I'm going on that ride," I said.

Cowboy winked. I wanted to cut the smile off his face. "What's that hanging around your neck?" he asked, stretching his arm out to touch it.

I grabbed it away. "It's mine." I tucked it inside my shirt.

"Never seen it before."

"One of my Ranger friends gave it to me."

"A dead one or a live one?"

"A loyal one."

"Nice. You want me to call Rory from the bar?"

"No. Don't spook her. I'll do it."

"I'm going to place some beers in a cooler. I'll meet you two out front," Cowboy said, strolling to the kitchen. *Shit.*

I threw my backpack and the duffel bag into the back of the van and put my shades on. I checked to make sure my Glock 19 was inside my jacket. Rory followed me back outside without a word. I opened the passenger side door for Rory. The dress moved against her body, a lacy eyelet piece, colored a soft purple. I had never known Anna liked to sew until I told her last week I wanted a special dress for Rory, and she volunteered to make something. Rory's eyes had danced with light when I brought the garment out of the bag this morning.

Rory turned to me, hesitating in the open passenger door, as she asked, "What kind of outing are we going on?"

"A date today. We're going for something to eat." I plastered a fake smile on.

"I graduated, hooray." She grinned as she climbed in. "Never ridden in the front seat before, either." Stretching out her hand, she bumped the Hula Girl, making her shake and said, "I remember you."

Cowboy came out the door carrying an ice chest, placed it in our vehicle and got on his chopper. Rory looked at me questioningly.

"Yeah, he's coming with us," I said.

Rory said nothing and folded both hands neatly in her lap, seemingly unconcerned. Did she trust me? Had she given up? Or had she become harder since coming here? All the possibilities bothered me.

Freight liners crowded the roads today, but I couldn't take chances passing the trucks with the van. No acceleration. It forced me to focus and keep my attention on the present instead of what I had to do. We'd both end up dead if I didn't. Cowboy kept pressing, pulling even, and then speeding up, trying to challenge me. Ridiculous. Race the Loser Cruiser? I was carrying precious cargo.

I saw the giant hotdog bun and fake oozing yellow mustard in the distance. Six years ago, it had made me smile, but today it didn't. The hot dogs weren't the draw; It was more the entire experience of eating there. Every place was a chain nowadays. This one wasn't—a genuine piece of Americana.

Rory's eyes kept looking side to side while waiting in line to order. Was she thinking of running? I wished she would, and then I wouldn't have to do anything. She ordered a strawberry shake and some fries at the window from a kid with a white and red striped shirt.

"My date will pay," Rory said. Smiling, she elbowed me. The shake wouldn't do her stomach any favors, but then I remembered what I had hidden in my jacket and frowned. My stomach was messed up too. Cowboy, standing behind us, ordered four dogs and chips.

We got the food to go. "Too crowded and no tables available," I told Rory, carrying the bags to the vehicle. We drove back toward the club and pulled the van into a secluded spot about ten minutes away from our property, with Cowboy following. It was a remote place I'd been to before, set back from the road, with desert shrubs, grasses, and small pines. Rory would run if she had any idea of what was about to go down. We strolled toward the clearing with the food and the backpack. In the distance we saw a couple of mules grazing.

Cowboy grinned and hummed as we walked. "He sure is happy today," Rory said. "I have to go to the bathroom, Sir."

"I'm sure you'll find a place." I pointed to a group of trees that provided coverage. Full of dark secrets, and by tonight they'd hold another one. I watched her hips sway as she walked toward the trees and disappeared.

"Doesn't she look pretty from behind? Easier with the dress. I don't think she'll mind this time, do you?"

Cowboy asked, laughing.

I wanted to kill him. I would if he went anywhere near Rory. I spread the cover on the sandy soil with short grass peeking through, then removed the food from the backpack. The sound of a thousand bees filled my head. The noise was deafening. Cowboy cracked the top off his beer, launching an explosion, creamy suds flooding out. He took a gulp. Foam dripped on his red pullover. "I gotta go too," he said. "Ain't that a bitch. Just when things are gettin' interestin'." He crouched down. "Let me leave my bottle here." He placed his beer on the blanket and headed toward the pine trees.

I kept an eye on Cowboy. I wanted to make sure he didn't go anywhere near where she'd walked. The buzzing sound was louder, my Glock heavy in my jacket. I clutched the drug in my hand, and took the lid off the shake. Less than thirty seconds to decide. Everything in slow-motion. It was possible she wouldn't come back. Rory was witchy, could sense things. I looked up as she flashed a Miss America wave, short stubs of hair aflame creating a pink halo. I held my breath, hand hovering over the brown beer bottle and the large white cup, deciding which one I would betray.

I dumped the contents and rearranged both drinks to how they looked before. Exhaling, I shoved the empty vial back into my pocket. Decision made. Either way, one life would be over. Mine.

Rory sat down and drank the shake. Minutes later, Cowboy sauntered back. "Let the party begin," he said, picking up his drink and downing it. He inhaled one hotdog, started on the second, then began sliding the chips on his tongue, a conveyor belt. He reached for another beer, staring at Rory.

"I'll build a fire," I said, selecting some kindling from the ground.

"Why bother? We won't be here that long, and it's too hot," Cowboy said, staring at Rory, ketchup oozing out of the corner of his lips.

"The sun is setting, and a fire would be wonderful," Rory said.

"Ain't you two a couple of romantics. How's that milkshake, Rory?"

"Delicious. Want a sip?"

"Nah, enjoy," Cowboy said, smiling his crocodile smile. "I'll find enjoyment in somethin' else in a little while."

"Rory, go find some wood for the fire," I said, pointing toward a small thicket of trees.

"It's creepy there. Like someone's watching."

Cowboy laughed. "I'll go with you, if you want."

"That would be even scarier. I'll go by myself," Rory said, walking and picking up branches as she went.

"A smart mouth who'll benefit from punishment," Cowboy said. He frowned and rubbed his stomach. "I don't feel well. I ate those dogs too fast." He looked at Rory and then back at me. A minute later he coughed, his blue eyes widening in surprise. He drew a gun from his cut and pointed it at me. "You did something stupid, WM, didn't you?"

"No, you did. You didn't tell the truth about her. You betrayed the club and expected me to go along with your lie."

Cowboy lifted the gun. "You're doing this for nothing. I'm gonna take her out." He aimed at Rory, his hand trembling. Twenty feet out at the edge of the tree line, she picked up a branch. An easy shot for Cowboy under ideal circumstances. His face crumbled. "Hard to kill my kind," he said, bending over, dropping his arm and stumbling to his knees, the Luger falling from his hand to the ground. He fought for consciousness, folding over the blanket and reaching for the weapon. He mumbled something, dragging the gun to his side and clutching it in his fingers.

"What did you say?" I crouched down next to him, bringing my ear to his face.

"She's not what you think."

"I know she's running," I said.

"More to it."

"What?" But there was no answer, and no way to get him back.

Rory returned, carrying small sticks and dumping them in a pile. Soon, the sound of snoring was interspersed with the sounds of the birds, crickets, and crackling flames. "He must be tired," she said. She ate the fries and continued to drink the milkshake.

I took the maps out of the backpack, unfolded them on the blanket, and ran my fingers along the red lines as the sun warred with the purple sky. "You're not going back," I said, meeting her eyes, "And neither am I."

"Never?" she asked, eyes enormous and fearful. The flames reflected on her skin, and the lengthening shadows from the trees grew on the ground. The scent of charred wood reminded me of how she used to smell.

"I can't go back if I don't turn you. I can't do that, and I won't. I'm making the U-turn you suggested weeks ago."

"Are you sure?" She turned her head, looking over at Cowboy, and whispered into my ear, "You could say you did."

"He can't hear you. I drugged him. And I refuse to lie. There's no going back."

"We could go back when he wakes up," her voice quaked. "I'll do whatever you need me to. None of it matters anymore." Tears formed as she said it, "I can't go back to Vegas now, anyway. That life's gone."

"Why would you ever go along when you haven't so far?" I asked, bending over Cowboy, reaching under him and into his jacket and taking the keys to the bike and his phone. I was determined to find out everything he had been up to.

"I'm stronger now," Rory said.

"You're not cut out for this life. And as you pointed out to me, you deserve better than this." I removed my colors and draped them over Cowboy's sleeping form.

"Maybe I don't," she said. "It's all my stepfather wanted me for, and you've got to learn how to face your fears."

"Not this way, you don't. You got away once. You realized you had to save yourself. You're getting away from this too. I'm tired of running from my memories by hiding with the Knights, aren't you?"

"You're right," Rory said and walked over to Cowboy. She pulled the gun out of his hand.

"What are you doing?" I asked.

"I'm giving Cowboy what he deserves. And making sure he never hurts anyone again." Rory aimed the Luger at Cowboy's unconscious body.

"No. Stop, think." I reached out to her. "This will stick with you forever. Give me the piece."

"You said he was bad." Her eyes burned bright with tears. "I'm saving other women. He needs to pay for hurting Turk too. For once, I need to be powerful."

"This isn't the way, and shooting an unconscious man isn't powerful. Cowboy did evil things, but we don't have all the facts. Don't do this."

She looked back and forth between Cowboy on the blanket and me. I had to convince her. "Haven't you ever read the Two Wolves story? An Indian legend?" She shook her head no. "A long time ago, a grandfather told his grandson a story. 'We have two wolves inside of us fighting, one of fear and hate and the other of love and peace.' The grandson asked, 'Which wolf will win?' The answer, 'The one we feed.'"

Rory brought her arm down and handed me the gun. "Cowboy talked about it too, our shadow selves." She stared out in the distance for a moment. "Can we get some of the others out who want to leave?"

"Who?"

"I…I think Anna wants to go."

"Anna? She can leave anytime she wants to. She's retired. She could've left four or five years ago. Who else?"

"Rose and Lily?"

"Did they say they wanted to go?"

"Not really…but how can they be a couple while working for the Knights?"

"Truth, no one cares about them as long as they do their jobs. They seem happy with the Knights, and they'll leave together when they're ready."

"There must be some who want to leave."

"All of them came willingly. You're the only one that didn't, as far as I know. I think someone forced Cowboy to take you by threatening his brother's life."

"Who?"

"I don't have the answer for that. Remember when

you said I'm not strong and smart enough to fix everything?" I shoved Cowboy's gun in my cut. "You were right. Getting my friends killed is proof of that. I wanted to play hero and rescue another unit. I should have known it was a setup. Drove the vehicle right into an IED blast. My best friend Chet, along with three others, died because of my actions."

"I didn't mean it that way."

"Chet used to wear a silver feather around his neck." I removed the feather from under my shirt, so she could see it. "His parents said he wanted me to have it. Today seemed like a good day to put it on."

Rory's eyes bored into the feather. "You didn't *play* the hero. You *are* one. Heroes don't win every battle. It takes someone special to fight for others like you're doing for me. I need to tell you something too."

"I'm listening." I held on to her.

"I did something before I came to Vegas." She touched the feather on my neck. "I started a fire. It got out of control, burned some trailers to the ground. Everyone got out, but the cops are looking for me."

"Why did you do it?"

"I mentioned my stepfather, doing some things…without my permission."

"You didn't provide details," I said.

"It's painful to talk about. The truth both my parents made my life a living hell." Her eyes were dark. "One of the trailers, it belonged to them. I couldn't stand it anymore. They did things to hurt me. The last year I was there, I found a stray cat someone had left. He followed me home and I named him Smoke. I took care of him, brought him to my room at night or whenever the weather was poor. They let me get attached to him. After six months, one evening Smoke didn't show when I called. My mother said not to bother." Rory's eyes watered. "They said they were tired of having him in the trailer and dropped him off at a shelter."

"Assholes. Did you try to find the cat?"

"I contacted all the nearby shelters, the weird thing was, none of them knew anything about it. My parents refused to tell me what happened to Smoke, no matter how I begged. Things spiraled further down after that, and when I tried to tell my mother exactly what my stepfather was doing to me, she stopped me. Called me a troublemaker. I realized she wasn't going to help me, and that's when I decided to leave. I created an older version of myself with all that entailed and left before my senior year. Went to an ashram to study Buddhism. The fire was a diversion, something to keep them busy and to burn up what mattered most to them…things."

"You did what you had to do and got away."

"You don't think I'm a bad person?"

"No. A good move to leave. Impulsive, though, setting the blaze. You were lucky no one got hurt. From my own experience, you can't run forever. At some point, you're going to have to go back and face what you did. The past isn't finished just because you say it is. Not that simple."

"I love you, WM." she whispered, taking my hand and drawing a heart into my palm with her finger. She then held the feather hanging on my neck while still sitting on my lap. "The gift from your friend. It's a reminder to live your life. My angel wing bracelet symbolized freedom and gave me the strength to leave my abusive home too. It was the only thing my real father left me." The fire cast an orange light on her face.

"I'm sorry I couldn't find it. Searched everywhere. I was going to give it back. I think Cowboy might have taken it."

"I have it here," she said, reaching into her jeans. "I took it from your room for comfort after Cowboy and Louie attacked me."

I slipped it over her wrist, smiling. "Now you can fly free," I said, standing up and bringing her to me. I held her hand high, the blossoming butter moonlight and orange flames reflected on the dangling, metal angel-wings as they flew out against the sky.

A smile spread across her face. "Have you ever heard the expression 'feathers appear when angels are near?'"

I gripped her shoulders and brought her toward me. "I don't doubt it. You're my angel, Rory, who guided me to the light." Then I whispered in her ear. "My real name's William McKnight."

Her eye's widened as she looked up at me. "Is it…Irish?"

"Yes. And you? What's your actual name?"

She smiled. "It really is Rory. I only made up a different last name. I'll use your last name now. Rory McKnight," she said. Then she poked me as she grinned. "I'm Irish too."

We stood together in the silence of the night. But I had more to say. I held on to her tight, the words coming out: "I'll take you back to the hotdog stand and find you a ride with a friendly family. It would be best if you got away from Vegas. The Knights and police will come looking for you."

"I don't know…I'm not sitting in a car with crying children and yelling adults. I was a crying child and lived with yelling adults. I'm done with that"

I let her go, as much as it hurt me. I turned to the fire and stomped it out, before pouring water on top. "I'm giving you a duffel bag." I picked it up off the ground. "There's a phone number inside, an ex-Ranger buddy. Call him. He'll help you, make a license and other new ID. Rory Riley is dead now. There's enough money in there to carry you for a year or even two if you're frugal." I kissed her, not letting my lips linger, as I passed the bag.

"Couldn't you come with me?" she asked, holding the bag and one of my hands. She looked up at me with those green marble eyes.

"I'm not a simple man. Truth."

"I'm not a simple woman, Sir."

I looked down at our connected hands. "Are you sure about this? I thought you wanted your freedom."

"Freedom exists if love is present." She reached up and touched her lips to mine, before whispering, "Nothing happens by chance. We belong together." She leaned against my chest, her words wrapping around us. "I was desperate, and Cowboy tricked me into coming to the Knights. You were desperate and needed to find a reason to leave. I provided this."

"You did." I recognized our truth.

A large black bird flew above us. *Caw, caw, caw*. Another one joined, making two. We looked up as shadow wings spread wide and touched, the birds soaring like one, creating a silhouette against the creamy moon and star-filled sapphire sky. We held hands and walked toward the bike. Together.

Epilogue

Friends, Family & Foes

"What do you think, Patrick?" Evan asked, looking through the branches.

"Is Rory safe, or do you want to pinch her?" Michael asked, using his hand to brush away the bugs.

"Don't act the maggot," Patrick said. "She's my daughter. Stop talking about her like she's candy you're fixing to thieve."

"It looks like the Cowboy fella is passed out on the ground. A perfect opportunity," Michael said, holding the binoculars.

"How're you feeling, Michael, after the beat-down he gave you?" Evan asked.

"Not bad, considering he knocked out two of my teeth. Took offense at me in his office, it seems. Accused me of giving your daughter a gun. Like I would ever do such a thing when it's me they'd blame."

Patrick chuckled and looked through his binoculars. "Yer man is taking the other biker's cycle and Rory. They seem to be packing up the bike."

"What do you want to do?" Michael asked, looking at Patrick.

"Let them go." Patrick said. "We'll follow and make sure all is grand. She'd be wise to dump this man. Not sure about him."

"He's helping her escape. If you ask me, he's a nice one," Evan said. "See them lob the gob?"

"Would you want your daughter mixed up with a manky guy called Whoremaster?" Patrick asked. His face turned red. "How do I know he won't put my daughter on the corner the first time he needs to make some coin?"

"Don't judge the poor fella. He was good to Rory at the club. Could be the leather-coated lad won't be so keen on having a father-in-law in the IRA either." Michael snorted.

"What makes you think he's going to marry her?" Patrick said. "Hardly seems the marrying kind."

"You never know about love," Michael said.

"What do you want to do about Angela and George?" Evan asked.

"I'd like to kill both of them. Not proper guardians if they drove my daughter from her home. But I can't do anything yet."

"Hard to believe Angela would work with the Brits and turn you in. She's hardcore IRA," Michael said.

"I think it's George working against me, not Angela. She just enjoys the juice a bit too much. Maybe we take care of George. But first, my daughter. Let them fly out of here, and at the right time I'll make contact. It might take time to sort it out."

"An apple doesn't fall far from the tree, they say." Evan snickered.

"My daughter's life isn't a joke. I know a frame job when I see one."

"Your girl will be shocked to find you're alive," Evan said.

"Yes, I told Angela to tell her I died in an explosion.

Didn't want MI6 to get hold of her. My daughter's likely to be bull-thick. Donkey years since I laid eyes on her."

"I like her haircut," Evan said.

"Mind yer business. She's wearing the bracelet, a link to our past and our future. My daughter has to believe in *me,* and all of us, to join our cause."

"You're right, or at least give us access to what's on her wrist." Evan nodded in agreement.

"Let's move. They're getting ready to close down camp," Patrick said. "We need to get in position to tail her."

"Good, I'm going to the jacks," Evan said.

"They shipped them in for you, did they?" Michael laughed.

"Be quiet, the lot of you, and move," Patrick ordered.

****

Cowboy was in his office, on his cellphone. "Stop callin'. I figured out who you are. No sense threatening my brother anymore, 'cause I know your brother's out on parole."

Pause.

"Oh yeah? You do that and I go to the cops. Give them pictures of you with your stepdaughter. My guy found them on the internet. Damn awful what you did to Rory, you perv."

Pause.

"You better get hold of your brother, 'cause you're going to need him if I ever catch up with you. You still there, George?"

Click.

"Motherfucking perv," Cowboy swore glaring at Louie.

"I can't believe WM's gone," Louie said. "Even if he did leave you a bag of money to cover your losses, and the title to his bike. Turned in his colors too."

"Goddammit, Louie, what WM did is serious business." Cowboy shook his head. "He took the girl. Rory belonged to the club. He fucked up his computer too. Worm can't tell where WM's headed. Must be using a burner 'cause we can't trace it, or my phone either. And there's some things on my phone I'd rather him not see. WM's only gone a week, and earnings are falling like a brick thrown from a high rise, fast and hard."

"What you gonna do about it?" Louie asked.

"I got Worm acting as Whoremaster for now," Cowboy said. I'll find WM eventually. I'm also searching for George. If it wasn't for him threatening my brother, all of this would never have happened. I wouldn't have lost my key man over it."

"Can't believe what went down with Turk." Louie poured himself a shot of whiskey. "That other car clipped him, not me. Two guys in a Black Escalade with funny plates, blue and red with lots of zeros." Then he added, "Could be WM loves her."

"Sexually infatuated, I understand. WM had no right to take her. I'll hunt them both down. Together, apart, wherever they are." Cowboy put the cigarette out. "Nobody makes a fool of me and gets away with it."

"He'll be troublesome to hunt down."

Cowboy's eyes got darker. "They can't stay lost forever. Don't forget I got Worm. He can hunt anyone down with those computers of his, and Rory didn't make a friend of him." He chuckled. Cowboy picked up a hunting knife. "Remember Rory's friend, Sarah, from the yoga place? Maybe I'll visit her.

He brought the knife down and plunged it into the top of his wooden desk. "The perv is going to pay, and so is Rory and WM." Picking up his beer, Cowboy downed the remainder of the can and crushed it on his forehead, his blue eyes shining in anticipation.

****

"What am I going to do if this cretin comes after me?" George asked. He paced back and forth, forehead sweating, tapping on the glass display case in the second hand store, to get their attention.

"Don't worry, George, we'll protect you, even if you are a perv pedophile," Jack said, laughing. "Blimey, this has turned into a bloody mess. But you know, brilliant stuff to flush out Patrick Kelly with. That's the name he's using now. No more Campbell."

"Definitely the ticket if we don't have another way," Nigel said.

"Yes," Oliver said, "The Real IRA boys have no patience for child abusers of any sort. Have quite a record of killing them."

"What the fuck. You guys promised," George said. He took his glasses off and cleaned them with the bottom of his lint-bald sweater, then paced back and forth, walking around boxes of old newspapers. "You agreed I'd have protection. That I'd get paid. And that I could have Rory." His voice climbed decibels higher.

"If the other plan hadn't got botched, then yes," Jack said.

"If we can use Cowboy to help us locate Rory, so much the better," said Jack. "Kelly's never paid his due for the attack on MI6, due to Her Majesty's Pleasure. Too bad the daughter never made her debut as a sub at the motorcycle club. We were going to be guests, yes?"

"Yes, I worked it out," George said, nodding his head up and down.

"Her Majesty's special foreign intelligence agents fucking his precious daughter would be perfect punishment for Patrick Kelly. Funny, the girl shares the father's first name," said Jack, "A boy's name at that."

"A shame we have to start all over again," said Nigel.

"The deal stands, George. You'll have her, but you do what we say, and we do what we want with her, until the father comes to us," said Jack. "And another thing. No more whining."

"Right, put a sock in it, George," said Oliver

"And clean this dump up," added Jack.

A word about the author…

Kay Freeman was born in Buffalo, NY, USA and moved five times before graduating from High School. A perpetual outsider, she immersed herself in books. Now she lives in Wilmington, DE, and loves writing about damaged characters transformed by love. Kay has over three hundred hours of yoga teacher training and completed a ten-day Vipassana Meditation Retreat. The motivation to write her novel came from that experience. The heroine of the story, a yogi, also meditates and the protagonist, an MC member is haunted by memories of Afghanistan. Kay's brother-in-law, a Marine, Vietnam vet, and a lifetime member of the Warlocks Motorcycle Club, inspired the creation of this character. Truth Moon is Kay Freeman's debut novel.

Follow Kay Freeman at:
https://linktr.ee/kayfreeman

Or her webpage:
https://www.kaylaafreeman.com/